AMANDA'S WEDDING

Jenny Colgan was born in 1971 in Ayrshire.
After Edinburgh University, she worked for six
years in the health service, moonlighting as a
cartoonist and a stand-up comic. She lives in
London.

Also by Jenny Colgan

TALKING TO ADDISON

LOOKING FOR ANDREW McCARTHY
(to be published in September 2001)

COSMOPOLITAN

- ■ *The magazine for fun, fearless females*

- ■ *Relationships, careers, advice, real life stories, news exclusives and celebrity interviews*

- ■ *Shopping, fashion directions, best for less high street buys*

- ■ *Beauty advice, glamorous products, plus health tips*

If you like **Amanda's Wedding**, the bestselling book of 1999, you will love **Talking to Addison**, a hilarious novel about love, flatmates and Jaffa Cakes.

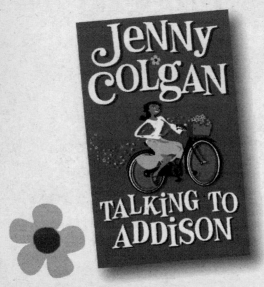

And don't miss her latest book,
Looking For Andrew McCarthy,
a must read for any 1980's chick.

See inside this issue of
Cosmopolitan to find out
about special offers and
fantastic discounts on these
irresistible books...

HarperCollins*Publishers*
77–85 Fulham Palace Road,
Hammersmith, London W6 8JB

The HarperCollins website address is:
www.fireandwater.com

This edition printed for Cosmopolitan Magazine, 2001
1 3 5 7 9 8 6 4 2

Copyright © ﾠ y Colgan 1999

Jenny Colgan asserts the moral right to
be identified as the author of this work

This novel is entirely a work of fiction. The names,
characters and incidents portrayed in it are the work
of the author's imagination. Any resemblance to actual
persons, living or dead, events or localities
is entirely coincidental.

A catalogue record for this book
is available from the British Library

ISBN 0 00 763492 7

Typeset in Garamond 3 by
Palimpsest Book Production Limited,
Polmont, Stirlingshire

Printed in Great Britain by
Omnia Books Limited, Glasgow

JENNY COLGAN

Amanda's Wedding

HarperCollins*Publishers*

Acknowledgements

Thanks to: Robin Colgan, Ian Wylie and Dr Andrew Teverson for their helpful remarks at an early stage; the amazing Ali 'don't mess with the' Gunn, Nick Marston, Carol Jackson and all at Curtis Brown; Rachel Hore for her brilliant editing, Anne O'Brien, Jennifer Parr, Fiona McIntosh, Yolande Denny, Julie Cass, Yvette Cowles, Alex Young, Dan Moore, Claire Round, and the team at HarperCollins; Salty Sandra McKay, Susan Hoyer, Andy Kennedy, and the Westminster red-hand gang for their support; David Knowles for the extra two months; Fiona Hastings, much missed, for suggesting it; my parents for not asking about it, and Jill Edwards.

For Andrew McConell Scott

One

Most of the really messy things in life don't actually have a beginning — they kind of bear down on you over years, like the consequences of not cleaning your bathroom floor (stickiness, cholera, etcetera).

This one did, though. It definitely did, and I remember it extremely clearly. Well, in a fuzzy kind of way.

Thank God — it was my bed. So: (1) I was actually in a bed, and (2) it was mine. I was beating the odds already.

I prised open one very sticky eye and attempted to focus it, to try and work out where the smell was coming from. I appeared to be jammed between the wall and an extremely large and unidentifiable chunk of flesh.

The chunk of flesh was connected to lots of other chunks, all in the right order, but I didn't notice this until after I'd sat

1

bolt upright in terror at a potential *Godfather*-type situation in my bed.

Everything seemed weirdly out of proportion. Maybe I was still drunk. I pawed at the sticky stuff at the corner of my eyes. No, something was very wrong.

An inappropriate hand was slung across me. It appeared to be about the size of my stomach, and my stomach is not renowned for its tiny-ness . . . A thought began to worm its way into my head.

I knew that thought and tried to avoid it for as long as possible, but alongside my hangover voice that was howling 'Fluid! Fluid!' the thought whispered, 'Oh my God . . . it's Nicholas . . . Again!'

I grimaced like I'd just swallowed something nasty — which, let's face it, I probably had.

Slowly creeping my way off the end of the futon, and feeling worse and worse, I crawled into the kitchen in search of aspirin and Diet Coke. Fran, of course, was lying in wait. She didn't live here, but she made herself more at home than I did. Her own place was a three-foot-square studio which induced immediate Colditz fever, so I'd got used to her wandering in and out.

'Good morning!' trilled Fran, bright and breezy. She must have been putting it on. Through a strange fog — which I supposed was the alcohol in my system filling me right up to the eyes — she actually looked quite good. I couldn't focus on her mass of fuzzy hair, but I did notice that she was wearing one of my T-shirts, not quite covering thighs that didn't even meet in the middle. I hated that.

I summoned all my energy to pipe, 'Hello!'

'Hungover?'

'No, no, absolutely fine. I've just suddenly developed a taste for a half-bottle of warm, flat Coke, OK?'

'Oh, *right*.' There was a pause. Then she said, 'I take it you'll be wanting two glasses?'

'Aaaaaaargh!' I put my head down on the kitchen unit.

'Mel. Mel Mel Mel Mel Mel!'

'Urgugh?'

'*Nicholas* . . . !'

'Uh-huh . . .'

'*Twice* . . . !'

'Aaaargh!'

Fran backed away.

'I know, I know, I know,' I admitted. 'Oh my God. Shit. SHIT! I think maybe I'll just move house, starting now.'

'In a towel?'

'You're right – all my clothes are in my bedroom, and I'm never going in there again! Why don't I start a fire?'

'Well, it's a bit risky, and I don't think Nicholas would fit in a fire engine.'

'That's OK! He could die! In fact, that would be good!'

Fran poured us both a cup of tea and looked sorrowfully at me. 'Come on, don't worry. Look on the bright side.'

'There's an eight foot tall accountant in my bed who smells like a polecat, whom I have now woken up with TWICE, thus ruining ANY potential excuses – and you're telling me to look on the *bright* side?'

'Ehmm, how about . . . if you spill any tea on the towel, it won't matter, because you'll have a towel handy? OK then . . . ehmm . . . it means you're not the type of girl who has one-night stands?'

'Oh God, WHAT am I going to do? Is Linda around?' Linda was my dumpy flatmate. I only saw her about once a fortnight. Possibly, she hid from me.

'She scuttled past about twenty minutes ago. She looked pretty tired. We might have been a bit noisy last night.

3

Wasn't Nicholas trying to pretend he could play the trumpet?'

I grimaced. 'That wasn't a trumpet.'

Fran grimaced back at the memory. 'Bloody Amanda!' she said. I nodded vehemently. Whenever anything *really* bad happened, Amanda was *always* mixed up in it somewhere.

Fran, Amanda and I were at school together in Woking, one of those dreary endless London suburban towns, not city or country, just lots of people hanging round bus shelters wondering if they were missing something. I'd met Fran when she ran past our house, aged four, chasing my older brother with a cricket bat.

Amanda lived next to us, and the three of us walked to school together for years, Amanda usually in possession of the latest Barbie-doll outfits, and extra sweets from the man at the corner shop with slightly dubious tendencies. Despite her blue eyes, strawberry blonde ringlets and general air of pinkness, she was pure evil, and played Fran and me off against each other with the talent of a Borgia poisoner.

Our biggest wish as children was to grow up famous and be on *Celebrity Squares*. Twenty years on, we were all still following this wish: Fran in the time-honoured method of going to drama school then hanging about for years and years and years, usually round my flat. I'd decided to do it by marrying someone very handsome and famous. I kept a close eye on *Hello!* magazine to check out when celebrities got divorced. Amanda, however, trumped all of us totally while still at school, by getting her dad to invent a new way of opening milk cartons or something, and suddenly becoming utterly stinking rich.

We didn't really notice at first, just that all through the

4

last year of secondary school she kept sighing and talking about how boring everything was – but then, we were teenage girls. Only when we saw the new house, with the pool and the built-in bar, did we realize something was seriously up. Her dad had left her mum by this stage and was too busy chasing totty our age to really care what we did, so we had big parties, shopped, and got tipsy in the new jacuzzi with the gold taps: it was a fabulous year.

Eventually, Fran went off to the Central School of Drama to pretend to be a lizard for three years. Amanda was heading for Durham University and, not having much imagination, and rather less sense, I applied there too.

I hardly recognized Amanda when we went up on the first day of freshers' week – mainly because her hair had changed colour and she talked differently. She gave me a lift up in the open-topped sports car her dad had given her for getting into university, and cut through the town like she owned it.

I knew when she dumped me in my seven-foot-square midden in the nasty students halls with damp running down the walls and shouted, 'There you are, darling! See you around, yah?' that somehow things had changed. Things had. She never spoke to me again, except once every six months when she'd condescend to take me out for a drink to remind me how wonderful everything was for her. I don't think her glittering success meant as much to her if she didn't have someone to look down on, and that was my job. I fell for it every time; the next day, she'd ignore me in the corridor.

If things were fair, I reckoned, it would all go wrong for her one day. As things were, she got a good degree and, as a result of her blondeness, qualified for a job in PR, and now was invited to lots of show-biz parties. I got a terrible degree, probably something to do with the bile marks on the paper, and ended up reading copy for a boring stationery company in Holborn.

But I still saw her. Every so often she'd phone, Fran and I would go see her, she'd gloat, and we'd get her to pay for all the drinks. And that's how it had started last night, when the phone rang.

'Melanie, *darling*.'

I've finally worked out that *darling* is PR code for *inferior acquaintance*.

'Hi, Mandy.'

She hated that.

'Listen, how about you and Francesca and I meet up for a drinkey tonight . . . ?'

Tonight? As if we had nothing better to do.

'I have news!' she trilled.

'Really? What?'

'Oh no, this is definitely drinkey kind of news.'

'OK. Fran!' Fran was lying on the sofa drawing a moustache on herself. 'Fancy a drink with Amanda tonight?'

Fran made a snarling noise, shook her head violently and contorted her face into that of a cougar, which apparently they teach you at drama school.

'Great,' I said down the phone. 'We'd love to. Where?'

'The Atlantic?' she simpered.

No chance. Cocktails and nob-ends. Plus, she lived in posh North London and we lived in Kennington, one of the nice but scruffy ends of South London, so it was like trying to arrange an inter-galactic alliance. I parried with the Ship and Shovel – both dirty and potentially dangerous.

'Oh, for goodness' sake, Melanie. All right, the Ozone then.'

'I'll raise you to the Pitcher and Piano and no further.'

There was a sigh on the end of the line. 'Well, if you

must . . .' She pouted audibly, which had zero effect on me as I don't have a penis.

'What did you do that for?' groaned Fran once I got off the phone. 'She'll only have been promoted or been asked out by some poof in a West End musical or something.'

'You never know,' I said. 'Maybe something's gone horribly wrong. Maybe she's up the duff by some sailors, and we, as her oldest friends, are the only ones who can truly comfort her. Heh heh heh.'

'Did she have an up-the-duff voice on? Or perhaps a twee gloaty voice?'

I thought for a minute. 'Ehmm, twee gloaty voice.'

'Well, that's it then. Sean Connery's son has asked her to lunch. And we're going to have to listen to two boring hours of how fantastic everything is for her, and we'll be so bored we'll get accidentally drunk, then she'll drive off somewhere much more exciting, completely sober, and we'll stay and get totally plastered out of bitterness and self-loathing, and hate ourselves for days.'

'Unh huh. So, what are we going to wear?'

Amanda flounced into the bar on time. She was a three Ps girl – pert, pretty and petite.

'Darlings, hi!' she crowed across the bar. I forgot: when she got posh, she also got *loud*.

'White wine OK?'

'Special Brew for us, Amanda,' shouted Fran. 'But in a glass.'

Amanda finally wandered over with the drinks, after checking to see if she knew anyone, perched down on her perfect arse and turned to us with a smile like a morning weathergirl.

'What's your news, then?' I asked helpfully.

'You'll never guess what, girls!'

'Ehm, you've won the lottery, for double world fairness? You're actually a man? You're pregnant by forty sailors?' Fran said the last bit under her breath.

'I'm ENGAGED!!!'

'Oh my God! Who to?' we yelled simultaneously.

'You know him, Mel. You remember – Fraser McConnald, from Durham.'

'Fraser who?' said Fran.

But I remembered. Sweet big gentle Fraser, with the scraggy hair and old clothes. I fancied him madly, he ignored it, so I followed him around pretending to be his mate instead. Not one of my proudest moments. God, did this girl have to win *all* the time?

'You and Fraser! Arse Bastards!' I said. 'And also, I mean, wow, you're getting married! Congratulations, that's wonderful! God, and *quick*!'

Fraser never did anything quickly, I seemed to remember. I had a flash of him mooching about the college, trying to find somewhere to sit down and stretch out his incredibly long legs.

'Oh, I know.' She displayed the ring on her perfectly manicured finger. 'He says I just swept him off his feet! Hee hee hee!'

Swept him off his feet? Or ran him over with a steam-roller? Fraser didn't even *like* being swept off his feet, I thought mutinously. Fraser liked striding about in the hills and reading *Viz* magazine and failing his engineering exams.

'I remember him,' said Fran, '. . . a couple of times when I came up. Lanky bloke. Lank. He didn't seem like your type . . .'

'Yes, well,' simpered Amanda.

'How did you meet him? Chess club?'

'No, actually, it was the funniest thing . . . I was purring . . .'

'What?' I said.

'Oh, my job, darling, you know.'

Grrrrr.

'I was working for these clients from Edinburgh who are launching some ancient castles guide. Anyway, who should I see in the portfolio brochure but my old friend from university, Fraser.'

I didn't point out that she can't have said two words to him the whole time, as he blushed a lot, and wore the same pair of Converse trainers every day for three years.

'Anyway, so I thought I'd go see him for a drink —'

'Hang on,' interrupted Fran, 'what the hell was he doing in a brochure? Was it a brochure for Converse trainers?'

Amanda tinkled her tinkly laugh. 'No, actually — and you'll think this is just mad: me, little Amanda Phillips from Portmount Comprehensive . . .'

Uh-oh.

'What?' demanded Fran.

'Well, actually . . . he's a laird!'

'A what?!'

I knew, though.

'Oh, I know, isn't it cute? Well, it's like a lord — only Scotch!'

'Is this true?' Fran looked at me.

'Ehm, I knew his uncle was. Maybe if his dad died, I suppose . . .'

Amanda looked at me in shock. 'Melanie, you knew all that time and you didn't tell me!'

'Amanda, you met him once at a party, and you said he smelled funny.'

'No-o, that can't have been me.' She laughed again. '*Anyway* –'

'Did he smell funny?' Fran asked me.

'Only when it rained.'

'*Darlings*!' said Amanda, with an edge in her voice. 'This is my BIG NEWS!'

We settled down, and her coy smile came back.

'*Anyway*, by sheer coincidence I spoke to the castles people and they gave me his mother's number, and she had his home number and it was just across London, so we got together and we had so much in common; we laughed and laughed . . . Then we went off to look at his land deeds, then one thing led to another at the Caledonian Ball . . .'

'*What* a coincidence!' said Fran.

'. . . and now I am going to be Lairdess Amanda Phillips-McConnald!' finished Amanda, all in one breath.

There was a silence.

'Hey, his name's Phillips too?' said Fran.

'No, no! You see, I'm keeping my name *and* taking his name. It's a feminist statement really. Didn't you see me in *Tatler*?'

Fran said later my eyes were like saucers. So she asked, 'Is he rich?'

'Don't be silly, darling. What's in Scotland?'

'History? Great natural beauty? Mel Gibson?'

'Sheep and alcoholics, darling. No, he hasn't a bean . . . and there's a "castle" to do up – he couldn't pay for that looking at bridges all day long.'

Then Amanda went completely off on one about her interior design plans for the castle. I'd been there. (Fraser had asked a bunch of us along, but I'd tried to pretend it was a private outing for me alone.) It was really just an impressive exterior, two habitable rooms, and a Calor Gas heater, but

10

she clearly didn't know that yet, given the lengths she was prepared to go to to put metal walls in it.

'I thought we'd go for a cutting-edge, post-industrialist look,' she was saying.

I knew I had to say something – anything – at this point. So I followed my time-honoured rule of saying the first thing that comes into my head:

'Wow, so really it's like a class-weds-money type of thing! That's practically . . .'

I was going to say Hogarthian, but too late. I got a look that could peel an apple whole, and a very long pause. Eventually:

'Well, of course, us Phillips can trace our ancestry back pretty far.'

'What, to Woking?' said Fran.

'Ha ha, very funny.' She turned. 'Are you getting married, Fran? Oh no, I forgot, you're not seeing anyone, are you? Because maybe, if you ever do, we could make fun of you for a change.'

Fran raised her eyes to heaven and headed back to the bar for more drinks.

Tantrum over, Amanda leaned in chummily. 'So, you and Fraser were quite close, weren't you?' She smiled, as if to show that this *didn't* mean *ENVY ME! ENVY ME!*

'Not really,' I said, meaning: *Well, I fancied him and he completely ignored me*.

'Oh, you *must* come to the wedding. It's going to be absolutely wonderful. Daddy simply *insists* on making a fuss.'

Amanda's dad had been married about four times since we were sixteen. He got a discount.

'I'd love to.' I would be generous. She was the first of my friends to get married, and to a lovely bloke. Why shouldn't

11

I be happy? Without warning, a thought of Alex popped into my head, and I winced.

'Great! Oh, I'm sorry I can't make you a bridesmaid, but Larissa and Portia are *such* good friends from varsity, I just had to ask them.'

'Oh, *right* . . .'

'You will meet someone, Melanie, you know. Someone nice. Such a shame about Alex dashing off like that. He was a bit of a one, wasn't he? And of course so terribly well connected.'

Meaning what exactly? I put my drink down, rather too emphatically.

'Well, I don't care about that, and I don't care about Alex.'

'No, of *course* you don't,' she said, patting me on the hand in an infuriating manner.

I was constantly forgetting Amanda's true potential for sheer malice. Revising my earlier estimate, I hoped she'd have a poxy marriage and get divorced before we'd finished the cake.

Fran came back with the drinks, but Amanda immediately hopped up and said she had to be elsewhere. She shook back her blonde sheet of hair – rootless – and sashayed her pert little leather-trousered arse out the door to her latest-model convertible, mobile phone already clamped to her ear, waving merrily behind her, off to somewhere infinitely more glamorous and exciting than the pub on a Friday night.

Fran and I sat in silence for a bit, till Fran said, 'Sod that, then!' and we drank her white wine as well as ours. Then we had another one to cheer ourselves up, and then a couple more, and before long we didn't care that Amanda Phillips had found her handsome – if scruffy – prince and was going off to live in a castle. Much.

* * *

Much, much later we were yabbering nonsensically about the last bloke Fran metaphorically kicked in the bollocks and threw out the house – actually, when I came to think of it, she had *literally* kicked him in the bollocks, and he had limped out of the house of his own accord – when across the crowded pub I spied what looked like a familiar pair of knees. Following upwards, I deduced that it was in fact Nicholas, tallest accountant in the world. (How did I know him again?) Gosh, he was tall. I liked tall.

I tugged on Fran's sleeve. 'Look – 's Nicholas.'

Fran looked roughly over. 'Wanker,' she said.

Had Fran not said wanker about every bloke we'd mentioned for the last hour and a half I might have listened to her and saved myself some trauma. Instead, I waved at him in huge circular motions. 'Knickerless!' And I dissolved in giggles. He flew over and gave me a big kiss. Oh, we must have been old friends, then.

'Melanie, *fantastic* to see you. I've just been having another crazy night out with the accountants.'

I squinted to make out anyone else who'd been at the other end of the bar, but they all seemed to have mysteriously disappeared.

'God, we're mad. Can't see us getting home tonight without a police caution! Chaw chaw chaw!'

'Buy 's a drink, Nicklas! You're loaded!'

'Sure, babe.' And he did so with the fervour of a man who knew only too well just how much alcohol he usually had to get down a woman to get her to sleep with him.

In normal circumstances I would have run six miles from Nicholas, whom I had accidentally slept with at a party once because he was, er, very tall. He'd phoned me up constantly since and I'd realized that, tall though he might be, he was

13

also the most boring bastard who'd ever lived. In fact, he was the most boring *accountant* who'd ever lived. After the inevitable grilling I'd caught from Fran when he turned up to pick me up in stonewashed jeans and pink cowboy boots, I'd made Linda answer the phone for a month. Now here he was again, and he was desperate, and I was desperate for attention – a deadly combination.

Ensconced in a corner next to Fran – who looked half-asleep, but with a drowsy look that said she could still bite you on the face if you thought about trying anything – Nicholas started telling me all the latest pranks him and his fantastic accounting mates had been up to. By the time they'd finally got on the coach they'd hired to go see Bryan Adams, I was about to gnaw off my own hands in despair. With impeccable drunk logic, I decided I'd better kiss him to get him to shut the fuck up. It wasn't the easiest of tasks; almost on a par with climbing a tree. While pissed out of your head. So, once I got to the top, I decided I'd better stay until the tree fell asleep. I'd crawled from under the wreckage the following morning.

'So now what am I going to do?' I complained to Fran. 'There's a big stinky man in my bedroom, whom I hate, and if I go in and wake him he'll start telling me hysterical stories about tax again.'

'So?'

'So, ehm, could you go . . . like, ask him to move?'

'Me! Why me? You're the one with all his saliva! Anyway, plus, what if he's naked?'

'Oh, right, you've never seen a naked man before?'

'Not one that's six foot seven. It'll put me right off my sausage sandwich.'

14

Suddenly my ultra-loud doorbell rang, which made us both jump. Fran and I looked at each other and I limped dourly towards the door to stop the infernal noise.

WHOP! Straight out of my bedroom, an absolutely starkers, very hungover, six foot seven man ran full into me in panic, and it didn't look like he had the faintest idea what galaxy he was in.

'IS THERE A FIRE?!'

We stood for a while, looking straight at each other like rabbits caught in headlights. Then my psyche made an independent decision to turn me into my mother for as long as necessary.

'No, Nicholas, of course there's not. Go get dressed immediately! Now! – before I open the door.'

He blinked and retreated without saying a word, headed for the bedroom, then did a quick U-turn and made a bolt for the loo, where I could soon hear him having a six foot seven pee. Well, it was either him or a passing horse had got in there. So I had solved one problem – getting him out of my bedroom – and discovered another. Maybe I could keep him locked in there for ever and the neighbours would let us use their shower.

Finally, I opened the door, putting on an ingratiating look – not that the fat postman on the doorstep gave a toss.

'Parcel.'

I signed for it, trying not to get too excited, but this was one huge parcel. Perhaps I had a secret admirer who was sending me precious gifts because they were totally rich and also perhaps completely famous.

Fran wandered through to try and use the loo. The fat postman noticed *her* – every man noticed her.

'Hello, fat postman,' she said. Then, indicating the parcel: 'Hey, is that for you?'

I turned it over in anticipation. 'No, it's for Linda. Bum bum bum.'

'God, what is it – the latest in the Woodland Farm Princess Diana *Star Wars* plate collection?'

'No, too heavy.'

The postman wobbled off. As ever, we looked at each other, wondering how a man who walked ten miles a day could get that fat.

'Books?'

'Linda doesn't read books. She eats them.'

'Is that true, or is it just that you don't like her?'

I looked at my feet.

'It's just that I don't like her.'

'Well then, can we open it?'

'No, of course not.'

'Why not? She wouldn't mind.'

'Fran, I believe she might, in fact, mind.'

To be honest, I had no idea whether she'd mind or not. In fact, all I knew about Linda was that she worked in a bank – I couldn't remember which one – was an only child, and had inherited money from her grandmother to buy this lovely flat and cover it in pastel tat. And I had learnt all this from the flat interview, where I had tried to look unbelievably fascinated, thus moving in under false pretences – which was a huge relief, as at the time I'd been on the run from a cabal of physiotherapists who were terrorizing me out of my shared flat in Edmonton, a period of my life I normally only flashed back to at four o'clock in the morning, wide awake and sweating.

As if hearing our thoughts – or, more likely, she'd had her ear up against the door earwigging our entire conversation – Linda stomped out into the corridor from her big bedroom at the back of the house, managing not to look either of us in the eye, even while grabbing the parcel out of my hand. She was short and round, with a definite aura of moustache. As she stomped back to her room, Fran and I swapped our familiar 'Linda' look.

'Erm, guys . . . ha ha . . .' came a strangulated voice, 'can I, er, come out of the bathroom now?'

Fran raised her eyes to heaven. 'Any time you like, darling. We'll be right here.'

I started to giggle.

'Right, OK, right . . .' came the voice. Then there was a pause, during which we didn't move back to the kitchen.

Finally, the door started to open and Nicholas emerged, with a mass of tissue paper covering his genitals. And I mean a *mass*.

'Bwah hah! Corking night, eh, ladies!' he hollered, putting on a good front, I have to say. 'What's for breakfast?'

'For you, a number sixty-eight bus,' said Fran. 'They deliver.'

'Haw haw haw – I'll get my dancing trousers on and be right with you. And how are *you*, my darling?'

We both looked round, till I realized he was talking to me.

'Oh, you know, some variation of fantastic,' I said, hunched over, still in my towel. 'The negative one.' Suddenly I saw something on the floor which I hadn't seen previously. I picked it up. It was a postcard, and this time it was for me.

'Fra-an!' my voice quavered as I followed her into the living room. 'It's a postcard.'

'So I see. Oh, and look over there, Nicholas – it's a door!'

'Cwah cwah!' came the voice from the other room. 'Just wait till I tell the boys at work about this.'

I sighed. '*Look*,' I said urgently. 'Look who it's from.'

The postcard was of the Empire State Building, almost

completely obscured by a close-up of a woman's breasts. On the other side it said simply: *Darling, I'm so sorry – big mistake. I'm coming home. Alex.*

There was a long dramatic pause. Or, well, there would have been a long dramatic pause, except that Nicholas chose that moment to launch into the room wearing purple trousers (I hadn't noticed they were purple; the effect was like a terrible plum-canning factory accident), shouting, 'Hey, I know what would be *hysterical* – let's make some French toast!!'

Fran gave him a Paddington Bear hard stare. 'Go look for some chocolate, Nicholas.'

I was in shock, and scarcely noticed when Nicholas disappeared, then returned obediently with a dozen chocolate mini rolls. I was too busy staring straight ahead without blinking and trying to work everything out: Alex, Alex, Alex – my 'one true love', according to me. Alex, Alex, Alex, that 'low-level rat bastard' according to Fran and pretty much everyone else in the world.

The first time I ever saw Alex I thought, 'Phwoar, I'd like to get into his pants!' And he looked at me and thought exactly the same thing: it was a true meeting of minds. Oh! That shitty West London party (well, I should have known better than to go to parties in West London and expect to have a good time, but just that once it paid off).

I was searching for the more expensive beer that hosts hide at the back of the fridge, when:

'Is it just me,' growled a tall voice, 'or does everyone here look like they've got something uncomfortable up their bums?'

'That's *trendy*,' I hissed. 'You're supposed to be *envying*

18

them. They're only *pretending* not to be having a good time.'

'Ohhhhh, now I understand. Right. So I can either try and get out of West London . . .'

'Can't be done,' I pointed out.

'True . . . Or I could get absolutely wasted and do something awful which I could later abdicate any responsibility for.'

This was so pointed that I gulped and took a closer look at this six foot two, dark-haired, unruly-looking character with the most heavy-lidded, pointy-lashed brown eyes I'd ever seen.

'That,' I said, 'sounds like it would be *completely* out of character.'

Eighteen astonishing hours later, damp, grubby and absolutely starving, lying in an unfamiliar bedroom having my tummy tickled with a tea bag, I realized I was on to something.

A year later I was blissful, swanning around with Alex, who was trying to make it as something in the music industry. He knew everyone; we always ended up at a party and all his friends were louche, slightly dodgy but with terribly nice accents. I was with the band: it was great. He wasn't exactly the most romantic character on the planet, but I didn't care; here I was, Melanie Pepper, twenty-six and watching minor pop-stars throw up in the corner of filthy nightclubs. Life was cool.

More than that, though, I absolutely adored him. I loved his cool long floppy hair, and his sad brown puppy eyes, and was constantly trying to get him to notice me. I would jump up and down trying to reach him, and he would give me his big lazy grin and check out who else was in on the conversation. Occasionally he would indulge me with his attention, and I would be like one of those pathetically affectionate little dogs they're always rescuing on programmes about the RSPCA. Other times he'd flirt with women for ages and I would be distraught. In short, he was not that good a boyfriend, no doubt about it. But in his leather trousers . . . well, you know, a girl is a girl, and leather trousers and pop-star friends are leather trousers and pop-star friends, so of course I did what the cool girls should NEVER do, which is fall in love with the cool boys. It blows the whole thing.

Still, he'd been coming round. I'd notice the occasional look of tenderness on his face. Or he'd phone me, for no reason. Or come home early from a gig. He was coming round, I could sense it. He loved me. He even passed the 'Would you mind just picking me up some Tampax on the way over?' test. So I was just about to suggest that we . . . possibly . . . think about moving in together – not seriously or anything, just a casual moving-in thing because, after all, all that toothbrush expense just didn't seem worth it, ha ha – when he vanished. Off the face of the earth.

I waited for him to call one weekend and he never did. It was that simple. Assuming it was an *X-Files* type incident and could have nothing to do with me, I let twenty-four hours go by before I finally phoned his flatmate, Charlie, who lived in Fulham. Charlie wasn't best pleased to have to put up with Alex's shit, and too posh to be kind. He informed me wearily that Alex had gone to the States to find himself, and was sorry he hadn't told me but it seemed easier that way.

Not even a desultory note! Alex had dumped me by moving continents and leaving a message with a laconic friend!

For weeks I was too strung out even to cry. It felt like someone had scooped out my insides with a cold spoon. Fran was wonderful then; I'd never known anyone with a fuller range of colourful epithets and hexes. She spat venom for me; I sat in corners and rocked myself. I felt embarrassed just walking down to the shops for more crisps, with the sheer humiliation I felt must be written all over my face. It was pain like I'd never known, worse even than when I got the Spangles papers stuck up my nose (I was four; I'm not weird or anything).

As the months passed, everything had settled to the occasional dull ache, which I had most recently attempted to assuage with the guest now smacking his lips over the chocolate mini rolls as if they were caviar.

'OK,' said Fran. 'I'm just going to take this little piece of junk mail and put it where it belongs . . .'

I snatched it out of her hand.

'Come *on*, Mel. This is low-life trash bastard post. In fact, if you like, I'll even give you the honour of setting fire to it.'

'Hey, guys, what's going on?' said Nicholas the Intuitive, through a mouthful of chocolate mush. Apparently, if he didn't get 15,000 calories a day he'd die.

I opened my eyes.

'Look, I really don't want to be rude, but would you just GO AWAY!' I burst out, but I couldn't hold the moment. 'Ehm, it's just that Fran and I have this REALLY IMPORTANT THING to do that we've been planning for ages . . .'

'Yeah, it's called the Getting Away From Nicholas Thing,' said Fran, not quite under her breath.

'Sure, hey, not a problem, babe. How about I pick you up tonight at seven and we go for a ludicrously expensive dinner at my client's expense? Chaw chaw chaw!'

'Unfortunately this THING that Mel and I have to do

21

lasts for AGES,' said Fran. '*So* sorry. But you have to go. NOW.'

'Hey, cool your jets. No one ever said that Nicholas Snodley couldn't take a hint.'

I suddenly ran to the other side of the room and started de-alphabetizing Linda's CDs in case he tried to give me a kiss. Linda's CDs: *The Greatest Love Songs Ever – One*, *The Greatest Love Songs Ever – Two* and, for a bit of variety, *The Greatest Love Songs in the World – Ever!* And some dolphin noises.

'Mel, babe, I'll ring you soon, huh? About the Brian May Appreciation bash?'

'Absolutely,' I said. 'BYE.'

He went for playing it cool: 'Yeah, right. What's your number again?'

I meant to give him the wrong number, but in my confused emotional state got mixed up and accidentally gave him the right one.

'Ciao then, babes,' he sleazed, and, bending under the doorframe, he was gone. I swear I could hear the echoing 'chaw chaw chaw' down the corridor in his wake.

Out of the frying pan, I thought to myself, picking up the postcard again. I moved back and collapsed on the sofa next to Fran, leaning my head on her shoulder.

'Please, never do the Nicholas thing again,' she said.

'But it's so much fun for you.'

'Mel, you know I'd rather grate myself than see you go anywhere near that eight-foot pole of slime.'

I held up the postcard weakly. 'I missed him so much.'

'I know you did.'

'I still do.'

'I know you do. But what kind of man would do what he did to you without being a total bastard?'

'*I* don't know. Boys are weird.'

'Yes, they are. All of them. And they think we're weird. But some of them are nice-weird and some of them are not. Think of Alex as an Amanda of the boy world. He made you feel exactly the same way as that snotty cow did when she took up with all those nobs and dropped you like a stone.'

'And I still see her.'

Fran sighed. 'And she makes you miserable. Which means you probably won't listen to a word I say.'

'Probably not.'

'OK, well, fuck that for sisterly advice then. Any mini rolls left?'

We regarded the debris of tinfoil strewn across the floor.

'That boy frightens me,' murmured Fran.

I lay back on the sofa, groaning. 'Oh God. First Fraser, then Nicholas, and now this. I hope karma isn't true.' A thought struck me: 'You don't think Amanda's marrying Fraser just to fuck me off, do you?'

'Probably,' said Fran, stretching lazily and putting the TV on. 'Don't worry. If Alex is coming back, maybe she'll marry him instead.'

Neither prospect filled me with glee.

Two

I trudged back into work on Monday feeling low. I always felt low at work anyway, so fortunately nobody noticed. Which they could only have done if I'd actually talked to anyone, and I never did. So, just a typical week, really.

I had a dingy grey office with a dead plant and big piles of crap all over it where I was supposed to check copy for a stationery company in Holborn. It was a shitty job going absolutely nowhere, but it demanded minimum brain power and paid more than McDonald's, so I sat it out. In front of the office the secretarial staff tended to hover, sniffing suspiciously. Given that all I did in my job was read, whereas they typed and answered the phone too, they were very cagey about my presence — I swear I could hear them sharpening their extra-long nails whenever I walked in. Mostly, they ignored me. But even they couldn't ignore me for three whole days, standing peering out over Holborn Viaduct through my tiny filthy window which didn't open, holding a postcard and looking painfully wistful.

'What's the matter, love?'

Shirley was queen secretary, in her late thirties, with two-tone hair and attitude. Since Fran had given up on me in disgust, and Amanda would have said, 'Oh, petal, are you going to take him back? . . . Well, you know best, dear, but he is a Charterhouse boy and they really do have a reputation for it . . .' I was desperate for someone to confide in.

'I, erm, well, it's my boyfriend. Ex-boyfriend. Ehm, well, he left a year ago without telling me and went to America, and now he's coming back and I don't know what to do.'

'Got any kids?'

'Gosh, no.' I was surprised, and felt horribly middle class and at the same time cross that she thought I looked old enough to have kids.

''As he got any money?'

'I . . . well, not much really.'

'Tell 'im to fuck off then. Simple, innit? What's the point of having 'im 'anging around, treating you like that?'

That made perfect sense.

'Is that really what you'd do?' I asked.

'Every time my Stan pisses off, that's exactly what I do. He knows he loves me, see. So he always comes crawling back. And I make him pay, believe me.'

'Oh.' I was confused. 'So I shouldn't tell Alex to fuck off, just make him pay?'

'Up to you, love.'

'Right. Right. Thanks.'

Oh God, I didn't know when I was going to get round to picking up my dry-cleaning, never mind considering making a sensible decision about the bastard who tore my heart from its aorta, stomped up and down on it, and gleefully reduced

26

me to the sort of person who considered Nicholas a fantastic night on the town.

Preparing myself a cup of my delicious coffee made with three different sorts of powder scraped off the bottom of other people's catering tins, I switched on my voice mail, a wonderful invention which had saved me the trouble of ever having to pick up the phone and speak to anyone at work, thereby avoiding being asked to do any. I had five new messages. Gosh, that made me sound popular. I perked up a bit.

It occurred to me, as it had done every half-hour since Saturday, that Alex might have phoned. After all, I'd hardly been hurling myself up the career ladder since he left; he knew where to find me. I got excited all over again, and drank my coffee without tasting it (a vast improvement).

'Hello, Melanie darling, wonderful to see you two the other night – looked like you were on for a bit of a party after I left!'

Great. It was Amanda 'La la la, I'm marrying the man I love and we're having fifteen adorable NCT children and living in a whole house done in National Trust colours for ever and ever' Phillips.

I beeped over the rest of it. It was definitely too early in the day to deal with that.

'Mel.' Phew. It was Fran. She would tell me what to do.

'I've thought this over very thoroughly. If you take him back you will have to die. And ring me – we have to decide whether we're going to bitchtastic Phillips's engagement party . . . and then decide to go anyway, like we always do, and have a shitty time, like we always do.'

That must have been what Amanda's message was about. Could I handle her and all her posh friends – whom I would hate and therefore get drunk so as not to mind talking

27

to them, and then get too drunk and possibly end up getting off with aforesaid posh friends, thus maintaining the cycle of shame? Still, a party was a party, no matter how humiliating.

BEEP

'Melanie, yes, good morning . . . um . . . you wouldn't still have that brochure proof I gave you six weeks ago? The marketing chappies swear they don't have it, but it couldn't possibly still be with you, could it? I'll speak to you later then. Goodbye.'

Bugger it. My boss, Barney, was terribly polite, ethical, and saw the best in everyone. Therefore everyone considered him washed up and constantly took the piss. I looked in despair at my desk. Anything six weeks old had probably mulched by now.

BEEP

'Melanie, this is Flavi in marketing. We've had your boss on to us, and I really don't think . . .'

BEEP. I think, Flavi, that I've got rather more important things on right now, don't you? Like major emotional crises and stuff?

One message left. Did I feel lucky?

BEEP

'Mel! Great, hey, well, what a wild weekend, huh?'

The speed with which my stomach hit the floor on hearing Nicholas's nasal whine made me realize how much I really, really wanted to hear from Alex. Only to tell him a thing or two, of course. Or listen to him grovel. Where the fuck had Nicholas got this number anyway? I thought of Linda. She paid me back for not doing the washing-up in a myriad of different little ways.

'Anyway, yeah, I'm pretty busy with all my friends, right. We're off on some accountants' night out. God, they're

28

nutters! But, hey, I might have some time on Tuesday night . . .'

Nicholas, it's Monday now, you plank. Not that I had anything planned, but God, of course I'm not going to say yes at that kind of notice!

'. . . or Wednesday, maybe . . . We could go out somewhere nice. Hey, give me a ring, it's 555 8923 – just ask for Crazy Nick, they all know me here! Hyaw! Hyaw! Ciao!'

Ciao? Suddenly I felt as depressed as I've ever felt in my entire life – or at least, in a month or so. This was it then. I was going to get niggled at in a shitty job I didn't care about, go to my so-called friends' fabulous engagement parties, live with someone who thought hoovering was a positive life choice, drink sludge instead of espresso, and date men who said 'ciao' until I got too old and ugly to date anyone at all.

I slumped down on my desk – the enormous mounds of paper gave it a cushioning effect – and reached out to switch off the speaker mode.

'A new message has been added to your voice mail,' said the mechanical voice.

Immediately, I knew.

I pressed '2'. An annoying voice in my head was singing, 'He's coming home, he's coming, Alex is coming home, he's coming home . . .'

BEEP

'Mel, hey, it's me . . . like, how're you doing?' People in the background. I could feel that big lazy grin of his spreading over his face and therefore mine. 'It's four o'clock in the morning, we're just hanging out . . . where the fuck are we?' 'The Village' – American woman's voice. Dirty. 'Yeah, it's absolutely brilliant and I am cummminngg', he started to sing, 'hooommmee tooooo yewwwww.' There was laughter in the background, a couple of 'whoops', then a pause, then: 'Hey, babe – I'll be at Heathrow. Today.' And then he hung up.

Oh. Oh! Chuffing hell. Every cell in my body renegotiated itself, and I shivered all over. Oh God. How was I going to cope? I would have to clean my bedroom for a start. And buy new pants. And start cooking again, boohoo. Could I reduce the size of my arse by – when? When was his today? Was it today or was it tomorrow? Piss! I started panicking. Why couldn't he tell me when his stupid flight gets in? He obviously hadn't been promoted from the space cadet corps.

Of course I would have to go. It never occurred to me otherwise. The adrenaline was coursing through my body: I felt as if I'd won; like I'd beaten America, his wanderlust and, well, any other lusts he might have experienced in passing. He was coming home. I was practically jumping up and down on the spot and decided to walk out immediately. Who would notice? Hey, it wasn't like I walked out over emotional crises a lot! Well . . . maybe occasionally.

Alex was coming back! Alex was coming back! He loved me! He loved me! I looked pitifully at the beautiful hand-written note my boss had left me vis-à-vis the delicate diplomatic situation between us and the marketing depart-ment, and decided to leg it. I took a deep breath, strode out in front of the secretaries, and announced, rather too loudly, 'Oh God, meetings all day. Ha! You know what it's like!!!' – then bolted, leaving them behind, hissing slightly. Free!

All the way to Heathrow I bounced up and down in the carriage like a toddler. Terminal Four was mobbed and I wan-dered off to buy myself a load of make-up and some magazines – who knew, he may be some time. I was just considering buy-ing some shampoo and washing my hair when it hit me.

He'd phoned at nine o'clock. From New York. At 4 a.m. his time. And now it was twenty past eleven. Half past six in the morning? He probably hadn't even gone to bed, never mind got up, packed, swallowed his hangover, got to the airport, checked in for two hours, got on the plane, watched a couple of films, got drunk again and got here. Yes, it appeared I might well have time to wash my hair.

I was back in the Land of Alex; the place that made me go completely out of my fucking head.

ARRRGGGH. I was the skeggiest creature in the universe. No one in the world could ever have been such a twat before. I counted it up on my fingers. The earliest he could possibly be here would be 6 p.m. I twisted about in an agony of indecision. A part of me wanted to wait, right here. A part of me wanted to get on a plane and jump out and meet him halfway. NONE of me wanted to go back to the office with my tail between my legs. What I really wanted was to turn back time and have none of this ever happen. Simultaneously clenching my buttocks and hopping up and down, I wondered what the hell to do.

Of course, when in doubt, one should always phone one's closest confidante for their deep love and support.

'I would say the best thing to do now is break into airport security where they keep all the confiscated firearms, confiscate one and hit him with a sniper bullet before he can make it to baggage control.'

'Frraaannn! I've got to wait all day and I don't know what to do!'

'Grow up? Sort your life out? Start making some conscious decisions about yourself?'

'I thought I'd read some women's magazines,' I mumbled.

31

'Oh, now there's a good idea for someone as sad as you. They're full of articles on "How to keep that pathetic cheating low-down pigdog in your life happy".'

I snuffled. As pathetic as I was, it made sense to play up to it.

'Don't try that snuffle bollocks on me. I refuse to be sympathetic because you're welcoming back into your life a man who is only going to cause you pain – and you are entirely to blame.'

I said 'bye' and wandered back into the terminal feeling utterly lonely and unloved. That was a feeling I found was helped by being surrounded by young couples fleeing into each other's arms and long-lost family members kissing, hugging and crying all around me.

But when he got off that plane . . .

I decided to take in the entire airport experience, make it a positive thing. I went and had my hair done – not cut, just done, which made me feel like a TV weathergirl. I quite liked pretending to be the kind of person who had their hair done, however it may have clashed with the ladder in the inside leg of my tights (you could hardly see it). There isn't that much you can do with a heavy scrunch of unshiny brown curly stuff, but they tried their best and made lots of interested-sounding noises when I mentioned I was here to pick up my boyfriend from the airport as he'd been in America.

I kept getting flashbacks. That time he walked into my office at eleven o'clock in the morning, straight past the vulture brigade, into the office, pulled down the blind, and gave me one right there. The time we got absolutely rollocksed and tried to break into St Paul's Cathedral. That time the central heating broke down and we both refused to get up and get any food and stayed in bed for fifteen hours and we both peed out of the window . . . That time he 'went to comfort an old friend' for three days and I never found out who, or where . . . That time I met his mum and dad – oh no, I never did.

I blocked out the bad thoughts from my head, and decided that this time there were definitely going to be ground rules. If he wanted to come back, it was going to be on my terms. This time, Fran would be proud of me.

OK: we'd have lots of togetherness. No more him vanishing with the lads . . . But then, what if I was just being all clingy and wouldn't leave him alone and he got really, really bored and I did too and we ended up just staying in and saying things like, 'Err, do you want to go to the cinema then?' 'Errr . . . don't mind . . .' 'What do you want to go and see?' 'Don't mind . . .' until we both killed ourselves! Maybe nitch that one then.

OK, we'd have lots of open public affection. Not snogging, necessarily, but a bit of hand-holding wouldn't go amiss, so he didn't look like my cousin from the attractive end of the family if I ever met anyone I knew.

And he could at least try and get on with my friends. Although they all hated him.

I phoned Fran again.

'Leave me alone. You are no longer my friend. You fraternize with the untouchable ones.'

'Fraaan.' My genuine panic was beginning to show through.

'OK. Here's one test. He's been away for ten months, right?'

'Yep. I've had my hair done.'

'Oh, that's pretty subtle . . . Anyway, he's been away for ten months. After vanishing completely and never contacting you again . . .'

'Apart from the postcard.'

'The postcard you got two days ago when he remembered

he'd left Charlie in the shit and needed to find somewhere else to stay.'

'Mmm.'

'OK. Those are the facts. You are dumb enough to be there waiting for him. As a hypothetical test, one might think it would be the least little considerate thing he could do to buy you a present, right?'

'Oh, Alex doesn't really believe in giving presents. He thinks it's bourgeois.'

Now what was she sighing for?

'God, Mel, what are you doing? Tell me you're not putting him up.'

'Mmm.'

'Fantastic. Have you told Linda about the new addition to your jolly little Kennington family?'

'Oh, she'll be fine. She won't say anything.'

'That means the same thing, does it?'

I was getting too upset to talk. I mean, what did my best friend since age four know about my life anyway?

'Mel, you know I wouldn't say anything if I wasn't worried about you and if I didn't care about you, don't you?'

'Yes,' I mumbled ungratefully.

'Give me a ring when he gets in then. When's that going to be?'

'Ehmm, anywhere in the next fifteen hours.'

'OK. Cool. Bye.'

It was true. Alex did a horrid, horrid thing to me. It's just, oh, Alex's problems — where to start? Public school, weird distant parents who divorced early, that whole deal. I was psychologically-tastic when it came to Alex. When I'd met him he'd just emerged from his last finding-his-own-anus phase in Goa. Well, I wasn't going to be his doormat any more.

Oh good, only six hours to go.

Wanting to avoid another ear-bashing, but desperate for someone to talk to, I phoned Amanda. Some bloke picked up the phone.

'Hello, is Amanda there?'

'No, she's not. Can I take a message?'

I recognized that accent!

'Frase! Hi, it's Melanie!'

There was a pause.

'Melanie . . .'

'Melanie Pepper. You remember! Mel!'

Jesus.

'Oh, hi, hi there. Yes. What are you up to these days?'

Oh, I'm just sitting in Heathrow Airport, where I've turned up fifteen hours early by mistake, having my hair set and waiting for my selfish ex-boyfriend who left me in shit nearly a year ago, and whom I still haven't got over, to – possibly – return from America, having walked out of my job this morning with no explanation.

'Oh, you know . . . usual stuff.'

'Right, great.'

God! Could we be any more scintillating?

'So, congratulations!' I said heartily. 'You're marrying my old buddy!'

I tried to imagine him bending over to kiss Amanda, but I couldn't make it fit. His curly hair would fall in her eyes. She'd hate that.

He laughed nervously. 'So it seems.'

'And you're a laird!' I added, helpfully.

'Yes, right, yes. Anyway, can I give her a message?'

'Ooooh . . . no message, actually. Just phoned for a girlie chat.'

'Right. OK. Bye.'

35

I often had romantic dreams of what it would be like to bump into an old crush from the past, when their eyes would be opened and they would see me anew: suave, sophisticated and thrillingly desirable. Although played out in a variety of exotic locales, the two things the fantasies had in common were that they normally included the crushee remembering who I was, and then giving a shit. Me, and my hair, were starting to flop.

Stuff it. I was going back to basics. I called my mum. I owed her a call. Well, about nine, actually. My mum was sweet – really sweet; I mean, she bakes – but definitely a traditionalist in every sense of the word. She had looked like Miriam Margolyes since even Miriam Margolyes hadn't looked like Miriam Margolyes. I was convinced that really she was only about forty and deeply frivolous but put an old mum costume on every day and got the rolling pin out. It was the only way to explain me, anyway.

'Hi, Mum. How are you?'

'Melanie, I've just this second been talking about you.'

Given that talking about me and Stephen, my elder brother, was my mother's favourite thing after baking, this wasn't surprising. Other non-surprising things she could have been doing: watching television, playing bridge, talking non-stop to my father, who could only grunt. I seldom spoke to him on the phone, as the grunts couldn't be accompanied by comprehensible gestures (macaroni cheese; beer; remote control – really, my dad's Homer Simpson without the deep self-awareness) and was therefore pointless.

'Is it true what I hear – that Amanda Phillips is getting married to that nice young man you brought home?'

'Yes. Oh, and Alex is coming back.'

'Well, he was a lovely boy. Scottish, wasn't he? Such a nice smile. And so well behaved.'

'He's not four,' I said crossly. 'He doesn't have to be well behaved. Anyway, Alex is coming back.'

'. . . it's sure to be a big wedding – that family never do things by halves. You should see the new swimming-pool extension Derek's put on the manor house. Of course, I haven't seen it, but apparently it's nearly as big as the house!'

'That sounds great. Anyway, Alex is coming back.'

'Are you going to be a bridesmaid? Maybe there'll be more polite Scottish boys there and you could meet a *nice one.*'

My mother didn't mince her words.

'I'm not going to be a bridesmaid. I might not even get invited. But I'm at the airport . . .'

'Of course you'll get invited. Great little friends at school, you three were. How is Fran? Met a nice man yet?'

'No. But . . .'

'Well, maybe the both of you can go to the wedding and *get lucky this time*. OK, darling, have to go, I've got bath buns on the go, and you know their temperementiality. Speak to you soon. Bye, darling.'

It drove me mad when my mum used the word *temperementiality*. It wasn't even nearly a real word. She did it to annoy me. Perhaps, I thought, musing on the conversation, she did everything to annoy me. That would explain a lot.

One of the cleaners, whom I'd noticed earlier for some reason, came past and caught my eye. He stared at me, a tad suspiciously, I thought. I wanted to run up to him and explain that, yes, I did have a home; no, I wasn't a terrorist (though I'd be strangely flattered if he thought so), but really I was choosing to be here to make some friendly phone calls, shop for consumer goods and WAIT FOR SOMEONE WHO LOVED ME, DAMN IT! So I grinned ingratiatingly. I checked the ongoing ladder in my tights. Shit. Where on earth was I going to find a pair of tights in an airport shopping mall?

37

Another three hours and I'd thought 'stuff it' and done the whole credit-card thing. I was top-to-toe coiffed: hair, Clinique lipstick, new top, poncey pants, hold-ups (the nineties girl's compromise, as far as I was concerned) and, sadly, the same old flat shoes, as even I couldn't bring myself to go that far. Unfortunately, the perfume ladies didn't see the shoes in time, checked out the posh togs and did a mass ambush on me, so I smelled like a tarts' annual general meeting.

Another two hours and I had managed to spend more than the clothes' total on coffee and nasty Danishes, and I was sitting uncomfortably, staring out of the window and reading 'What your man really means when he shags all your mates and has started to look at the dog – is this how the new soft new lad has to express himself?' I was ready to a) kill myself; b) go play in the arcades; c) buy the damned shoes. I'd been tempted to try and make friends with the cleaner, but he'd wandered off shift, still staring at me and shaking his head.

So I bought the shoes. Then I went and played in the arcades.

Five hundred years later, it seemed a reasonable time to start going to meet planes. I bought a toothbrush and toothpaste, and prepared myself.

Four New York planes later, and my fixed smile was starting to look a bit desperate. How did travel reps do it? Must be the drugs.

I started to think that maybe I'd missed him. Maybe he'd disembarked already and was on his way somewhere – he'd phoned one of his mates and been whooshed off in a taxi to some expensive postcode. Maybe he'd walked past while I was looking at the girl carrying the enormous stuffed elephant. Maybe when all that bloody coffee made me go to the loo again. Oh Christ. More than a whole day in an airport for absolutely nothing.

My anxiety levels were reaching their peak and I was about to put a call out for him over the intercom so I could at least attempt to head him off, when, at last, at last, at last, he loped out of the by now extremely familiar automatic doors.

My stomach hit the floor. He looked gorgeous. I arranged my face into a suitably affectionate, wry look and pointed myself in his general direction. He didn't see me (it must have been the hairdo), so I ended up having to run after him in my new super-sexy high-heeled shoes and attack him from behind like a mugger.

He jumped round as if he was about to kung-fu me, then gradually took it in.

'Mel!'

I was out of breath from running and out of breath from seeing him.

'Heh . . . heh . . . Alex!'

He gathered me up in his strong arms and gave me a huge movie-star bear hug. I wished the cleaner was still around to see.

'You . . . you complete and utter fuckhead,' I choked.

He buried his face in my hair.

'God, I missed you.'

Three

All the way back on the tube we yabbered and yabbered, genuinely thrilled to see each other again. He told me about his trip across America: the larks he got up to in New York; the English pop-star he bumped into in a deserted part of Montana and what great mates they became; his awful jobs and the amazing characters he'd met. His voice had taken on a new American tinge. I didn't mention the fact that I hadn't changed jobs, or flats, or, despite appearances, got it together at all since he went away, instead embroidering wildly the love lives of several mutual acquaintances, some boring parties and a hilarious imaginary cat of Fran's (I was getting desperate by that stage). Neither of us mentioned the inauspicity of his leaving; it was as if he'd simply been away, perhaps on business, perhaps for a fortnight, perhaps in prison.

We turned up at home at half past midnight. The flat was ominously quiet, which meant that Linda was wide awake, listening to our every move. However, it was a special occasion, so I pinched her bottle of vodka anyway, called in sick with a midnight vomiting fit (unpleasant but effective), and fell into bed with my big – OK, slightly smelly – darling, who managed to make me buzz all over before passing out for fourteen hours.

The following day I watched him sleep, and the time just drifted by. Maybe they should put beautiful sleeping males in airport waiting rooms.

He woke up dazed, stared at the ceiling for a second, then rolled over and grabbed me with a grin.

'Oh, Mel, darling. I will be yours for ever . . .'

This was more like it.

'. . . if you'd make me a bacon sandwich. Two bacon sandwiches. And some fried eggs I am *starving*.'

'That', he said twenty minutes later, after I'd emptied the fridge of Linda's food, 'was the best bacon sandwich I have ever had. Americans just cannot make a bacon sandwich. They put it in brown bread and cover it in crap.'

'What, like vegetables?'

'Yeah!'

'You're right – bloody Americans and their healthy eating! That's why they're all in such fantastic physical shape.'

He giggled, then took my face in his hands. Here it came.

'Gee, Mel, it's good to be back. Americans . . . they never mean what they say. I never feel I can talk bullshit with anyone as much as I can with you.'

'I think that's possibly the nicest thing anyone's ever said to me,' I said gravely.

He laughed, and ruffled my hair.

'I mean . . . I behaved like a complete dork, Mel. I'm sorry. I really am. What I did to you, it really bit. You know, I had no idea what I was doing. With all my parents and stuff . . .

42

I can find it really hard to open up . . . and I got scared. I was so worried you were going to . . . just ignore me. Which I would probably have deserved.'

'Yes, you would.'

'You're special to me, you know.'

'I do know. And if you ever EVER do anything like that again, I'm going to impale a testicle on each arm of a pair of scissors and start snipping.'

He winced. 'Is that nice?'

'You'll see.'

And that was it. I was very happy.

The next week passed in a blur – a dirty-sheeted, stupid, giggling, New York-time blur. I finally got it together to go into work, but was so glowing and smiley that I got away with more murder than usual. Even the secretaries couldn't hurt me. No one in the world had ever been as happy as us, ever, and in fact could have no idea what it was like. I floated around, occasionally stopping to pity people for not being as happy as me.

At home, I stopped answering the phone and made Linda do it, which was mean of me as she hated doing it and my friends hated speaking to her. Fran eventually stomped round in a fury, having gleaned, accurately, that things weren't exactly going the way she'd planned. This surmise was confirmed when she came to the door and Alex opened it, clearly in possession of both kneecaps.

'Hey there, Fran,' he said winningly. 'Good to see you again.'

I wondered what she was going to do. For a moment she looked as if she would completely ignore him, then she shook her mane of hair and smiled.

'Hello! Great to see you – you complete bastard! How nice!'
she said, walking straight past him to kiss me on the cheek.

Alex grimaced at me, but I shrugged. Even if I hadn't been
able to give him a hard time for what he'd done, I had no
objections to Fran doing it.

I put the kettle on. From the other room I could hear Fran's
trained voice, devastatingly polite.

'So, did you stay in lots of interesting places . . . cocksucker?'

'Well, yeah,' Alex stammered. 'Yeah, I moved around a
bit, saw a few states. Bumming around, mostly.'

'Really? How unusual . . . for such a rampant arsehole.'

'MEL!' shouted Alex, coming through to the kitchen. 'How
long do I have to put up with this?'

'As long as it takes . . . buttcheeks.'

'Buttcheeks? That's complimentary, surely?'

I blushed. 'Shut up and take in this tea. And try and make
it up to Fran.'

'I didn't do anything to Fran.'

'What, you want to get on her bad side? Be nice.'

He sighed, hung his head, and we carried in the tea.

'I like knobchop's new fake accent,' Fran said to me. 'Do
you remember when he came back from Goa? He talked about
his karma all the time and wanted to be a hippie. Gosh, wasn't
it jolly funny! What a wankfox!' And she laughed a tinkly
little Amanda laugh.

'Fran, give me a break!' said Alex. 'I'm sorry. I'm sorry,
goddamnit.'

'Gimme a break! Ah'm sawry, gawdamnit.'

'Oh, for God's sake, stop it!'

'Stawp it!'

'OK, OK, OK.' He got up and made to leave the room.

Fran wasn't finished. 'So what are your plans now, worth-
less anal wart?'

He looked at me and then at the floor.

'To make it up to Melanie and never leave abruptly again and be a good human being and find a good job and become respectable, SUH!'

Fran nodded slowly, winked at me, and smiled at Alex, who gradually sat down again. Then she launched into filling us in on the gossip. It looked like things were going to be OK.

And they were. Alex and I swanned about London, doing all the things we normally couldn't be bothered with, like Art and Culture, for example. I cooked us fabulous meals, to which I politely asked Linda. However, she didn't seem to fancy them. She'd had another big parcel, anyway, and stayed in her room a lot, not really giving me a chance to thank her for doing the washing-up.

Alex did have some plans. This pop-star bloke was apparently lined up to get him some work here in the record business, so it was all going to be cool and he might even try and get a band together. I nodded supportively . . . For the moment, I was simply happy to keep playing Hide the Trousers and didn't really care.

Eventually, I phoned Amanda back about the party. OK, I was happy, but it didn't stop me feeling an urge to get a gloat in, given half a chance.

'Darling, hi. I've just got a call on the other line – give me a second.'

Crap. This meant she must already have heard and had gone into defensive mode, which meant I wouldn't have the satisfaction of relaying the news.

'There,' she said, 'now what's all this about Alex? I couldn't believe it when I heard. Really, Melanie, haven't you ever thought of playing hard to get?'

Every time.

'No, it's great,' I said. 'We're really . . . happy to be back together, get everything sorted out, you know. We worked out we wanted to be together.'

'Oh!' she squealed. 'Tell me you're going to get married too! We could have a joint celebration.'

She knew damn well I wasn't.

'No, of course not. That's for grown-ups. Which reminds me, we're coming to your do on Saturday night.'

'OK . . . well, Alex will know everyone, I suppose. You know it's black tie?'

'Uh huh.'

'OK, darling. Well, improvise as best you can. Must dash! We've got a Teletubby stuck in a lift! Bye, darling!'

By the following Saturday, I knew for a fact that everything was all right with the world and I was ready to hit Amanda's engagement do. I had it all worked out. No doubt there'd be a lot of nudging. Someone might even say, 'Hey, it'll be you two next!' and I'd blush modestly and do a shy smile, and Alex would look at me tenderly and say, 'Well, you never know . . . maybe one day, if I'm lucky!' and that'd get all round the party and I'd be the queen! By the time my imagination had supplied a huge circular staircase down which we could descend to mass applause, I had to pretend to be Fran and tell myself not to be so silly. But, oh – look how wonderfully compatible we were! We hadn't fallen out once, all week. He'd grovelled, he'd done his bit. He was home again, he was beautiful, and he was mine. Everything was brilliant.

Amanda's party turned out to be a pretty swish affair. Fortunately, what with all the shagging and healthy gourmet meals, I could get into last year's grey silk frock. And if I kept my right-hand side to the wall, the wine stain scarcely showed. Alex had shoved on his usual T-shirt and jeans, but looked gorgeous anyway.

I'd begged Fran to come, but she'd absolutely declined, on the grounds that I would be snogging Alex all night and everyone else would be horrible.

The party was in an exclusive club on the Thames: all noisy gravel and ginormous bouquets of unnatural-looking yellow flowers clustered around a bunch of braying men and sharp-lipsticked women. Everyone was taller than me and knew everyone else, and before I was two steps through the door, my carefully groomed confidence started to plummet, until once again I was Melanie Pepper, unruly loudmouth of 2C, worrying about puppy fat and what would happen if George Michael didn't want to marry me after all. (Well, who knew?)

This was definitely not my race, this mob of anorexic, complacent, poshtastic freeloaders. I caught sight of myself in the enormous gold-tinted mirror opposite, surrounded by the glitterprati. I looked like I was wearing my mother's shoes, en route to the dentist.

I turned round for the consolation of having the handsomest man in the room on my arm. But my heart sank again. How could I forget? Alex's hair flopped! He went skiing! His parents couldn't remember his first name! He was One of Them! Even before I had grabbed my first free glass of champers (*Don't grab, Mel*! *You have a right to be here, remember*?), he was practically being mobbed.

'Al! Al, darling! Where *have* you been?'

'Alex! Sara said she bumped into you in LA – had a few fantastic days, I hear?'

'Oh, come over and see Benedict and Claire – we haven't seen you since the pool party!'

I too had been at the pool party, having a thoroughly miserable time. I too hadn't seen any of these poncey poseurs since then. I pretended to look politely interested and waited for Alex to re-introduce me.

'Guys, you remember Melanie, don't you?'

A blonde horse glanced at me cursorily, and I wished — for God's sake! — that my name was a little less common.

There was a short pause in the conversation as they gave me simpering nob smiles and enquiring looks, then they fell back into loud guffaws as Alex recounted his adventures yet again, cast me one apologetic glance, then hurled himself into dissecting the rugby season and knocking back the 'poo.

So much for the grey silk dress. The entire circle, defying the laws of physics, appeared to have its back to me, and I felt out in the cold. Deflated, I wondered what had happened to my fantasy big night at Amanda's party. I would have made my excuses and left, but there was no one to give my excuses to. So I wandered off, pretending to be in search of a toilet, and wondering whether or not to go and have a little cry by myself.

Weighing up my options, I spotted Amanda. After all, she was the hostess, she had to talk to me! I wandered up to her group in my best 'I'm not at all desperate to talk to anyone at this party, ha!' manner.

'Hello, darling!' air-kissed Amanda. For once, her shallowness was pitched at precisely the right level for me, and I was extremely grateful for it. She was wearing a Barbie doll-sized dress made of some pastel, girlie, lacy thing that was almost, but not quite, see-through. 'That's flaunting it a bit when you're meant to be celebrating your union with someone you'll love for the rest of your life,' I thought nastily as a waiter did a full body-swerve trying to make out her nipples — but I decided not to mention it.

'Ehmm . . . are you having a nice party?' A stunning social opener from me.

'Darling, it's fantastic! There's a *Hello!* photographer here.'

There was social success, and there was social success.

Amanda was looking even tinier and more cutesy than ever. Her sly little features glowed in the gold of the room as she checked her reflection again in the mirrors and – I swear to God – simpered at herself.

'Ho!' I said heartily. 'Maybe he'd like to photograph me and Alex, back from the grave!'

This was meant to be a weak joke, but as I would so patently never be *Hello*! magazine material, it just came out as a bit sad.

'So, tell me all about it!' pouted the minuscule radiant one, while doing a quick scan of the room to make sure no one could see her talking to me.

I did start to try and explain, but other people's happy love lives are so unbelievably boring – we shagged, we stared deep into one another's eyes and, hey, we had this really funny private joke whereby we turned the pillowcase into a singing animal – and Amanda hid her boredom less than most. It also didn't help that the other half of this indivisible team was guffawing his head off, miles away. I found my voice trailing off into a litany of hmm, so, it's great, yeah, fine. Then there was a bit of a pause. My shoulder was being looked over. I knew I should have paid my homage and left by now, but I could hear big roars of laughter from Alex's clique – laughter I simply could not share (I was tending towards the melodramatic by this stage) – and my options remained either clinging desperately to Amanda like a limpet or bursting into tears in the toilet.

'So,' I stalled, 'where's Fraser?'

'Hullo thair,' lilted the Scottish tones behind me. I turned

49

round, with the only genuine smile of pleasure I'd felt all evening. He must have remembered me after all.

'Frase!'

Despite the kilt, however, this character wasn't Fraser. He wasn't even looking at me – he was looking at Amanda, who returned a rather icy stare. I felt a complete fool.

'Angus,' pronounced Amanda beautifully, 'have you met my old schoolfriend, Melanie? Melanie, this is Fraser's baby brother.'

I looked at him like a surprised fish.

'Hullo there,' he said again.

A rather ruddy-faced boy stared back at me. He was as tall as Fraser, but didn't share any of his features. His hair was reddy-brown, and he had freckles. Hmm.

'Hello,' I said casually. 'Are you the best man?'

Whoops. Patently not the thing to ask. Ongas, or whatever his name was, blushed to the roots of his – almost ginger in this light, really – hair and mumbled, 'Ehm, well, I don't think so . . . erm, no.' Amanda looked cross. 'Well, we had to make all these decisions for the church and so on!' This was so meaningless I took the point and didn't enquire further. Amanda had, however, managed to say this in transit and had already made her exit, leaving us with 'Unpopular at Parties' syndrome. We both knew we were the leftovers, so we certainly didn't want to be speaking to each other, but we didn't have anyone else to talk to.

'So, what do you do, Angus?' Jesus, I sounded like the Queen.

'I'm a mechanical engineer.'

'Oh, like your brother?'

'Ehm, no, it's a bit more boring than that.'

As if in cruel mockery, this remark was punctuated by yet another enormous laugh from Alex's group, who were

50

obviously having the best time any one group of people had ever had, in any place, ever. Someone had a napkin tied on as a blindfold, I noticed.

Another long pause. Every fibre of my being screeched for Fran to mince in, or for Alex to run up declaring, 'I'm so sorry to have been parted from you, my darling. God, these awful bores, they just won't leave me alone. Come, let me ravish you in the gazebo, you amazing raunch-puppet.' Maybe then I could find out what a gazebo was.

'So, did you come down from Scotland?' This remark was pointless before it came out of my mouth, judging from the kilt. Actually, I was dying to ask why he and the lovely Fraser clearly didn't get on, and why they had fallen out, but looking at his face as he failed to hide his disbelief at the idiocy of my remark, I decided against it.

'Yes. Yes, I did.'

We dabbled, excruciatingly, in the myriad available modes of transport from Scotland to London, before lapsing, once more, into an uncompanionable silence. Finally, I decided that Tears in Toilet beat this hands down and, preparing to make my exit, I laid down my last small-talk tool:

'So, what do you think about your big brother and little 'manda then?'

Suddenly he faced me full on and, for the first time, managed to look cold and cross without going red. His eyes were a very bright blue. Out of nowhere he said, 'I think he's being a twat. And I'm sorry, but I think your friend is a witch. Excuse me.'

I really looked at him then. So much for party chitchat.

'Care to elaborate?' I asked, in what I hoped was a casually wry manner, and not the kind of thing middle-aged women said when their husbands announced they were having an affair.

'She treats our mother like a skivvy, she treats Fraser like dirt, she treats that bloody title like a cure for cancer, and she wants to re-do the old place like some fucking King's Road bam-pot house. So, I apologize, but I'm not quite in the mood to meet her pals. Excuse me.'

And with that he stomped off, deserting me! Bloody hell, what a pig.

Secretly, I was quite impressed. It was kind of true. Amanda was a witch. Fraser was being a twat. But even so! There was I, trying to be nice to the poor bloke, who obviously didn't know anyone. He'd hardly needed to be so rude as to march off at the first opportunity. He could have at least waited for me to do so first. I stared after him, then examined the chandelier very hard in case anyone thought I was staring at someone who'd just walked away from me as opposed to doing some hearty chandelier-spotting.

Well, at least there were deliciously expensive hors d'oeuvres. I stuffed my face and wished I'd brought a magazine – I could almost enjoy myself.

Alex's group were by now completely plastered and utterly hysterical over nothing – well, not nothing, something about a chap called Biffy and an imaginatively cruel PE teacher – but, to be honest, I couldn't follow the details. Alex slung a drunken arm round me and hollered, 'Totty!' I pretended to laugh and inadvertently caught Fraser's brother's eye. The look on his face plainly showed that he thought we were all a big bunch of wankers. Over in one corner I could see Joan, Amanda's distinctly tipsy mother, pawing Alex's old flatmate, Charlie, who was clearly drunk himself but doing his best to reciprocate. It was not a pretty sight.

The speeches came and went as a welcome distraction, because everyone had to be quiet, and not just me. Fraser was eloquent, Amanda fluttered and blushed attractively.

Then Amanda's dad said something, but God knows what – it was lost in the car crash of his new-posh and Estuary vowels. And then they brought on an Irish samba band, which was apparently the latest thing on the snooty party circuit. There was a mass screeching noise as three hundred people who could all ride horses scrambled for the dance floor. I decided to feign illness.

I sat down and tried to look pale and a bit brave, hoping someone would come up and ask me what was wrong and I could complain of feeling faint and not wanting to ruin anyone's night, thus drawing lots of sympathetic attention to myself. I was sitting there for quite some time until – AT LAST! – Alex came up to me when the crowd had dispersed on to the dance floor, and grabbed me under the arms.

'Having a good time, pumpkin pie chicken thing?'

I struggled to escape. 'Mm hmm . . .'

He ignored this blatant message of despair and started to tickle me.

'Come on, come dance with me.'

Perhaps the evening could be salvaged after all. However, my image of a romantic smoochy dance-floor show of togetherness in which I could show everyone (well, that poxy brother of Fraser's) what a successful character I was lasted about two seconds, till I remembered that Alex was one of the world's all-time worst dancers. He counted out the beat, wrongly, while bouncing from foot to foot. Not only this, but he was so pissed that he got distracted and forgot who he was dancing with, so that he was bouncing around the room like Tigger before he takes his medicine, while I was left bopping along on my own, like a girl in a Human League video. I checked the clock and it was only midnight.

Cursing the fact that I didn't go with the feeling ill thing twenty minutes ago when I could still have caught the tube, I leaned over and, gently but firmly, grabbed Alex's attention.

'I'm going home.' I smiled sweetly.

'What?'

It was impossible to hear a damn thing.

'I'M GOING HOME! I'M HAVING A SHIT TIME AND I'M GOING HOME!' I hollered, exactly as the music stopped, and everyone turned around to play 'Spot the Harpy'. I flinched, tried a half-hearted grin, and decided to scram.

'Thanks, Amanda, it was wonderful, lovely to chat, speak to you soon, bye!' For once, I was the one doing my socializing on the run.

Heading out the door, an extremely puzzled and drunk Alex staggering behind me, I practically bumped into Fraser, who'd been saying goodnight to guests.

He looked at me for a second, quizzically. Fuck it. I wasn't going to remind him yet again how insignificant I'd been in his life.

Alex scrunched warily ahead down the gravel drive. Of course, the pre-booked taxis wouldn't turn up for hours yet, so it was a mile-long walk down the drive, then out into fucking Fulham to try and catch a black cab on a wet Saturday night just after pub chucking-out time.

'Melanie?' I heard behind me as I stomped off.

I turned round. He was wearing the same kilt as Angus, but with a less porcine effect, and his curly hair had fallen over his eyes from dancing. I resisted the urge to run up and give him a huge hug and rub him painfully on the head to show him how pleased I was to see him again.

'Hi,' I said, coolly. 'Ehm . . . great party.'

'I suppose. Yes. Yes, it was. I'm sorry I didn't recognize you on the phone.'

So, bring it up again whydoncha?

'Oh, no, I didn't recognize you either,' I stuttered. *That's why I shouted out 'Frase!'*

'Well, I suppose it's been a while.'

'Yes, it has.'

'So, I'll see you around then.'

The beautiful grounds were quiet. Silhouetted against the big house, taller but less of the long streak of piss he used to be, Fraser looked both extremely familiar and, now, extremely foreign to me.

'No doubt.' Scintillating.

'C'mon, darling!' hollered Alex, sounding a bit worried. I smiled weakly at Fraser and followed him down the path. After being hustled out of the building, he wasn't sure whether or not he'd done anything wrong – and neither was I. After all, who was I cross at? Him? His friends? My parents, for not being better off? My parents' distant ancestors, for not being friends with the king? I could see his fuddled brain trying to work it out. Fortunately, he plumped for the former, to be on the safe side.

'Are you OK?'

I had to work out my strategy quickly. What I wanted to say was:

'No, I hate your friends because they're all horrible to me. Well, they're not even horrible, they just ignore me because I didn't go to the right school and have a crap name, so actually I'm jealous more than actual dislike, but I don't like it, waaaaaaah.'

Being an independent nineties girl with her own opinions, though, what I actually said was:

'Yes, gorgeous, I just couldn't wait to get you home – I had to get you out of there somehow.' And I added a girlish giggle for effect.

As the blazing golden lights of the illuminated mansion

dimmed behind the trees and I looked at my big, strong, placated, slightly wobbly man, I felt better again.

We spent a wonderful Sunday morning in bed the next day, 'nursing' his hangover. Then – after he saw I wasn't too interested in dissecting what a fantastic night it had been, 'particularly the bit when Barfield stuck the napkin up his arse, ha ha ha!' – he went out to see his mates.

I lolled around with the papers all day.

Back late, he barged in loudly, waking Linda, probably, and certainly me. After bouncing around the kitchen looking for something to eat (I never seemed to have any food in the house after my first week of being a show-off chef, so God knows what he found, although Linda was looking, if anything, even more fucked off these days, so it might have been that. You'd think she'd like having a man around the house – God knows, I did), he came in, sat on the end of the bed, kissed me squarely on the nose and announced, 'Hey, guess what! I've found a flat! Or rather, I've found my old flat – Charlie's forgiven me and I'm moving back in with him!'

I sat up. I hadn't rationally thought about it, but now he'd told me, I realized that I had planned our future out, after all, in my head. We would go find a room together somewhere nice, and eventually get our own place, once he had this music company job. Or we would both stay where we were – Linda wouldn't mind. Perhaps she'd even move out – oh no, she couldn't, it was her flat. Either way, I hadn't seen us being apart so soon, nor the decision so gleefully made on his part. Despite it being only two weeks, waking up next to him every day already felt a necessity of my life, something I didn't want to do without.

'Ermm, great!' I said casually. 'So, is Charlie still living in . . . ?' As if Charlie and I had had tons of in-depth chats about our personal lives.

'Fulham, yeah. It's a great flat.'

'But it's bloody miles away! And it's in West London . . . you hate West London!'

'Well, I can't stay here pestering you for ever, can I?'

Actually, that's exactly what I'd been planning on.

I pouted prettily, in what I hoped was an appealing manner. 'I wouldn't mind.'

He looked at me and ruffled my hair again. But not as enthusiastically as before.

'It'll be fine. You're still my favourite pumpkin, aren't you?' I was. We dived under the bedsheets. End of matter. Well, apart from when I got up to get a glass of water at three o'clock in the morning and found myself inexplicably staring at my reflection in the kitchen window and starting to cry. I went back to bed and tried to forget all about it, clinging on to him in the night.

Four

Fran popped by on Monday evening before we went to the pub.

'Enjoy the party then?'

'Ha ha. You were missed.'

'Yes, only by you and Alex's ghastly mate Charlie, who seems to think that because I didn't go to public school he has God-given leave to put his hand on my arse every time he's pissed.'

'Ah, well, there's good news about Charlie . . .'

I told her everything. All I needed her to say was, 'Mel, just because he's moving out doesn't mean he doesn't love you. He's getting his own space together, that's all, so that wherever you do end up, you'll have chosen it yourself and everything will be absolutely fine.'

'Oh God, Mel!' she yelled. 'He needed somewhere to crash, he was worried about coming home alone, he wanted a bit of shagging attention . . . America probably wasn't half as much fun as he's telling everyone it is – I mean, does he have a job from his great pop-star mate yet? Honestly, how can you let yourself be taken advantage of like this? Aren't you worth more than this? Aren't you?'

Linda walked into the sitting room. Her fat face fell.

'Ehmm, I didn't know you were having people over.'

'Yeah, you know Fran, don't you?'

'Hello! How are you?' perked Fran, taking a momentary break from her onerous shouting duties.

'Fine.' Linda retreated. I heard her head out of the door with some elderly voices.

'Shit! Do you think those were Linda's parents?'

The door slammed.

'God, I feel awful. And it's Monday today. Sunday is parental visit day. Everyone knows that!' I was grumbling to myself. 'Why doesn't she tell me these things?'

'Isn't it written up on the calendar?'

'Who the fuck keeps a calendar, for fuck's sake?'

Fran pointed out the large thing covered in kittens on the back of the kitchen door. I thought that was Linda's idea of changing artistic taste. In big pink letters, it said 'parents coming today' under the date. There wasn't another single thing in the whole month.

'What is the matter with that girl?' I cringed. 'Why can't she just go out with her friends and get rat-arsed like everyone else?'

'Does she have any friends?'

'No. Don't think so.'

'Do you ever think of asking her out with us?'

I couldn't stand Fran pulling this saint act.

'You ask her!'

'She's your flatmate!'

This was getting childish, so I just sighed and made a

60

half-hearted flapping motion which was supposed to mean OK without actually committing myself to anything. Alex temporarily forgotten in the light of someone else's troubles, something else occurred to me.

'I wonder what's in those enormous parcels she keeps getting.'

'So, to make her life a complete misery, why don't we snoop amongst her stuff as well?'

'You started it!'

'Did not!'

'Did too! When Nicholas was here!'

'Oh.'

We looked at each other enquiringly.

'Well . . .'

'That would be extremely . . . naughty.' Fran giggled nervously.

'Well, I've already ruined her day . . .'

We looked at each other and both leapt out of the room.

Linda's sanctum was possibly the most spotless place I have ever seen. Even the teddy bear looked like he'd been through teddy grooming school. Everything in it was either pink or peach, and the wall managed to be both, with the help of the type of nasty border normally only seen in motorway hotels. There were frilly things everywhere – tie-backs, potpourri holders, ornamental pigs. It looked like the wet dream of a seven-year-old girl.

'Wow,' said Fran, picking up the matching brush set from the glass top of the dressing table, under which rested a doily. 'Miss Havisham's cleaning rota's certainly improved.'

I couldn't see the parcel I was looking for and headed towards the cupboard. Fran picked up one of the Laura

Ashley pinafore numbers Linda favoured and flounced round the room singing, 'I'm Linda, and I couldn't be sorrier for breathing! Sorry, please pay some rent, how about five pence a month? I'm just going out now – oh, of course, I never do . . .'
I grimaced.

Suddenly, the phone rang. We both jumped out of our skins, as if we'd been caught doing something very wrong. Which, of course, we had.

'You answer it!' I hissed, absurdly, to Fran, and snatched the dress off her. Wrong-footed, she did as she was told.

I went to hang the dress back up and, as I did, I noticed the box peeping out of the back of the cupboard. Feeling thoroughly low, I picked it up anyway.

Inside there was layer upon layer of chocolate: everything from little Flyte bars to enormous, one-acre Galaxys, and those huge Toblerones you can only get in Duty Free. Some were just empty wrappers, strewn about in a most uncharacteristic manner.

'Chuffing hell!' I exclaimed, as Fran walked back in.

'How did you know that was Nicholas from all the way in here?'

'Look at all this!'

'Oh my God. Eating disorder city. Jesus!'

'I know. She just gets fatter and fatter. She must eat in secret all the time.'

'What are you going to do?'

'What am I going to do? Oh, take full responsibility for it, obviously. I don't know! We don't even say good morning!'

We looked at each other.

On the overwrought bedside table, beside the crocheted tissue-box cover, there was only one picture, of Linda – a chubby child – standing next to a vicious-looking pony.

Oh God, what was I going to do – mention it to her?

D'oh! What did advice columns say? Leave some handy leaflets lying about. I didn't know if they did ones that said, 'We were snooping in your room and found something you're obviously desperately trying to hide.' Go down the pub? I tried to judge a tasteful length of time before suggesting this. Fran gave me a look that plainly told me it wasn't long enough.

'Huh? Sorry, I was just thinking about Linda.'

'So what do you think we should . . .'

'I have absolutely no idea.'

Pause.

'I suppose I could try and be nicer to her,' I offered.

'Well, you do live together.'

'So do you, practically, and you're not nice to anyone.'

'That's because most people are boring. But Linda's like, you know, *sick*.'

'OK, OK already.'

I hoisted myself up and went and tackled some of Alex's and my washing-up. Well, it was a start.

'So, ehm, that was Nicholas on the phone then?'

And not, say, Alex (who was out buying furniture), having had a big change of heart and begging me to move with him to Fulham.

'Yes. You appear to be in demand.'

Well, hooray!

'However, I told him you weren't available, so he asked me out instead.'

Boo! OK, I may have despised the guy, but I'd like to think he could tell me apart from other members of the same species.

'Huh. Did you say yes?'

'What do you think?'

'I think you said yes, you would smoochily love him forever

63

and ever, and did he have any more of his hilarious accounting stories?'

'Oh, and also he said you may have to test for some disease or other.'

'WHAT!?'

Fran gave me the finger and laughed evilly.

'Melanie, given that you're probably the only person who's ever gone to bed with him, I wouldn't worry too much.'

The brief tension gone, I told her about how awful the party had been, which I knew would please her. She was particularly interested in Angus.

'Sounds intriguing. Was he handsome?'

On the sniff, as usual.

'Ehm, I don't know. Have you seen that film *Babe*?'

'He looks like a pig?'

'Hear me out . . .'

'Farmer Hoggett?'

'No! You know the dog in it who goes bad and bites people . . . ?'

'He looks like a dog?'

'Well, he has an air of wounded nobility.'

'In dog form.'

'Ehm . . .'

We both sighed.

'God, there really are no men left,' exclaimed Fran for like the billionth time.

I couldn't help it, but I must have involuntarily made an Amanda-type look, because she pretended to knee me in the tits. She didn't quite pretend properly and unfortunately did hit me in the tits. Fran's always played rough.

* * *

Linda came back eventually, on her own. We both stiffened. As usual she headed straight past the sitting room for her bedroom. I held my breath, terrified she was going to find something out of place. Maybe she had a hair taped over the doorframe and some talc or something, and now she was going to kill us . . .

Fran gave me a meaningful look, so I heaved myself up again.

'Erm, Linda, do you want a cup of coffee?'

There was silence from beyond. No doubt this was a terrifying and unprecedented advance on my part. I felt horribly embarrassed and ashamed. Finally:

'No, thanks.'

'I think you've only got half a pound of sugar left anyway,' whispered Fran meanly.

'OK!' I shouted. 'We're off to the pub. Do you want to come?'

Linda came out of her room and looked at me, her pale eyes suspicious.

'Why?'

'Ehm, no reason . . . you know, Monday night . . .' I trailed off weakly.

'No, thanks. I'm going to clean my wardrobe out.'

'Ohhh – I mean: Oh, right, have fun!'

Then Fran and I fled to the pub to meet Alex and Charlie. 'Amanda & Fraser Ltd' had generously deigned to join us: the presence of two good-looking West London boys had obviously upped our social desirability somewhat.

Walking into the pub, I shot a sidelong glance at Fran. It was not looking good. Amanda was sitting in the middle of the three men, showing off in her pertiest manner. Fraser was watching her dutifully – or staring at her adoringly, I couldn't make out what was true and what was bitchiness on my behalf – and Alex and Charlie were sniggering and nudging each other.

Alex gave me a kiss, and I went to get some beers, while Amanda said something and everybody laughed. I looked at the beautifully cut profile of the man I loved and suddenly felt empty, even when he yelled, 'Mel, gorgeous gorgeous thing, get over here and sit on my knee immediately.'

How could he be so sweet and still want to move to Fulham with Charlie? I sat on his knee and tried not to mope, but it wasn't easy.

'So, anyway,' Amanda was squawking, 'I spoke to the designer and she says she's never seen such a tiny waist! They're going to have to do it all by hand specially, and it's going to cost an extra two thousand pounds! Can you imagine!'

'Bloody hell!' said Alex dutifully.

The other boys nodded blankly. That infuriated me: they listened to her because she was pretty, but they wouldn't know what a wedding dress cost at gunpoint.

Then she gave Fraser a look and snapped her fingers. He immediately got up and fetched her another drink. Fran and I looked at each other in amazement.

Anyway, to make myself sound at least vaguely interesting, I spilled the beans about Linda. Fran looked disapproving, but only because she didn't think to tell it herself. Everyone was enthralled, so I tried not to embellish too much. Well, everyone except Fran, who was being disapproving, and Charlie, who was staring at Fran's breasts. And Amanda, who was attempting to tell a rival story about her suspected anorexia, which she was trying to make sound like a pretty cool disease.

Suddenly, Angus walked in, and it was like a chill hit the air. Fraser smiled anxiously in welcome, while Amanda gave him a very tight look out of the corner of her beautifully made-up eyes and deliberately smiled without smiling.

'Oh, hello, Angus,' she said. 'So glad you could make it.'

'Aye.'

Good God, what was he, an extra from *Cold Comfort Farm*? Angus sat down stolidly.

Fraser looked around. 'Does everyone know Angus?' Everyone hummed and pretended to – even if (like Fran) they'd never clapped eyes on him before – so we didn't all have to go round and introduce ourselves.

I'd gotten to that delicate part of sitting on somebody's knee when I'd forgotten to balance my toes on the floor and they now had an extremely dead leg which they were being too polite to tell me about.

'Hey, elephant baby, darling, obviously I adore you, but if you don't get off my knee now I'm going to collapse and die,' my beloved announced loudly.

Amanda brayed with laughter, as she was the dictionary antonym of an elephant, whereas clearly, I was the synonym.

There was nowhere to sit, so I edged to the end of the group, red-faced but pretending to take it as a joke, next to the naturally red-faced Angus who was staring surlily at a pint of English bitter. This was a bad ploy, because by the time I re-emerged from my mild and unnoticed strop to re-enter the conversation, the conversation was away from my nutsoid flatmate altogether and back on to bloody *weddings* again.

'So,' Amanda was saying, 'we're going to hire out the entire castle and have heather and haggis and tartan swathing and pipers . . .'

'. . . parading out of my arse,' a voice said quietly in my ear, in a not bad approximation of Amanda's posh squawk. I giggled before coming to my senses that it had

67

in fact been uttered by Angus the Sulky. No one else had noticed.

'Hello there,' I said, warmer than I had intended.

'Hullo.'

'Good time on Saturday?'

'Hmm,' he said, with a pointed look at the intended duo.

Our fast becoming habitual embarrassed silence stole over us.

'So, are you older or younger than Frase . . .' As soon as I asked the question I remembered I already knew. God, my small-talk radar was getting worse all the time.

'Still younger.' He almost half smiled. I briefly wondered what he'd look like if he really did smile.

Someone set another drink in front of me, and I smelled Alex's aftershave and closed my eyes.

'Oh, have you two met?'

Alex and Angus shook hands in that wary fashion blokes do when the girl they're going out with introduces them to another bloke.

'Hi. Err, you're Fraser's little brother?'

Well, of course he was. D'oh!

'Yes. Yes, I am.'

'You were at the engagement party, weren't you? Brilliant night, wasn't it?'

Then quite an odd thing happened. Angus and I exchanged glances, and I almost smiled.

'Yes. Yes, it was quite something.'

'So, what are you doing down here then? Working?'

'Yes, I've got a short-term contract in Docklands. If I like it I might stay . . .'

'Bet you miss the sheep in hoochter-choochter land though, eh?'

I cringed.

'No. Actually, I've met plenty of woolly twats since I arrived.'

Double rude! Yikes! Fortunately, Alex had already turned back to Charlie to make some other sheep-related remark and had missed it. But I was shocked, and puzzled: why did this ginger bloke hate us all so much? And if he did, why was he here?

Nothing happened to change my opinion as the evening wore on. Angus seemed staggeringly unimpressed by Alex's American stories, which I still found funny, even though I'd heard them several times. More pints were consumed, more chatter went round, and he didn't feel the need to offer a single comment, make one remark, or laugh – not even when Alex got on to the time he decided he was going to become a rodeo star!

I looked around for Fran. She had managed to get herself completely cornered by Charlie, whose eyes were as round as Fran's nicely shaped baps. He'd got her up against the wall at the back side of the table, and everyone else was in that mildly blootered universe where they didn't notice much around them (except Amanda, who was drinking Aqua Libra, but never noticed anyone other than herself anyway).

'Darling,' he was slurring, 'you're absolutely top totty . . .'

'Fuck off, Charlie.' Fran sounded dangerous.

'Come, give Charlie a little kiss –'

He reached out to grab her. Fran put her arms up and, without meaning to, slapped him in the face. The atmosphere turned suddenly.

'I say, did you bloody slap me, you bitch?'

That posh charm was obviously spread pretty thin.

Fran drew herself up to her full height, looking like she was on fire with humiliation and rage.

'No, but I fucking should have done, you wanker!'

'You fucking little bitch!'

Then, and I mean it, he really looked as though he was going to go for her. Everyone watched like they were caught in a sci-fi time freeze, except for Fran, who seemed to be moving backwards in slow motion. Then suddenly there was a flash of ginger as Angus leapt up, grabbed Charlie's arms, and in one movement threw him against the wall with the full force of his body.

'STOP IT!'

There was a long pause. For some reason, rather a lot of people seemed to be panting. The landlord was heading ominously in our direction, and Angus and Charlie were staring at each other very intently.

Alex leaned in. 'Come on, Charles, leave it,' he said softly.

After an agonizing wait, Charlie lowered the eye contact, put his fangs away and stomped out of the pub. We were all looking at each other, half worried, half thrilled to bits with excitement.

'Well, what a cunt!' said Fran. And that was a word we never, ever used.

Outside, Charlie was obviously wanting to go, but Alex was hovering to see me.

'Ehm, I'd better take Charlie home. I'll stay there tonight.'

I didn't want him to go, especially not with that . . . git.

'Good night then,' said Alex, and he walked off supporting Charlie.

The rest of us stood around wondering what to do next. Fran thanked Angus, but it seemed almost distasteful to mention it; like he had seen her being raped or something. Fraser was wandering over in our direction, looking concerned and worried, when Amanda grabbed him firmly by the arm, turned round and cheerily said, 'Well we'd better go!' as if

70

they'd just spent the afternoon touring the village fête. As she hustled him off to her car, Fraser looked over his shoulder at Angus, who was standing looking a bit embarrassed, and gave him an awkward grin meant to convey shame, apology, pride and general goodwill all at once. Angus gave him one back, and they suddenly looked very alike.

'Right! All back to mine then?' I said, as usual. Fran and I were dying to discuss it, obviously, but it would be a lot easier if Angus didn't come . . .

However, he was already striding off in the opposite direction.

'Oh, look at him,' said Fran, as he headed off towards the tube. 'He's my pig in shining armour. My Lone Rasher. My ginger . . .'

'Shush, Fran. He bloody sorted that out, OK?'

'Oh, for God's sake! I've had enough hassle tonight already, don't you think?'

Now Fran was in a mood.

'Come on, Franster, don't bother about it. That revolting prat mauling you – bleurgh . . . Come on back, have a glass of wine, stop worrying.'

We piled back to the flat, managing for once not to cackle on the stairwell. Fran was still a bit shocked, so I sat her down, poured her a big glass of whisky (yes, it was the one Linda had won in a raffle, but it was medicinal) and let her tell me about it all over again as if I hadn't been there.

I couldn't stop thinking aloud.

'It is good news for me, though,' I added, after what I thought was a considerate length of time.

'What?!'

'Well, Alex is hardly going to move in with Charlie now,

is he? Now he knows he's practically a rapist. Hmmm, maybe we'll get a place of our own . . . move in properly.'

'Oh, well, I'm glad my being nearly pawed to death is going to help out your domestic arrangements.' There was a glint in her eye. 'Do you want me to go down to King's Cross and turn a few tricks? Then maybe you can get a joint mortgage.'

'No! I was just saying . . .'

'If he moves in with Charlie —' Fran was showing her teeth, always an ominous sign — 'if he moves in with Charlie, after all this, you'll chuck him, won't you?'

Fuck! Moral dilemma-tastic!

'He won't; that's what I'm saying.' I was pretty blithe about the whole thing.

'But say he did.'

'He won't.' For God's sake.

'In a hypothetical universe, you'd chuck a bloke who moved in with the person who molested your best friend.'

'Are you emotionally blackmailing me? And anyway, technically, he didn't molest you.'

The second I said that, I realized what a dreadful thing it was to say and that I was the worst feminist of all time. We were shocked for the second time that night, and now I was behaving worse than Charlie. Suddenly I felt drunk and tearful and terribly tired.

'Let's not talk about it any more,' said Fran after a long silence.

I pulled out the spare mattress and we went to sleep in silence. For once, Linda should have been proud of me.

Five

Next morning we staggered around pretending to be more hungover than we really were so that we wouldn't have to talk to one another.

Fran had an audition, and I wished her good luck with it then set off for work. My boss was waiting in my office. That could not possibly be a good sign. I couldn't remember him ever being in there before. I hoped he hadn't been pawing through my desk: it was full of 'I love Alex' doodles.

'Ah, yes, good morning, Melanie.' He smiled at me, even more politely than usual. He was about five foot tall, but perfectly in proportion: you always had to resist the urge to pat him on his bald head.

'Erm, mm, there's been the most terrible fuss with marketing about the new brochure. Apparently the word "Fabricon" has been misspelled throughout.'

I sighed. 'It's a made-up marketing word though, isn't it?' I pointed out. 'It doesn't matter how you spell it, it still means sod all. I can hardly check it in the *Oxford English*, can I?'

'Nonetheless –' oh no, he was sounding pompous – 'nonetheless, it was the brand name of our latest product and was already on £45,000 worth of marketing literature. Which should be £48,000 worth, if we hadn't missed the window in the production schedule due to your – and I'm sorry to have to say it – frankly substandard work.'

Suddenly I felt incredibly small. *Substandard work?* Yup, I was back in the lower fourth. But this time it wasn't my lack of comprehension of wave motion that was the problem, it was my own sheer laziness. I ran through all the possible options in my head, and chose the worst, nastiest, most pathetic one of all.

'God, I'm sorry. It's just . . . well, my flatmate has bulimia, and it's been a really difficult time.'

I looked like I might, possibly, burst into tears. I was scum. I was lower than scummy scum scum. Truly, that should be a sackable offence.

'Oh, gosh, that must be really difficult for you.' My boss looked so heartfelt and sensitive and upset I nearly started crying for real. 'My sister had that.'

Shit! That was it: hell, handbag, me, en route.

He put a hand on my shoulder. 'I think it's just as hard for those around the person, sometimes. It's so frustrating, isn't it?'

I nodded plaintively, and embellished it a little. We revelled in our mutual caring personae for another ten minutes, and I reckoned I'd just about got off scot-free when he said:

'I'm really sorry, Mel, and I know this isn't going to help, but marketing have asked if you could move downstairs into their office – so you can all work a bit closer together, as it were. You're going to be in their department from now on.'

He looked genuinely regretful. It was all I could do to speak, so I just nodded woefully.

'We'll get your stuff moved down as soon as possible. My dear, it's been a pleasure working with you.'

It couldn't have been, but I accepted the outstretched hand numbly, a billion growing threads of horror spawning through my head. The marketing department! Oh God, they had orange walls down there! And they used the term 'conceptual'! And now I would have to get drunk at the Christmas party and make a fool of myself! Oh no – I did that already. Anyway, it was going to be work, work, work all day from now on, just like real people had to! I groaned heartily to myself. The phone rang.

'Well, I can see you're busy, so I'll leave you to get sorted out.' My boss got up gracefully and floated off on his little handmade shoes.

It was Fran, of course.

'Well? Have you spoken to him?'

'Fran! I'm being shifted! They're putting me in marketing!'

'Oh my God, is that good or bad?'

Fran had no concept of what goes on in the world of work. To her, corporate affairs meant copping off with City blokes.

'Well, I'm going to have to work all day and never talk to you again surrounded by a big bunch of people who think it's really cool to be in marketing, and sit in a cubicle, not in an office, and suffer the smell of other people's baked potatoes at lunch time and hear their constant boring chatter about focus groups, and have people watching what I'm doing all the time and making bitchy comments about how I never wear anything orange . . . But apart from that it should be fine.'

'Oh, OK. Anyway, have you spoken to Alex yet?'

'Fran! This is IMPORTANT!'

'More important than your boyfriend moving in with a rapist?'

'Yes, actually!'

There was a bit of a pause. Fran couldn't see anything in life more important than the vagaries of our personal lives, and normally I agreed with her. So finally she must have sensed this was pretty bad.

'I'm sorry. Have you been sacked?'

'No, I haven't been bloody sacked. Oh, forget it!'

'Are you going to make less money?'

'Fran, I'll speak to Alex now, OK?'

Damn. Still, at least she didn't get the audition, or she'd have told me. I lived in constant fear that she would get unbelievably famous and never hang around with me ever again, and I'd be the old sop in the bar telling strangers boring stories they didn't believe about how she used to be my best friend.

I was pretty upset and frustrated and tired and pissed off, and the last thing I wanted to do was phone Alex and ask difficult questions. I wished he'd phone to tell me how he'd seen the light about that creep Charlie last night and beg to come and live with me instead, as he loved me SO MUCH. Then I caught a glimpse of my unhealthy pallor and dribbling mascara in the window and realized that: (1) I was actually crying a bit, and (2) if I were Alex and saw me, I'd run ten miles.

Fortunately I'm not, because the phone rang, and it was him.

'Hey, sweet chops.'

'Hey, nasty friend-chops.'

'God, yes, Charlie was a bit pished, wasn't he?'

'He really upset Fran, you know.'

'Fran? That girl eats Charlies for breakfast. If ginger boy hadn't leapt in, she'd have gnawed his nads off.'

This was undeniable.

'Are you still going to live with that wanker?'

'Well, it's either that or trail through *Loot* for the next two months and end up in some Turkish bedsit in SE13.'

'But Fulham . . . it's Tosserama over there.'

'Oh, they're not too bad once you get to know them.'

'But I can't get to know them! They're all ice weasels!'

He sighed. 'Is this about the public school thing again? Are you getting all chippy?'

'Yeah, right, like I want a private income, a cushy job in publishing and long flicky blonde hair.'

'Oh, come on, Mel, stop being daft. Anyway, I need to live somewhere. I mean, it's not . . . it's not like we could live together or anything.'

I paused, that one instant too long.

'No, of course not.' Oh God, that didn't even sound like my voice.

There was a bit of a silence. Then he said, 'You know, I'm sorry I hurt you when I left. But it was because of things like this. You always want to push too fast, pumpkin. I mean, I've only been back a fortnight. Can't you, like, chill out?'

'Right. Right then. Ehrm, I'll phone you later.'

'No, Mel, don't be like this. You'll upset yourself. All I'm saying is that there's no rush . . .'

I hung up. Oh, bloody bloody hell! Maybe I should just get a T-shirt printed: 'Incredibly needy woman; gets very upset without constant attention and immediate commitment. Histrionic tendencies. Unable to live independent life without man. Disloyal to friends. Bursts into tears over nothing.'

I burst into tears.

I knew it had only been two weeks, but it hadn't really,

if you counted the year before he disappeared which now appeared to be my fault, but anyway . . .

My boss floated past again.

'Oh, my dear girl, I'm so sorry. Marketing will be absolutely fine, you know – they'll love you. Don't think of this as a setback, think of it as an opportunity. There there.'

He actually had a spotless handkerchief.

'And don't worry too much about your flatmate either.'

I struggled to remember why I might worry about her, and fortunately did.

'You can't take all the responsibilities of the world on your shoulders, you know. I tell you what . . .' He looked mischievous. 'Go on, take the day off. I won't tell a soul.'

I faked shock, but with a wounded little half-smile to show my complicity.

'I know, normally something I'd never do. But go on. I reckon you need it.'

Truly, the sweetest man in the world. He even walked me to the door, talking loudly about some imaginary new project. I felt an odd sense of *déjà vu*, then escaped to the fresh air – hooray!

A free day in London when I was feeling totally depressed and my boyfriend was moving to Fulham. What to do? Well, I could go shopping, I supposed. Or perhaps I could go shopping. I decided I was absolutely depressed and therefore deserved shopping and should go at it with a clean conscience. Linda hadn't put the rent up for two years, so actually I was fairly solvent. Even though I hadn't shaved my armpits and didn't have my shopping underwear on, I headed for Regent Street.

They'd put the Christmas decorations up, which made

me realize it was only November. Months and months and months of winter to go. Oh, and Alex was going to leave me because I was a needy cow. And my best friend hated him. And my rival was getting married and going to have a perfect life. And she had size three feet! I nearly started blubbing again in the middle of the street, but pulled myself together in the usual way (imagining our school bully walking past, having become really successful, seeing me, and laughing), and headed for Dickins and Jones. The smell of perfume was instantly reassuring.

I wandered around Hobbs, thinking that it really was time to change my image and become a classy girl. But it was no use wearing brown with my brown frizzy hair and brown mousy eyes and brown freckles: I'd just look like one long walking poo.

Over in the sale section I started picking up bits and pieces, including a ridiculous pair of pink mid calf-length trousers a size too small for me because they were £79.99 reduced to £14.99 and, who knew, they might just make me look instantly fantastic. I don't know quite why I thought I suddenly resembled Fran, who had wonderful elongated limbs that were angular and gawky when we were small but were now wildly desirable. Anyway, it was hot in the changing room, and I kept falling out of the curtain trying to wriggle those things up my leg. By the time I had wangled myself into them and examined my overstuffed posterior in the mirror, I was feeling about as thoroughly foul as a person can without actual physical illness.

'Look at you!' I was saying to myself. 'You're miserable, so you come here and dress your legs up like two big fat pink sausages! What is the matter with you?'

I stomped out to see if the full-length mirror was going to help – chuh huh – and gazed helplessly at my dishevelled hair, sweaty red face, lumpy hips and the way my eyes appeared to have disappeared, as if in protest at all the crying, leaving behind only black smudges of mascara.

'Oh well, at least Alex isn't likely to walk past,' I thought, to console myself.

Angus walked past.

Slouching in what could only be described as an anorak, at first I thought he was going to miss me. Then he looked up and saw me in the mirror. For a second he seemed almost jolly, but he soon remembered himself – and my status as friend-of-Amanda-lover-of-Alex – and walked over stiffly.

'Hullo again.'

'What the hell are you doing in women's pants?' I hollered, using the well-known 'aggressive' technique to try and cover my embarrassment.

'Trying to buy my mother a birthday present. What's the matter with you?'

'Nothing. I'm FINE.'

'I like those trousers.'

'Bog off. Oh God, I'm sorry.' I was suddenly tired of being mean. 'I didn't really mean that. I've had a shitty day, then I got the day off and I thought that would be cool, but it's pissy and I'm FED UP.'

'Oh.'

We stood there, me in ridiculous pink trousers so tight that I couldn't get the zip done up, him in his anorak.

'Would you like a cup of tea and a bun?' he offered politely.

I snuffled a little. 'Yes, please.'

We sat together in the café rather awkwardly, surrounded by rich shouty women. I wondered if people were looking at us and speculating on what kind of relationship we had: I always did. Or maybe it was obvious he was my non-friend's fiancé's bitter little brother.

I looked a bit more presentable after I managed to get rid of the worst of the mascara with a wrinkle-creating rub, brushed my hair upside down, and shrugged back into my navy blue trouser suit – the one that almost made me look like my arse didn't stick out, although it did make me look flat-chested, and if I buttoned it up it was a bit Pee-wee Herman.

'Do you usually buy your mother lingerie?'

'No, I was just pissing about. I never know what to get her, so I drift about hoping something fantastic will leap out at me – then end up getting her a bath mat or something.'

I knew that feeling. I didn't know how many Delia Smith books my mother could take, but she was bearing up manfully.

'Why don't you and Fraser club together; send her on a cruise, maybe?'

'I don't know . . . How much money do you spend on your mother?'

'Hmm, well, about thirty pounds, I suppose.'

'Oh.'

There was a long pause, during which I started to worry in case I'd insulted his mother: I knew what the Scots were like. And just what I needed, too: to upset someone else in the world. I was losing a popularity contest with the ebola virus.

He frowned. 'That would get her about halfway into the Camden canal then?'

'Well, she is a bit of an old boot.'

He laughed at my utterly shit joke, which made me realize that he was feeling as uncomfortable as I was.

'Yes, I don't spend thirty pounds lightly,' I went on.

'I know. I could tell by those pink trousers.'

I smiled for the first time all day.

'Oh, thanks for the fashion tip, Anorak Man.'

He half smiled.

'What?' I demanded.

'Oh, nothing.'

'What? Is it, like, a magic anorak?'

'No.' But he was grinning now.

'Yes, it is, isn't it? It's a magic anorak that gives you – oh, I don't know, a supernatural ability to notate trains.'

'Hff. Actually, my lovely anorak is North Sea standard issue. I had to go see the BP people today and they take you more seriously if they think you just got out of the helicopter.'

'Wow, you've been in a helicopter?' D'oh. Who was I – Amanda?

'Yes,' he said seriously, 'just like Noel Edmonds.'

'Well, I didn't know you got to go in helicopters. I thought you went down pipes and stuff.'

'I do. But I need a helicopter to get me to the pipes. And the pipes are underwater.'

I was impressed, but wouldn't show it.

'So what are you saying, that this is, like, your James Bond anorak?'

He stared me straight in the eye.

'Yesh, schweetheart, thish ish my James Bond anorak.'

And, weirdly, that was the moment I fell in like with Angus McConnald.

An hour and a half later we'd bought his mother some hideous golfing memorabilia from the Disney shop. (She golfed. I'd wondered if maybe this was an obligatory Scottish thing to do, but apparently it was a real hobby.) And I'd bought some comfortable size fourteen navy blue trousers from Racing Green, which proved I was getting old, but I had to buy something.

A boy who liked shopping? I'd cheered up considerably, as I must have appeared to the world like the kind of girl that boys liked enough to go shopping with, even if they were a bit ginga. And we chatted easily about everything under the sun – except when we passed an enormous crystal display in one of the glassware departments. A young, smartly dressed couple were looking at it and checking things off on an enormous list.

'Marcus, you must hurry up and choose the place settings,' the girl was saying bossily. Marcus, who looked exactly as he must have done at the age of six, only larger, pouted and turned red.

Angus leaned over to me.

'Does everyone in London look up new minor peers five minutes after their fathers have died and move in on them like piranha fish?'

I turned to him in surprise. 'Do you know him?'

'I know the type,' he said darkly, looking at the girl. That pissed me off.

'Well, excuse me. I didn't realize it was international sexist day. And for your information, the answer is yes. I personally am killing time with you on my way to seduce Prince William.'

'Huh!' he said. Then, less grumpily: 'I didn't mean it like that.' Then he clammed up like a, umm, clam.

Still, it was time to go home anyway, and I really felt quite relaxed.

'It was good to bump into you,' I said lamely at the tube station.

'Serendipity.' He grinned through his anorak.

'Oh, a word with lots of syllables in it! Was that meant to turn me on?'

God, WHY did I say that? Angus turned red and neither of us knew what to say.

'Erm, no, no, it wasn't. I'll . . . see you later.' And he scuttled off into the crowd.

'Angus!' I yelled after him.

I caught a glimpse of his neon orange trim bobbing up and down towards the tube, then just in time he turned round.

'Thanks,' I shouted. 'Thanks for last night. Fran was really appreciative.'

He grinned again, infectiously. 'At your lady's service, ma'am,' he said, bowing low in the middle of Piccadilly Circus.

Alex had left a message saying he'd gone to the football, so I looked almost as mournful as Linda when we came face to face in the hall. Then I remembered my niceness campaign.

'Hey, Linda, how's it going? Off out?'

God, could I say nothing right?

'No, eh . . .' she hesitated, 'I was going to watch *The English Patient.*'

This girl was so weird. But, what the hey, there was more to life than drinking, uncommitted men and falling out with all your mates, so I joined her and slumped down with a large glass of white wine (it doesn't count as drinking if you're in watching TV).

I spent most of the film trying to figure out why Kristin Scott Thomas got to be Kristin Scott Thomas and I had to be me, until I happened to glance at Linda. Her whole face was overflowing — tears, snot, the works.

'Are you OK?'

'It's so saaad!' she snortled.

'But you've seen it like two hundred times. What, are you thinking, "Hey, maybe he's going to make it to the cave this time"?'

'Shut up. It's my film and you don't care. Nobody does.' She stared down at her toes, her face looking like it was melting. I had noticed a Kit Kat wrapper in the bin earlier, which didn't seem excessive, but who knew?

Oh God, situation. If Fran were here she'd say something smart and buck-upish, but it was only me. Someone once said that only the young can afford to be selfish, which gave me about two and a half more years. I didn't want to cope with this now.

'Are you OK?' I asked again. 'Do you do this every time you watch this film?'

She sniffed loudly. 'Maybe. Where's Alex?'

That put me off a bit. 'Ehm, he's at the football with the boys. He's moving in with Charlie, in Fulham.' That ought to cheer her up.

'Oh.' She looked at me through her thick spectacles, all steamed up from crying. 'Oh . . . you'll miss him.'

'Yes, yes, I will.'

Good Lord, we were bonding.

'We're still seeing each other . . . It's just till we find somewhere for both of us, know what I mean?'

She nodded her head vaguely. Oh no, I hoped she didn't find anyone else to move in, that would be rubbish. But when I looked at her I realized she wasn't listening at all; she had re-immersed herself in the drama. Which part was she playing in there, I wondered, behind the thick specs and the psoriasis. How much didn't I know about this totally rotund person whom I live with? Then I thought, sod it, and

– having (correctly) ascertained that there was no possibility of further Ralph Fiennes butt shots – lost interest in direct proportion, made myself some tea and had an early night for once. Well, it had been a big day.

Six

The following morning I awoke with the realization that: (1) for once, I didn't have a hangover, which felt weird, and (2) bugger it, today I had to go to work in marketing. And (3) Fran was pissed off with me, and (4) I would have to pretend to Alex that everything was FINE, and I'd never pressure him again, and (5) Alex wasn't lying there beside me, begging me not to get up, holding me to him, smelling good. Where the hell was he?

Was it raining? Oh, good.

I trudged into the office, almost but not quite late, in an insolent fashion. There were already strange men around my desk fiddling with my dead pot plant. Barney, wisely, was nowhere to be seen.

'So I'm moving already, am I?' I remarked to the builders (wryly, I thought).

'Don't worry, love.' The bigger of the two chaps looked at me with pity, as if they cleared out people's desks every day, which they probably did. God, they must be human misery experts. I thought he was about to say, 'Worse things happen at sea,' but he didn't.

'We'll have you out of here in no time.'

If only. Suddenly I realized that his mate with the funny ears and what looked like Copydex stuck to his chin was reaching towards my emergency didn't-get-home-but-had-to-go-to-work-drawer, the contents of which included knickers, tampons and the numbers of several reputable clinics.

'Errm, I'll get that,' I screeched, in what was patently not a casually helpful tone of voice.

The first guy gave the ear guy a 'seen it all before' look.

'Actually, love, we don't need to open the drawers to move the cabinet.'

'Right, OK, right.' Bugger it. I looked around for something else I could pretend to be helping with, but decided to settle for the 'I've just remembered something incredibly important' look and dashed off.

On the way downstairs to the marketing department, I paused to say goodbye to all my friends in the publishing unit, then I remembered I didn't have any.

'Off so soon?' I heard from Shirley.

'I thought she was part-time anyway,' said someone else and I made a face at her (to myself, obviously; I had no intention of getting my eyes clawed out with long fake fingernails with jewellery in them), and disappeared down to the bowels of the building.

The marketing department had been painted again – mmm, lime green and turquoise, how wacky. Somebody here wanted you to think of your job as fun – or else. Already I was scared.

'Hi there — you must be Melanie!' gushed someone who sounded so pleased to see me I assumed she must be a long-lost relative who thought I was rich. 'I'm Flavi!'

This was Flavi, prize bitch, with whom I'd been having a voice mail argument for nearly a year? Well, there you go. She looked like an over-made-up perfume counter assistant.

'Brilliant to see you! Are Tony and Elvis bringing your things?'

How does she know their names? I wondered nastily.

'Yes, I think so. I saw them upstairs . . .'

'Great, great, we have a space for you over here.'

Stop being so nice to me! What was this, first day at Malory Towers?

I moved to the space and looked at it, not quite sure what to do. The bloke to my right in the cheap suit and chains gave me a cheery Cockney nod. I recognized his face from various indistinct but possibly naughty photographs that got pinned up on the noticeboard after the annual Christmas party. No doubt I would recognize other parts of him as well. He was about twenty-one, skinny as a whippet, with plastered forward hair, shiny and heavy with gel.

On the other side, a sweet-faced chubby girl gave me a half-smile half-grimace, and I realized she was probably reflecting my own expression. Out of the corner of my eye I noticed a run in her tights and warmed to her.

'Hello there!' I said heartily, putting a brave face on it, like I did in the majorettes when they picked Amanda to lead the marching band. Cheery Cockney lad gave me a smirk.

'Alwight, dorlin? Wot you in for then?'

'Five to ten, unless I behave myself.'

'Roit,' he said, with an odd little sidelong glance. He was obviously wondering if I was trying to be a smart arse and, if so, what I was doing trying to usurp his position.

I turned to the left, but the girl with the ladder in her tights was obviously having a deeply personal conversation on the phone. Huh. I busied around tidying things up – like that was something I usually did – so Flavi wouldn't come over to see how I was doing. When lunch time came, *at last*, I went out to find a payphone. Well, I didn't want to look too bad on my first day.

As I walked out into the freezing afternoon, I didn't even want to think about where Alex had spent the night. Last time I'd phoned Charlie's house, he'd been six thousand miles away.

And he hadn't even called me, the bastard. I was ready to get deeply upset when I remembered that Elvis and Tony had had the phone disconnected all morning, so he couldn't have got in touch even if he had wanted to. *If* he'd tried, I thought grimly. But I decided to give him the benefit of the doubt, and tried my house first. Surprisingly, Linda answered the phone. I really didn't want to talk to her. After a quick mental battle with myself as to whether to just say 'Sorry . . . long number' in a dreadful Chinese accent and hang up, I asked for Alex, without identifying myself.

'No, he's moved his stuff out. Melanie, is that you?' she asked wonderingly.

'No! Sorry! Bye,' I said, and put the phone down, slumping against the wall. He'd moved his stuff out. Another fucking moonlight flit. Where had he gone this time? I wondered to myself. China? Tibet? He could stick that North Pole up his arse, see if he could find himself with that. Fuck! How could he?! Again?

I noticed a particularly virulent prostitute's card stuck up in the phonebox. A woman was bent over with her wrists tied to her ankles. Above a childishly written phone number it said: 'Melanie, new to the area, submissive – loves punishment. Will service your every need.' It was a sign. Definitely a sign. But what could it mean?

I had a disconsolate sandwich and wandered back to my new home, where the rat-faced man to my right was vigorously enjoying a ridiculously stinky hamburger. Small pieces of lettuce and indescribable goo were dripping on to my . . . what looked like my . . . well, anyway, an enormous bunch of flowers dumped straight on to my desk. My mind went through the options: David Duchovny; the cast of *ER*; Alex, from the North Pole . . .

Out of the corner of my eye I noticed the girl with the ladder in her tights trying to weep inconspicuously.

Very carefully, I picked up the bouquet. 'Hey, pumpkin,' it said on the card. Terse as ever. I relaxed.

'Sending flowers to yourself again?' coughed Ratto, mildly spewing me with burger phlegm.

'No, actually, they're for you. Oh, have you got a boyfriend called Alex as well? What a coincidence!'

'Think you're funny?' muttered Ratto, and returned to his mastication.

I turned to the girl.

'Are you OK?'

'Yes, I'm fine,' she whimpered, clearly not fine. 'It's my contact lenses.'

The man with Copydex stuck to his chin eventually came downstairs with my phone sorted out. The voice mail appeared to have been switched off, and when I looked up Charlie's number in the phone book it had been scrubbed out furiously – although whether by me or Fran I couldn't say – so I was stuck sitting there, still vainly tidying, till it rang.

'Hey there.' Alex spoke softly. The tone of his voice made me soften.

'You've moved your stuff,' I said.

'Well, there didn't seem to be any point in hanging about. That flatmate of yours was giving me the evil eye.'

'Really, she's cross-eyed. She was really giving me the evil eye.'

'Ah.'

There was a pause.

'Did you . . .'

'I got . . .'

We spoke simultaneously.

'I got the flowers. Thank you. They're gorgeous.'

'I wanted to apologize. I didn't mean to hurt your feelings, and I should have phoned you when I stayed at Charlie's last night. I just don't want to take anything too fast. But, you know, we've got so much time. To get back together. For everything.'

'I know.' I sighed. 'It would have been daft. Far too quick. Etcetera.'

There was a silence, then he spoke tentatively.

'Friends again?'

'Just friends?'

'Oh no. And will you come and visit me in Fulham?'

'Nope.'

'Not even if I beg?'

'No, but you can try a bit of begging if you like.'

'Please!' he yelled. 'My darling Melanie, pearl and pumpkin of my life, take the immortal trip on the District Line and enter my realm of joy.'

I giggled.

'Nope.'

'Tonight?'

'Nope.'

'So I'll see you around six?'

'Nope.'

'Excellent. See you later then. Bring wine.'

He put the phone down and I smiled to myself.

''Oo's that, your lesbian lover?' said Cockney Boy.

'Yeah. Actually, it's your mum.'

'Fuck off.'

There was still Fran to deal with. I caught her at her house, or rather her bedsit. She lived sparsely, not far away from me in Kennington.

'Franster?'

'You've got your ingratiating tone on. Let me see: you want me to sponsor you on a round-the-world bike ride for badgers? You need me to donate some bone marrow? Or has Alex moved in with that creep Charlie and you haven't done anything about it?'

'Ehmm . . . are those all the options?'

'Yup.'

'I'm sorry! I couldn't, not for that! He wouldn't understand! Oh, Fran, don't make me . . .'

'God, what is this, *Sophie's Choice*? OK, fine. You want to go out with a wanker that lives with another wanker, then fuck it, that's how it is, flowers or no flowers.'

'You know about the flowers?'

'What? Yeah, I got a big bunch, from Charlie. Odious little creep.'

'Ohhh. I got flowers from Alex.'

'How nice. They obviously bought them in a job lot.'

'Hmm. How big was your bouquet?'

'ENORMOUS. What about yours?'

'Average. Average to good.'

'Ha ha ha. Listen, bloody Amanda phoned me again.'

'Wow, now she's falling in love with you.'

'She just wanted the gossip on Charlie. And she wants to know if we'll help her pick out a tiara.'

'I'd rather eat my feet with a spoon.'

'Me too.'

Seven

We were sitting in an All Bar One, after spending six hours with Amanda trying to choose a fucking tiara because her mother was in the Priory, a drying-out clinic so exclusive that Amanda managed to make it sound like an absolute honour to end up there, and her bridesmaids were all in Barbados or somewhere. Not only had I been forced to make admiring noises in Amanda's direction as she tried on four thousand identical filigree things that cost more than I make in three months, I'd had to stop Fran from shoplifting out of delirious boredom. It had been a tiring day.

'So, 'manda, when's your hen night, then?' asked Fran.

Unusually, Amanda didn't immediately start talking. Instead, she blushed.

'Ehm . . . I'm not sure I'm going to . . . you know, nothing big.'

'But you just said you wanted to do everything properly!'

I said, the implications not hitting home. 'You can't get married without a hen night!'

'Ehm, yes, I know . . .' Her voice trailed off. 'Ectually, ehm, I am having one, but with a few close friends from varsity.'

I was genuinely shocked.

'What?!' said Fran. 'When? Why didn't you invite us, you bitch?'

'Ehm, it's in a couple of weeks. Look, I'm sorry. I didn't want to hurt your feelings.'

Yeah, right . . .

'. . . I'm sorry. But, you know, I didn't invite you because you'd probably get drunk and cause a fight. You two are always getting into trouble. I mean, aren't you, darlings?'

She gave a little laugh.

'Fraser and I, well, in the position we're in now, we have certain friends and, anyway, we're going to Quagli's, and that's so expensive, and then Yanna's, and, well, it's just going to be my close friends really. You do understand, don't you?'

'Close friends! Amanda, you came crying to us when you had two periods three days apart in primary seven!' Fran was furious. 'And when Daryl Stobson said you'd gone up the bikes with him and everyone believed him, we convinced them all otherwise for you, even though it was true!'

That was true?

'Oh, for God's sake, Francesca! Can't you see that this is exactly why I'm not inviting you? What if you started coming out with that kind of . . . crap in front of all my friends? You'd completely show me up. We're just . . . Things are different now.'

'No, they're not,' snarled Fran. 'You're still the spoilt little cow you always were. God, I pity Fraser. Come on, Mel, we're off.'

96

She dragged me up by the sleeve.

'Are . . . are we . . . still invited to the wedding?' I couldn't help asking, pathetically, as we left.

'Yes. But then everyone is,' sneered Amanda, turning away from us.

Outside, I could see Fran's nostrils flare like a horse.

'That stupid cow,' I said companionably.

'Oh, who gives a fuck!' said Fran. 'It's not like I even want to go to that poxy wedding anyway. What do I give a toss for? Prats in cravats? Some chinless wonder whose life she's about to make a complete misery?'

'Fraser's not a chinless wonder.'

'Yeah, right, and Alex isn't a complete piss weasel.'

We walked along in grumpy silence for a while. Then a brilliant idea occurred to me. Really, a brilliant, brilliant idea.

'Of course,' I began subtly, 'we could always . . .'

Fran looked at me sideways. 'What?'

'No, no, you probably wouldn't like the idea.' Heh heh heh. My reverse psychology skills were second to none.

'OK, cock that then.'

We marched on in silence.

I started again.

'We could always' – it came tumbling out – 'ask Angus if we could go to the stag night instead, and really piss her off.'

'My reverse psychology skills are second to none,' said Fran. 'But, you know what?'

'What?'

'Oh no, you wouldn't be interested . . .'

'What?' I said.

'That is not at all a bad idea.'

'Thank you,' I said proudly.

'We could annoy them big time. In fact, a few little words in Fraser's ear . . . Maybe we should let him know what little missie is really like before he gives her a castle and stuff.'

I looked at her, shocked.

'What, like, talk to him about Amanda?'

'Why not? You're his friend, right?'

'I suppose so.'

'And if you saw a friend about to be eaten by a crocodile, you'd warn them, right?'

'Hmm.' It sounded a bit dubious to me.

'A big, poisonous crocodile, Mel!'

'Do you get poisonous crocodiles?'

A look at Fran's face convinced me that you did.

'Well,' I concurred, 'then, yes, I suppose I would.'

'Jamesh Bond?'

'Hullo thair, Moneypenny.'

'You know the Evil One, whom that brother of yours insists on marrying?'

'The person of whom you speak is not unfamiliar to me.'

'Well, I have a secret mission for you that could piss her off mightily.'

'Tell me more.'

I explained her treacherous betrayal, and he instantly saw no trouble at all in inviting us to Fraser's stag night.

'Even though I'm not best man, I'm still doing all the organizing. McLachlan can't sort his way out of a paper bag, as you'll see when you meet him.'

'Are there going to be strippers?'

'Why, do youse two want to do it?'

'Do you think Fraser would approve?'

'Och, you know my brother. He'll be hiding under the table anyway. Yes, there might be a stripper, but nothing, you know . . .'

'What?' I asked innocently. I could sense his pink face getting even pinker over the phone.

'Now, stop being a naughty girrul. It'll be fine. Saturday night, starting at the Princess Louise. And tell that skinny pal of yours not to get into any more fights.'

'Ha! You tell her! Then I can watch her kick your head in.'

Alex was faintly perturbed that he hadn't been invited to the stag do and we had.

'You don't even know him,' I pointed out. 'You've met him about twice.'

'I know Amanda and her friends.'

'Well, go to her hen night then.'

'No thanks. Bunch of screaming Harpies. Why aren't you going?'

I rolled my eyes at him.

'Long story. OK, look, why don't you tag along with us? No one's going to mind.'

Except Angus, who inexplicably hates you, I thought. Oh yes, and Fran, who barely tolerates you.

'Well, OK then,' he said diffidently, as if we'd all been begging him to come for hours.

He stretched his legs out on the chaise longue. Charlie's place, while lovely and clearly very expensive, was done up in boy-meets-mother style. Soft furnishings – no doubt spares from the country – shared house room with mountain bikes; expensive and overwrought stereo equipment rested on expensive and overwrought occasional tables. Over it all was a faint aroma de rugby kit. Still, I was making the two-hour trip to West London more and more often, as Alex showed a marked reluctance to cross the river now he didn't absolutely have to. It was Sunday afternoon.

Charlie walked in and ignored me as usual.

'Splinters!' he hollered at Alex.

'Fishcake!' returned Alex, and they burst out into hearty guffaws.

'I've got tickets to Twickers on Saturday.'

Alex leapt up. 'Fantastic! How'd you manage that, you old bastard?'

Charlie tapped his Huguenot nose. 'It's who you know, innit?' he said in fake Cockney.

'That's Fraser's stag night,' I said.

Charlie's heavy half-shut eyes lit up. 'Stag party! Wo ho ho!'

'And you are NOT invited,' I added.

'How do you know? It's a stag party. Blokes, beer and birds, way hey!'

'Because I'm going, and Fran's going and – oh yes, a whole bunch of other people who actually know the groom.'

Charlie was obviously ruffled by the mention of Fran but merely swept through to the kitchen saying, 'Totty at a stag party? Shouldn't be allowed. Sounds like absolute crap, if you ask me.'

'Shall we go out for lunch?' I asked Alex pointedly.

Alex gave me a hangdog look and trailed out the door after me.

'Got you by the apron strings there, hasn't she, matey boy?' I heard as we left.

*   *   *

'I don't think,' I said, walking down the street, 'that I could dislike that boy any more than I do. He's such an . . . an oaf.'

'Charlie is not an oaf!' said Alex, looking cross. 'And he doesn't like you either.'

'Boohoohoo,' I said. 'The molester doesn't like me.'

'You get more like that friend Fran of yours every day,' he said.

We ate lunch reading the papers sullenly. Eventually, I kicked him under the table and gave him a grin. He grinned back and raised his eyebrows, and we returned to the papers in relative harmony, reading out our favourite small-time celebrity shagger-of-the-week stories, before Alex had to disappear for a tour in his friend Henry's new car — a two-seater, natch.

That friend Fran of mine was waiting outside my flat when I got back later that afternoon.

'I can't see why you won't just give me a key,' she huffed.

'I can't see why you think you actually live at my house.'

Fran slouched herself off the wall and deigned to mount the stairs to my flat. She still looked good being pouty, given that most of us had grown out of it at nineteen.

'Anyway . . .' she said, sitting down and lighting a cigarette. This was strictly *verboten* in Linda's house, but she didn't look in the mood to be trifled with. 'That molesting bastard friend of your very own personal bastard phoned me to ask me out for a drink.'

'What? Charlie? NO! When?'

'About two hours ago.'

'Jesus. So, this time he's going to buy you dinner before he attempts to rape you.'

'Looks like it,' said Fran, narrowing her eyes.

'God. That really takes the piss. No wonder you got the big flowers. What did you say?'

'I didn't say anything: he left a message asking me out. Well, I think he did. You know what posh boys are like. He said, "Maybe a drink sometime, right, yars, OK, right, yars, sorry, right, bye then, yars." So, statistically, it could have meant anything.'

'What are you going to do?'

'I'm not sure. I mean, I could tell him to take the phone, stick it up his arse and dial 999 with his prostrate now, or I could do it loudly in front of a lot of other people somewhere public.'

Now I came to think of it, this could be good. This could be very good indeed.

'Ooh, do the second one. Where's the most public place you could actually dump him?'

'Well . . .' She exhaled in an actory way and leaned forward. 'First I thought, what's the highest-rated TV show? Then I realized that what we'd have to do is qualify for *Stars in Their Eyes*.'

'Don't tell me . . . Sonny and Cher?'

'Keith Harris and Orville.'

'Yuk. Who'd be Orville?'

'Who d'you think?'

I winced. 'Well, I suppose he'd be used to it.'

'Quite.'

'So, you'd dump him on *Stars in Their Eyes*?'

'Oh no. We'd win that, bring out a cover record, get asked on to pull the National Lottery lever, and *then* I'd dump him.'

'Wow! An almost flawless plan.'

'What do you mean, "almost flawless"?'

I put my arm around her.

'I'm sorry, dear. But I don't think even the real Keith Harris could win that show.'

She sighed melodramatically. 'I know. Unless we were up against the fake Joe Dolce.'

'What's Plan B?'

She giggled maliciously. 'Plan B is the table next to Amanda's bunch of slavering Sloane witches at her hen night. I thought I'd do lots of shouting and maybe set things on fire.'

I loved that plan.

'Oh yes, please, please do that, please.'

'Unfortunately it's on a Friday night, and they're full up.'

'You checked?' I asked, full of admiration.

'Well, I'm not called . . .' she paused. 'What am I called?'

The man-chomping gonzo of South London, I didn't say.

'Ehm . . . no one calls you anything. Except Fran.'

'Huh. Well, anyway, so, plan C.'

'?'

'Keep reading the papers.'

'What?'

Fran lifted up her profile dramatically.

'I am going to shag him to death.'

Oh no. Fran had done this shag-to-death routine before. It was never pretty. It involved a man having a night he would probably never forget, with a woman he would never normally have a hope of scoring with – i.e. Fran – then having to follow her around in humiliation for weeks begging for a second chance. It had never failed so far, and was a punishment kept for the most flagrant transgressors.

'Are you sure?' I asked her. 'That's pretty serious.'

'It's poetic justice,' she announced sternly, reaching for the phone.

'Charlie! Hello there! How lovely to hear from you!'

I danced up and down furiously in front of her doing more and more elaborate vomit-miming. She reciprocated by making wanker motions in time with her talking.

'Yes, that would be super.'

I couldn't not laugh.

'Eight thirty? I'll see you there . . . OK, bye now.'

She put the phone down and I let out a suppressed snort of laughter.

'He's dead!' I said. 'You just killed a man stone dead!'

'I doubt he'll be able to even get it out of his pants,' said Fran. 'It's almost too easy.'

Next day I got in the lift by mistake before remembering my rightful place back in the lime green basement.

Cockney Boy was on fine form. 'Hey, snoots!' he yelled at me. I gave him my best contemptuous look. I was a bit worried that I was taking all my career angst out on him. Then I looked at the rash of unbroken pus spots under his shaving line and thought, well, if needs must . . .

'Snoots,' he said again, 'I got off with this girl last night, right. She was all over me.'

'I know,' I said, smiling sweetly. 'She's left some dog make-up on you.'

'Ha,' he said, without humour. 'Bet you just stayed in watching *EastEnders*, then?'

'Yes, I did, actually. I didn't know you had a part-time acting job as Robbie Jackson.'

He sneered at me and left me alone. On my right, Janie was red-eyed again. We hadn't got past the everyday stage of my asking her if she was all right when she clearly wasn't, to which she would vehemently nod while being on the brink of tears. I got her a coffee, and didn't get Cockney Boy one, and her eyes brimmed over at such basic human kindness.

At lunch time I took a book and a ciabatta roll – the cool effect rather spoiled by a packet of beef Hula Hoops – into an alcove I'd discovered behind reception. I was rather cross to find it already occupied. Janie was there, snivelling away into a disgusting piece of green tissue. I sighed and mentally abandoned my peaceful lunch.

'OK, tell me: what's the matter?' As long as it wasn't a lifelong infatuation with *The English Patient*, surely I ought to be able to do something. Oh God, I hoped it wasn't cancer or anything really tough. Or her parents dying – oh no! That would be awful. I cringed in anticipation. I'd always thought of myself as a kind person, but now I realized that was in fact a complete fallacy. I was really a path-of-least-resistance person. Damn!

Gradually, the sobbing started to slow down. I patted her tentatively on the shoulder, and said 'Don't worry!' encouragingly. This brought on a fresh wave. My sandwich began to fade away into some dried-out afterlife in my mind.

Finally she stumbled: 'It's James . . . my boyfriend . . . It's – boohoohoo . . .'

Oh well, at least it was something I could deal with. Not-quite-up-to-scratch boyfriends were my speciality.

'Right, tell me all about it,' I said. 'Has he moved to Fulham to live with someone you absolutely hate?'

'No,' she looked up, momentarily surprised.

'Whoops, no, that's me,' I remembered. 'Well, what's he done?'

'He wasn't at home last night . . . and he didn't even phone me.' The last part of the sentence was drawn out in melodramatic sobs.

'Ehm, so what?' I said gaily. 'Who are you, Ally McBeal?

It's not that much of a problem! He was probably just out for a pint or something.'

She sniffed loudly. 'Why didn't he ring me, then?'

'Why? Are you two married?'

'No.'

'Have you got kids? Pets? Lice?'

'No.'

'Well, why did he have to ring you then? You're both independent.'

God, this was good advice. I was brilliant at this.

She sniffed again.

'Did you phone him?'

'Yes,' she said quietly.

'More than once?'

'Yes.'

'How many times?' I asked, not wanting to know the answer.

'Oh, well . . . I pretty much just –'

'– pressed the redial button all night?' I interrupted.

She nodded mutely.

'Pfff. Bad news. How long have you two been together.'

'Six weeks.'

I heard *Psycho* music in my head.

'Oh . . . OK.'

I settled back into the potted plant. This story was obviously a long one.

It was, but nothing original. After being dumped by her fiancé well into plate-planning stage, she had clung on to any passing flotsam ever since. James was a stock-broker and sounded perfectly dull and nice and nothing to worry about.

'Nothing to worry about,' I said. 'He sounds perfectly . . . nice. And at least he's rich.'

'I know.' She pouted a little. 'When we get married I think we could get one of those nice houses in Clapham . . . if he ever speaks to me again.'

Hang on there, schizo girl!

'He doesn't know you're getting married, does he?'

'No.'

'Then for God's sake, Janie, leave him alone. He's going to do what he's going to do anyway, whether you're crying about it or not.'

She looked as if she was about to cry again.

'Come on. Stop it. You know it's true. Leave him alone. He sounds nice and you're going to drive him away.'

She sniffed in a final kind of a way and looked up at me.

'I know. I'm sorry. I just get a bit daft.'

'Huh! Don't worry about that,' I said heartily, trying to get my hand round to where my sandwich was.

'What about you?' she said suddenly. 'How's your love life?'

'Oh . . .' I raised my eyebrows quizzically. 'It's good. It's fine. No, really, I mean, it's OK, most of the time . . . Well, ha ha, you know how it is.'

'Oh well,' she said. 'Any time you want to talk about it, just let me know.'

Hang on, I thought. Wasn't this . . . I mean . . .

'Righty-ho!' I said. (I never say 'Righty-ho.')

I looked out through the atrium into the rain.

'Hula Hoop?'

'Thanks,' said Janie, and took four.

Eight

Alex phoned that night.

'Hey, pumpkin.'

'Hey yourself.'

'What are you up to?'

'Oh, you know, just hanging around the house in my black, silky, lacy underwear – oh, it's so warm! I must unfasten my negligée.'

'Yeah yeah yeah.'

'Oh! Is that the door? Goodness me, hello, plumber. Have you come to . . . clean out my pipes?'

'Mel, shut up for just one second.'

'OK . . . big boy.'

'Listen, ehm, Charlie really wants to come to this do on Saturday night.'

'No he doesn't. He said it sounded complete crap.'

'Well, when I got back on Sunday he said he really wanted to come, and could I ask you.'

'God, what's the matter with the boy, is he a Johnny No-Mates? Is this the first party he's ever been invited to? Hang on, no, I mean, is this the latest party he hasn't been invited to?'

'No, I don't know what it is. He just keeps pestering me, and I said I'd ring you, that's all.'

'Ah ha ho – I think I know.'

'What? What is it?'

'I'm not telling you. And no, he can't. He's annoying.'

'Oh, go on, Mel – please. Please. For a mate.'

'A mate? Who, you?'

'Well, you know what I mean.'

'You're my mate?'

'Yes,' he said. 'Your soul mate. Now, please, please can you get Charlie an invite?'

'Alex, is he going to chuck you out if you don't wangle him into this party?'

'Ehmm . . . yes?'

'Good. No, he definitely can't come.'

'I'll . . . do the washing-up.'

'I . . . probably wouldn't notice.'

'Oh, go on, Mel. It'll be a laugh.'

I sighed. 'Fine, fine, if it means that much to you.'

'Fantastic.' His voice turned curious. 'Why does he want to come so much then?'

Ha! I don't think Alex really needed to know that. Fran had obviously commenced the process.

'Ah,' I said. 'Well . . .' I said. Then inspiration struck. 'Apparently, Charlie's never seen a stripper before and there apparently . . . might . . . be one.'

'No, really? I've never seen one either.'

'Good God, what is the public school system coming to these days? Anyway, good. I'm glad you're happy. I'll see you on Saturday . . . unless you feel like popping round now . . . ?'

'Jeez, Mel, it's two hours away.'

'Oh! So it is. Saturday, then.'

'Bye, pumpkin.'

'Bye, sweetpea.'

I phoned Fraser to check the rapidly extending guest list was going to be all right. Angus had already OK'd our presence by threatening to withhold stripper privileges if we weren't granted entrance, so at least Fran and I were in the clear. Amanda answered.

'Oh, hi,' I said coolly. I was prepared for this. 'Is Fraser there?' Hee hee hee.

'Is that you, Mel, darling?'

Uh-oh: what was this, scary reverse psychology? Maybe she was planning on turning my legs into the legs of a chicken.

'I'm dreadfully sorry about the other day, darling. Pre-wedding tension and all that.'

I didn't know what to say. She seemed to have had pre-wedding tension for the last twenty-six years.

'Don't worry about it,' I mumbled.

'Darling, I'd love you to come to my hen party. Honestly.'

'But . . .'

'No, no "but"s, darling. Please, do come.'

'What about Fran?' I said loyally. Also I'd be too scared to go on my own.

She sighed. 'Yes, and Fran too. It's Quagli's at eight, a week on Friday. We'll squeeze you in somehow.'

'Have you been dropped on the floor and landed on your head?'

111

'No, darling, it's just . . . I thought . . . Oh, it would be so silly and embarrassing for you two to have to go to Frase's stag night. I mean, the humiliation . . .'

'Oh no. We're still going to that. It's going to be a right laugh,' I said.

'Darling, don't be a silly. It's for boys. They won't want you!'

I knew it! She couldn't bear not being the centre of attention for even one tiny microsecond.

'Can I speak to Fraser, please? And thanks for inviting us . . . eventually. It's a sweet thought.'

'Look, I'm only saying this to be kind . . .' she said nastily, 'but he doesn't really want you there. It's only because that retarded brother of his thought it'd be a laugh. Fraser thinks it'll be embarrassing too. You'll be the laughing stock.'

SHUT UP, WITCH! I badly wanted to say.

'Look, Amanda,' I said, as calmly as I could, 'it'll be fine. We'll all be fine. Don't worry about us. Can you put Fraser on the phone, please?'

There was a pause, and some frantic whispering. I wanted to hang up, but forced myself to stay on the line.

'Urr, hullo,' came a familiar gravelly voice.

'Ehm, hi, Frase . . .'

There was a bit of a pause. I could picture Amanda in the background, drawing her finger across her throat . . . dramatically uplit like the queen in *Snow White*.

'Frase, do you really mind us coming on your stag night?'

Fraser was obviously weighing up his options of girls plus stripper or nothing.

'NO. DEFINITELY NOT.'

The stern tone surprised me.

'DO YOU UNDERSTAND? DEFINITELY NOT, OKAY!'

Then he put the phone down. I hugged myself with glee.

112

We were going all right. Although I did find Fraser tricking his fiancée slightly worrying. I mean, I was allowed to hate her — I wasn't going to marry her.

I remembered I'd forgotten to ask him about Alex and Charlie. Oh well, surely they could blend into the background.

Finally, with the phone feeling welded to my ear, I managed to catch up with Fran, and told her what had happened. She was pleased.

'I'd have given anything to be a ghost and have crept into her room and seen her face when that happened.'

'Er, wouldn't you rather just be a fly on the wall?' I said.

'Would I rather be a fly than a ghost?'

'OK, can we have this conversation later? Because NOW you are going to tell me what happened with Charlie.'

She laughed evilly. 'Oh, my dear, I couldn't possibly tell you on the phone. Really, it was disgusting. Quite brilliant. Almost a shame to have to punish him, really.'

'But you're going to.'

'Sadly, rules are rules. And I'll see you on Saturday. Has he phoned up and begged to come?'

'Yup.'

'*Excellente!*'

Saturday was fast approaching, and I realized that I had no idea what to wear to a stag night. Cockney Boy was most surprised that we'd been invited to a stag, and even offered to teach me how to make a selection of suggestively named cocktails.

Janie was looking much better, apart from jumping six feet every time the phone rang and asking me whether I thought it was too early to introduce James to her parents.

I pondered this for a bit.

'Well, I've always found the will reading to be the only really safe time. That might just be the boys I know, though.'

She turned green, and I wished I'd kept my mouth shut.

I debated with myself whether to wear jeans, then decided against it, in case we ended up in one of those nightclubs that preferred cheap shiny Top Shop suits to real clothes. A good frock, however, was not the thing, as it would surely be raining beer at some stage. Anything tight or short was out, in case of stripper identity problems. And nothing too plain, or I might be mistaken for a dyke, which is why I had to come to the boys' night out. Yikes. That pretty much just left my bought-on-a-whim catsuit, so called because if I ever walked past any cats in it their fur went on end and they made a 'ssssssssssssssssssssuuuuuuuuu' noise.

Fran turned up, looking glorious in something dainty and impossibly trendy. This was getting worse. I picked my kilt up from the back of the cupboard. Fran shook her head imperiously. Just as I was hopping about in my black tights gazing at some weird Japanese kimono thing which had somehow turned up in my clothes, the doorbell rang again.

'Can you get that?' I said. 'It'll be Alex and Charlie.'

'Ah, my two favourite men,' she purred languidly.

Fran swanned out of my bedroom and I could hear rowdy voices. Oh well, she sounded like she was being civil. Then Alex's voice drifted into my room:

'PLEASE – look, will you just stop calling me a cocksucker?'

I grinned to myself.

They did sound noisy, though. Oh God, I hoped they weren't drunk already. That would be dreadful.

114

Finally settling on smart chinos and a flowery shirt, I shoved on some mascara and lippy and popped outside.

Alex and Charlie had hauled out one of Linda's bottles of wine and were debating in loud voices exactly which hilarious rugby song they were going to sing next. Uh oh. I looked at Fran, who nodded and raised her eyes. They were absolutely, gloriously, buggeringly drunk.

'BESTIALITY'S GREAT, MATE!' shouted Charlie.

To which Alex immediately responded:

'PUT YOUR LOG IN A FROG, MATE!'

'PUT YOUR GEAR IN A STEER, MATE!' hollered Charlie lustily.

'BESTIALITY'S GREAT!' they concluded together, holding each other up.

'Oh God,' I said to Fran. 'We can't take these two with us. They'll be awful.'

'You tell them.'

'Oh, why does it always have to be me?'

'Yeah, right, like I invited Charlie.'

At the sound of Fran speaking his name, Charlie fell to the ground and clasped her round the ankles. She kicked him.

I turned round to face the boys. They were both very red in the face, and the wine was sloshing around dangerously.

'Alex, you're completely pissed,' I said, trying not to sound too headmistressy.

'Jesus, gorgeous, you sound just like my old headmistress,' he slurred, wobbling backwards and forwards.

'You're not coming to this stag night like that!'

'STAG NIGHT! STAG NIGHT!' they started chanting. Charlie got up off the floor and looked around, puzzled. 'Are we there?'

'Oh, shut up!' My patience was gone, and I couldn't cope. 'You're not coming, so you might as well just fuck off.'

'PUT YOUR LOAD IN A TOAD, MATE,' started Alex inexorably.

'PUT YOUR GOO IN A ROO, MATE,' Charlie joined in.

'Oh God,' I said to Fran. 'What shall we do? Make a run for it?'

'Oh, good idea,' she said. 'Then when Linda gets back from Singles Night at Tescos she can find them prostrate in vomit and weeing on her carpet.'

'BESTIALITY'S GREAT, MATE! BESTIALITY'S GREAT!'

'Maybe we can take them outside, then lose them.'

'Good idea. Just as well you've already taken Alex's set of keys back.'

'Shit.'

'Look, let's go. They'll probably be all right.'

'SHE CAN SHOOT GREEN PEAS FROM HER FUNDAMENTAL ORIFICE!' shouted Charlie suddenly. Fran and I stopped talking and turned round.

'That's the wrong song, you twat,' said Alex.

'I KNOW!' hollered Charlie. 'Err . . . PUT YOUR POLE IN A FOAL, MATE!'

'THAT'S MORE LIKE IT!' yelled Alex. 'PUT YOUR STAFF IN A GIRAFFE, MATE!'

'Oh God.' I sat down, then stood up again when I realized I was sitting in the wine and spittle range of fire.

'This is great. This is just great. First, Amanda is never speaking to us again for going behind her back.'

'Yeah. One: who cares, and two: how is she going to find out?'

'Oh, probably shortly after these two get arrested and in the papers.'

'HAVE A SHAG WITH A STAG, MATE!'

'HAVE INTERCOURSE WITH A HORSE, MATE!'

'Then,' I went on, bravely, 'we turn up at this thing and get thrown out, and Angus and Fraser never talk to us again. So, in the space of a day I've managed to alienate about thirty-three per cent of all my friends. Not to mention Alex, when he wakes up tomorrow and I'm beating his face to a bloody pulp.'

'Why don't you do it now, when he won't notice?'

'What would be the point of that?'

'Come on.' Fran took me by the arm. 'Let's get this over with. Maybe they'll fall out of the taxi . . .'

'Yeah, and into another dimension. C'mon, you two, we're going.'

They started to sway towards the door.

'UP THE CRACK OF A YAK, MATE!'

'HAVE A FRIG WITH A PIG, MATE!'

And the four of us sang, going down the hall:

'BESTIALITY'S GREAT, MATE! BESTIALITY'S GREAT.'

We nearly got thrown out the cab, and it took all my conciliatory powers to get us to the Princess Louise pub, in Holborn. I shot a nervous look at Fran, but she appeared extremely cool, even though Charlie was trying to get on his knees in front of her to express his true and heartfelt devotion in loquacious terms. Every time he got too close she kneed him on the crest of his rugby shirt.

I took a deep breath at the door, squared my shoulders and headed in.

'Neh, it's a private party up there, mate,' said this extra-ordinary talking-monkey thing.

'Yes, that's right,' I said. 'Fraser McConnald's stag do.'

'That's Laird McConnald,' added Fran helpfully.

The monkey raised its eyebrows.

''Ere, are you the . . .'

'No, we're not. We're invited guests. Come on, Mel –' and Fran shrugged us through imperiously.

As in werewolf films, the inn fell quiet when we entered the room. Lots of young men were standing around having a perfectly nice comfortable drink, and here were two pairs of breasts all set to ruin it. A couple of the blokes even had cigars, if it could be any more Freudian. I wanted to turn on my heel, but, fortunately, Angus came to the rescue.

'Hey, hullose there!' He walked over, beaming. 'Glad youse could make it.'

His smile fell as he looked over his shoulder and cottoned on to the collapsing figures of Alex and Charlie.

'I'm sorry!' I said straight away. 'They were going to get thrown into the river in a sack and we didn't have the heart to leave them.'

Angus half smiled. 'Och well, they're here now, I suppose. Is he –' indicating Charlie – 'going to cause any trouble?'

Fran had somehow managed to conjure a cigar out of nowhere and was proceeding to look felinely wonderful with it.

'Oh no,' she purred. 'He won't be any trouble, will you, big boy?' And she winked at Charlie like some thirties vixen until his eyes popped.

Angus looked understandably confused then turned back to me.

'Can I get you a drink?' he said eagerly.

'Ehm . . . bottle of Budvar, please.'

'I'll have a long vodka please,' ordered Fran imperiously.

'A what?' I said, when Angus had gone to the bar. 'What are you playing at? Queen of all the Vamps?'

'Oh, go on, Mel,' she said. 'Look around. There's forty

118

blokes here and two of us. When's the last time I got off with a bloke?'

'Thursday.'

'He doesn't count. That was duty. And tonight he's hopelessly drunk, while I'm in the mood. I'm a prowling lioness. So stay out of my way.' She took a draw on her cigar and blew smoke rings at me.

'Huh. Well, my boyfriend's here . . .' I looked over. Alex was slumped on a sofa, stupefied. 'So I have to behave myself.'

'Do you?'

'Yes!'

Angus arrived back with the drinks, and Fran downed hers in one. Eyes shining, she looked around the room. 'Who's . . . that?' she said to Angus, eyes trained on a sweet-faced, wan young man standing by himself next to the punch, and helping himself liberally to it.

'That's Johnny McLachlan — he's the best man. Why, do you want to meet him?'

'Yes. Have him washed and —'

'Fran!'

Angus clearly thought we had both gone mad, but he beckoned Johnny McLachlan over anyway. Johnny McLachlan did a huge 'Who, me?' double take, and eventually sidled up, slightly hunched over.

'Johnny, meet two friends of ours, Melanie and Fran.'

'Hi,' I said.

'Enchanted!' exclaimed Fran. 'Now, tell me all about yourself and how you came to be darling Fraser's best man.'

'Aye, well, hullo,' said Johnny, in an accent so thick he made Angus sound like Princess Anne. 'Well, actually, like, Ah'm a geography teacher, likesay.'

'How fascinating!' Fran leaned over intimately. A sweat broke out on Johnny's forehead.

Through mutual eye contact Angus and I moved to one side.

'What on earth is going on with your friend? Is she on heat?'

'I think so.'

'Is she serious?'

'Serious? Well, if I were Johnny, I'd take out some life insurance.'

'Eaten alive?'

'Sucked clean.'

'Woo.' There was a pause.

'Oh, I remember what I came for,' I said.

Angus looked at me quizzically.

'The bridegroom? That whole wedding thing? Horseshoes and stuff? You remember!'

'Oh yes. I'm being a terrible host. Let me –' and he bowed and proffered me his arm – 'escort you to his lairdship's table.'

'You are too kind.'

Fraser was sitting on a large leather banquette in the corner, surrounded by some rather technical-looking young men, whom I assumed were fellow engineers. They all looked rather doleful, and not as if they were having a primeval bonding experience at all.

'Hey,' I said, still on Angus's arm.

Fraser looked up and grinned.

'Hey, yourself. Glad you could come.'

'Me too. Is it going to get you into trouble?'

'Och, Fraser's always in trouble – aren't you, lad?' said Angus, and the whole table burst out laughing. Fraser smiled ruefully.

'Of course not. Everyone is sworn to secrecy.'

There was a chorus of, 'Yeah, right!' and 'How much are you going to pay us?'

'Did you bring that terrifying friend of yours?'

'Yes. She's over there, being terrifying.'

Fraser looked over.

'Oh my God, poor wee Johnny. You haven't set her loose on him?'

'Nothing to do with me, I'm afraid. Apparently she's being a lioness tonight.'

Angus and he swapped a look.

'I was at primary school with Johnny. Haven't seen him much since then, but he qualified as oldest pal when I was looking for a best man. God, I hope she doesn't get her claws into him . . .'

In the corner, Fran was quaffing another martini, with one hand on Johnny's lapel. He was laboriously trying to explain something to her – oxbow lakes, probably, but I could tell she wasn't listening, just throwing her head back with raucous laughter.

'He's been married eight years and his wife never lets him out of the house. He only got to come here because I promised there wouldn't be any strippers.'

'Fraser, just how many lies did you have to tell to get this party together tonight?'

'I don't even want to think about it. Who's for another?'

'Way hey!' shouted the boys at the table, and bumped up to make room for me.

They turned out not to be doleful at all, just serious about deconstructing the *X-Files*, e e cummings, politics, stand-up comedy and the general state of the world today, at least in so far as it related to the world of engineering and *Dr Who*. Strangely, I found them fascinating and non-judgemental company; infinitely relaxing. Of course, not having to buy any drinks helped.

Every so often there would be a loud grunt or guffaw, as Alex and Charlie seemed to have descended to the level of bestial communications. But just as I was thinking how very, very fond of Fraser's friends I was, there was a muttering at the door. In walked a woman in a large coat, out of which was peeping a pair of open-toed stilettoes and fishnet tights.

All relevant political and cultural debate instantly went flying out the window. I suddenly had a lot less room on the bench as the testosterone level rose and the boys suddenly needed plenty of space to splay their legs wide open.

Behind the stripper was an enormous man who managed to make finding a plug point for the tape recorder seem imposing. Immediately, 'Hey, Big Spender' started up. Without removing her cigarette, the woman walked nonchalantly to the centre of the room and, showing no perceivable interest, slipped out of her coat.

The previously well-mannered and charming boys beside me turned into a host of baying beasts. The roaring was incredible, punctuated with wolf howls as the woman did a desultory shimmer to 'Spend . . . a little time with me.'

Eventually, she started to walk towards our table. An excited 'Way hey!' went up as she bent over to have her bra strap undone, with the bloke she approached only just able to restrain himself – after a sharp look from the bouncer – from pinging it. The bra went whirling through the air and landed near a surprised Fran and Johnny, who were snogging like they'd just invented it over in the corner.

The bra got a big round of applause, but all eyes quickly came back round to the main attraction. The boys' eyes were wide as saucers as the woman stifled a yawn, shot me a dirty look (I thought), and stuck her leg up on the table to undo her suspenders.

I stifled a yawn myself, and looked over to where I'd last left Charlie and Alex, muttering like two old alkies at a railway station. Alex was tottering uneasily to his feet, being egged on by Charlie. As I watched, hypnotized, ignoring the mounting hysteria behind me, Alex picked up the gold lamé-trimmed bra and put it on over his shirt, dancing along to Shirley Bassey. He approached Fran and Johnny, making lewder and lewder movements, while Charlie shouted encouragement. Finally, when all eyes had gone past her, the stripper turned round to see Alex rubbing her costume like a towel between his legs.

''Ere!' she shouted, which was enough for the bouncer to stop looking menacing and do some actual bouncing.

He walked over to Alex and put his hand on his shoulder. Incredibly drunk, Alex leered up at him uncomprehendingly. Charlie, however, was back on his feet again.

'Leave him alone!' he shouted petulantly.

The bouncer gave Charlie his best ominous look.

'Yeah?'

'Yeah! Or you can just . . . fuck off!'

There was an ominous silence, except for the inaudible noise of me attempting to disappear. Oh my God, he'd done it again. And I had brought him.

Very deliberately, the bouncer retrieved the bra from Alex's limp hand and laid it on the table. Then slowly, almost tenderly, he led both the boys outside. Nobody moved as some cartoon scuffle noises reached us from the other side of the door. After about three minutes the bouncer came back in, actually dusting his hands down.

'You coming, Leese?' he said.

123

Leese was already dressed – in her own terms. She stood in front of Angus while he paid her, then the pair left in a dignified silence.

I closed my eyes in horror. Nobody said anything. Then finally a lone Glaswegian voice from the back said plaintively:

'Well, I thought the bloke was a better dancer, ken.'

I opened half an eye. Fraser turned round, but there was a glint in his eye.

'You mean I brought a stripper to my stag night for a crowd of fucking poofs?'

The whole room guffawed with relieved tension, and new rounds were ordered in. I went up to Angus.

'Oh God, I'm so sorry. I mean . . . oh, they're just . . . I'm sorry.'

'I know what you mean,' he said kindly. 'Why don't you tell me all about it?'

'I will, I need to go see if Alex is OK.'

'Why? He deserved it.'

'No he didn't! It was just a prank.'

'Not to her it wasn't.'

'Oh well, you know what boys are like.'

'Huh. Not all of them.'

I could feel him watching me as I headed out the door. Fran and Johnny were now looking distinctly biological, and I averted my eyes.

Outside, everything was quiet. I couldn't see the boys anywhere, or even hear any muffled groaning. I pondered the situation for nearly half a second, heard a burst of boyish laughter from upstairs and decided to head back to where the warmth and beer were.

Inside, everyone's faces were looking redder. Fran and Johnny were nowhere to be seen, but the lads were presenting

124

Fraser with a blonde blow-up doll, which happened to look extremely like Amanda.

Blushing, he stood up as Angus sidled alongside me and pressed a bottle of beer into my hand, which I swigged gratefully.

'I wanted to say . . .' Fraser started manfully.

'Get yer tits oot!' shouted the Glaswegian wag.

'Shut up, Nash.'

I turned round to see who Nash was. *Gosh, he doesn't sound black*, I found myself thinking, then immediately felt like the stupidest person in the world.

'I just wanted to say,' continued Fraser 'that it's good to see so many of you here.'

'Apart fae yer best man!' someone shouted, and there was a burst of obscene laughter.

'Yes, well, apart from – ahem – Mr McLachlan, who seems to be otherwise disposed.'

'Aye, up the bits of some tart.'

'Hey!' I said to Angus. 'That's my friend they're talking about.'

'What, not your friend that was behaving completely like a tart?'

'Huh. Well, maybe.'

'OK, calm down . . .' Fraser looked slightly unsteady. 'I just wanted to thank you all for coming, and I know some of you came down a long way. Getting married is a frightening thing, although not as frightening as seeing you shower all in the same room at the one time.'

There was a friendly muttering.

'No, really. It's great to see you all. I'd like to thank my brother for getting everything organized, Mr Flaherty for the loan of his pub, and . . . well, just the whole big bunch of you lads.'

125

'And girls!' I squeaked.

'And honorary lads,' said Fraser, bowing in my direction. I grinned.

'So, get some drink down you. Oh, and sorry about the stripper . . .' he petered out.

'To Fraser!' shouted Angus.

'To Fraser!' said the company. I think I was the only one who noticed that he'd missed out the bride from the toast.

'To the stripper!' shouted someone else.

'To the dirty bint that's taken Johnny up the close!'

'What?' I asked Angus. 'Is that rude?'

'Never mind.'

We wandered back over to Fraser's table and rejoined the company.

The evening wore on – the landlord was an old drinking buddy of the McConnalds' father, and wasn't too bothered about licensing restrictions. I lapsed into lovely drunk time, where things just floated past, and I jumped in and out of different conversations at will. After dissecting the genius of Billy Connolly on one side, I tuned in like a radio to the other, where Angus and one of the Scottish boys were deep in serious conversation.

'Just talk to him,' Angus was saying.

'Look, I only met her once. She seemed all right.'

'She's not all right. She's a complete cow and she'll make his life hell. This is why I got you all down here – to persuade him not to do it.'

'What are you two talking about?' I exclaimed brightly.

'Nothing,' said Angus shortly, turning back to his pint.

'Have you met this "Amanda" that Frase is marrying?' asked the other chap.

'Course I have. I've known her all my life.'

Angus looked up at me.

'What's she like then?' the bloke asked.

I paused, not quite sure what to say. Idiotically, I suddenly felt quite loyal. It was all right for me and Fran to talk about Amanda having her gizzards ripped out by vultures, but with anyone else it wasn't really on.

'Well, she's . . . really pretty, and dead rich. She's nice.'

'Fair enough,' said the bloke to Angus. 'I'm not saying anything. You should never get involved in these things. My sister married this right bastard and she wouldn't be told anything.'

'What happened?' I asked.

'Oh, yeah, he turned out to be a right bastard. Left her with the kids and everything.'

'Oh, for God's sake, Mel!' burst out Angus. 'She's a complete bitch and you know it.'

I sighed.

'Sorry, forgive me if I'm being slow here, but you talk about her non-stop. I mean, why do you hate her so much? And Alex, and Charlie – well, it's OK to hate Charlie . . . But, I mean, when I met you, I thought you were really awful, 'cause you hated us all so much. But now I know you're not, you're actually really nice, so I don't understand it at all. Are you a secret communist? Do you hate posh people? You're posh anyway. Well, your brother's a complete nob . . . I didn't mean that last bit the way it sounded.'

'Have you finished?' asked Angus.

I thought for a second. 'Ehm . . . yes.'

He rubbed his eyes with the heel of his hands.

'Look,' he said, 'if I tell you something, do you promise on your life that you won't tell Fraser?'

The third bloke was still with us, unwilling to draw

attention to himself by getting up and moving away, but embarrassed to be listening to something personal. He was staring very hard at the ashtray.

'Maybe,' I said. 'Maybe on my dog's life.'

'Be serious. You don't have a dog.'

'OK, no, I promise.'

He looked away. 'I overheard her. On her stupid minuscule mobile phone. When she came up to visit our mum a few weeks ago and behave patronizingly towards her. She had to lean out of the window to get a signal, and I was in the next room.'

'With a glass up against the wall?'

'With the window open. Look, do you want me to tell you or not?'

'Yes please,' I said meekly.

'Anyway, she was talking to *Hello!* magazine.'

He paused dramatically. I looked at him like he was crazy. '*Hello!* magazine? That's it? You're trying to wreck their marriage before it even starts because of *Hello!* and its . . . its inane pictures of unhappy celebrities??'

He ignored me and went on.

'She was offering them the rights for the wedding. I heard her. She promised them she could "get Tara". You know, they love all that minor aristocracy bullshit. "Aren't Posh People Lovely? Here's a picture of one standing next to a horse." That kind of thing. Bitch!'

He grumbled into his pint.

'I don't understand,' I said. 'She was just trying to get her picture in the paper.'

'No,' he said slowly, as if I was an idiot. 'She asked them for £15,000 to let them take photos and have an –' he imitated her shrill tones – '"in-depth interview with me about the new castle . . . not much point talking to the aristo, darling — you know what they've got between the ears, hee hee."'

'Jesus. Did she get the money?'

He looked at me grimly.

'I don't know. Fraser certainly hasn't heard anything about it if she did.'

'No. You don't think she half-inched it do you?'

'You're talking about . . .' he turned away. 'You're talking about the woman who turned up, entirely by coincidence, in my brother's life a month after our dad dies, we're all completely fucking shell-shocked – still are – and guess what? He's blinking in the daylight and they're engaged. So she can get on the cover of fucking *Hello!* magazine. She's probably been through every Right Hon in the country. I think she's capable of it, don't you?'

'I'm sure that's not true,' I said, not sure at all. 'I'm sure she loves him.'

'Why? What, honestly, do you think someone like her sees in someone like him, apart from that stupid falling down piece of medieval crap in Kirkudbrightshire?'

I looked over. Fraser looked sweaty and dishevelled, and his curly hair was falling in his eyes. One arm was round his big pal Nash, the other round Amanda the blow-up doll, and they were all (the doll was faking it) singing 'Danny Boy' very very badly and making up the words.

'I think losing one member of her family's enough for my mum this year, don't you? That fucking title. Just because you're all modern women who can do anything, you think that kind of thing doesn't happen any more. But it does.'

He reverted to staring at his drink. His face was red. I stared hard at the table.

'I think we need another drink,' I said.

'I'll get them!' shouted the bloke at our table, jumping

up and rushing across the pub. We both looked after him, startled. As we turned round, Fraser and Nash made a bravura attempt at the high note at the end of 'Danny Boy' then immediately fell away as, silhouetted in the doorway, stood the very wan, very dirty Johnny McLachlan, looking for all the world as though he had, indeed, just been mauled by a lioness.

A roar went up, as Johnny dazedly walked back amongst the tables with his eyes wide open. There was no sign of Fran behind him. He sat down, heavily at the bar, his eyes red.

'A large one, please.'

There was a crash as Nash and the doll fell over laughing. Everyone in the room was guffawing and clapping Johnny on the shoulder. I suddenly felt very much the lone female.

I picked up my drink and headed off to the loo, and to look for Fran. It was like one of those Agatha Christie books, where the party gets picked off one by one. Everyone was extremely drunk now, and the whole scene was becoming confusing. I sat in the bathroom for a long time, fully dressed and staring intently at the dirty floor tiles while trying not to fall off the toilet.

I had no idea how long I'd been there when I heard someone get into the cubicle next to me.

'Fran!' I whispered urgently.

There was a long pause.

'Err . . . no. It's me.'

It was one of the brothers, but I couldn't tell which one. It sounded like Angus.

'What are you doing in here, you twat?'

'Oh, the boys loos are looking . . . pretty revolting. There's blood in them. Mixed with —'

'Oh, OK, I don't want to think about that right at the moment.'

130

'Sorry.'

'It's all right. Is that Angus?'

There was another pause.

'Erm . . . yes.'

'Oh. Look, I'm sorry about what I said. I'm really sorry. I didn't realize . . .'

'That's OK. I get a bit grumpy sometimes. I suppose it's because everyone thinks my brother's so great.'

I heard what sounded like a strangulated giggle, but chose to ignore it.

'Look, really I agree with you,' I said. 'I think Amanda's a cow, and you think Amanda's a cow, but your mate's right: there's no point in interfering, is there? People simply do things, whether you want them to or not. Tough. Who knows: maybe she's different with him than she is with everyone else on the planet.'

Suddenly the toilet next door flushed and the door banged. I gradually sat upright and let the blood flow back down from my head. Shakily, I opened the cubicle door. Shit.

'You lying fucker!' I yelled at him. I was furious.

Fraser was bright red. 'I just wanted to hear what you were going to say. What were you sorry about?'

'It's none of your fucking business was what I was going to say! I was talking to Angus, not you! What a stupid thing to do.'

'Right, just because you're too pissed to tell one voice from another.'

I stared at him. 'Oh, so it's my fault. What? I don't know. I don't know why I'm even having this conversation. I do NOT give a toss.' I headed out the door. He caught me.

'Look, I'm sorry. Please don't go.' There was a note of urgency in his voice.

131

'Fine!' I was on my high horse now. 'I can stay, go . . . I do NOT give a toss, remember?'

'Shush a minute. Please. I'm sorry.'

We stood there for a bit in silence. Then he set his lanky frame on the hand basins, his long legs kicking out in front. He got his arse wet, but didn't seem to notice.

'Is it true . . . ?' he faltered. 'I mean, do you . . . does everyone . . . ? Oh, fuck it.'

He took a deep breath and started again.

'Look, with Amanda and everything . . . I thought her and Angus just didn't hit it off. She point-blank refused to let him be my best man after he asked her why she was inviting all these people she barely knew just because they were famous.'

'Not Sean Connery's son?'

'Yes, people like that. Well, it's her job, isn't it?'

That sounded familiar.

'Ah mean,' he said quietly, 'you're practically her best friend. Don't you like her, either?'

His voice was so soft and sad I couldn't bear to hurt him.

'Sweetheart, she's not my best friend. I hardly see her. I hardly know her these days . . .'

I could tell by his face that that tack wasn't working. 'I mean, she's fine. Really, I've known her for ever . . . Look, do you remember at college, when I wanted to go out with Flattypuss Malloy? And you couldn't bear him because he had a lump on his neck?'

'It was gross! Really – especially from where I was standing.'

There was at least a foot's difference in height between us.

'And he was really nice after all?' I pursued.

'He was a lumpy bastard.'

'Well, sometimes people dislike other people without us understanding the reasons for it.'

'What happened to him, anyway?'

'I heard he painted a second face on it and rents himself out at parties.'

'Wow.'

We pondered that for a second. I looked at my reflection in the mirror. Either a mouse had walked across my face or I was having a seriously bad mascara attack.

I decided to make one last attempt.

'Look, when Amanda wants something,' I said, truthfully, 'she goes for it. She's completely single-minded and nothing holds her back.'

Quite unlike myself. I touched him gently on the face. His eyelashes cast a shadow on his cheek.

'So, therefore, she must really, really want you.'

He looked down at me with a wounded look in his eye.

'Do you really think so?'

'Yes, I do.'

He sighed.

'Do you love her terribly much?' I asked, suddenly longing for a bit of highly dramatic romance in my life.

'She's . . . you know, pretty and confident and, well, she knows lots of people and . . . stuff . . .' Fraser looked down. 'And, you know, she really wanted to marry me!'

'Was that so difficult to believe?'

He grinned. 'I don't know.'

We got a few limp 'Woah hos!' when we emerged from the ladies toilets together, but the single-entendre brigade was getting pretty tired, and the room was definitely a bleary party ready to go home. Fran was still nowhere to be seen, so I decided to brave it home alone . . .

I waved cheerily to Nash and found Angus in a corner, finishing a whisky contemplatively.

'I'm off,' I announced.

'Bye then.'

'Look, I'm sorry,' I said, for the second time that evening.

'What for?' he smiled wearily. 'We just had a discussion, that's all.'

'Yes, I suppose so.' I wasn't going to tell him about what happened in the loo . . .

'You never told me about . . .'

'What?'

'You never told me about Alex.'

'It's a long story.'

'So you said before. I've got lots of time.'

'Some other time then. Umm, when there's lots of it. And not tonight, when I have twenty-eight minutes and counting before I pass out wherever I am.'

I leaned in to kiss him good night. Unexpectedly, he put his arms round me and gave me a hug.

'Do you want me to come and find you a cab?'

'I'll be fine,' I said gratefully. 'This is Holborn, for God's sake – what are they going to do, sue me to death?'

'Goodnight then.'

I grinned, turned and left, before I could do something clumsy and spoil the moment.

Outside I spotted a cab and was just putting up my arm when I heard my name being called, weakly, from an alley.

Discounting the obvious, I assumed it was an evil spirit coming to reclaim me for the night, and jumped six feet in the air. When I saw the arm coming out of the alley, I discerned it was at least semi-human . . . I hoped.

I wandered over and crouched down beside the sorry specimen.

'Woooooah, Alex! I came looking for you earlier – I thought you'd gone.'

'I wasn't feeling too well.'

'What on earth happened to you?'

'Um, he hit me. Then I felt a bit tired and had a sleep. Then I woke up and didn't know what to do. And then you came.'

'That's because I am in fact an angel from God,' I said severely. 'Can you stand up?'

I wanted to work out how bad a state he was in. Still pissed, he had a gorgeous black eye coming up, but his nice patrician nose remained in a nice patrician state, and I didn't think he'd broken anything too major. I hoisted him to his feet.

'And also, I was sick.'

'Aha, so you were!' I said, noticing suddenly, but managing not to drop him like a stone.

'Charlie?'

'Dunno.'

'Fran?'

'Dunno.'

I sighed.

'Come on, you.'

I hailed the cab. The driver slowed down, saw me half-carrying a bloody, vomity war victim and speeded up again.

'Bastard!' I yelled after it. 'Poxy poxy bastard.'

One freezing November hour later, all my pleasant, muddled, drunken feelings had evaporated and I was cursing London, cursing parties, cursing cab drivers, and especially cursing the enormous stinky sack of potatoes I had been

135

delegated to haul around just because I was in love with it.

Finally we found a minicab driver too hashed up to care about the vomit – actually, judging from the smell of the cab, it was his speciality – and made it back to Kennington for 3.30 a.m. The entire building was silent and completely black.

Alex only wanted to get to bed, but he wasn't going anywhere near me in that state, so I dumped him fully clothed in the shower and turned the water on.

Instantly, he started to make a noise like a howling dog. I made a flying tackle through the air, which successfully cut off the howling, but not without pulling the shower curtain down. It fell with a huge clatter as I stood there, hand over his mouth, tilted at a horrible angle and getting soaking wet, with the curtain over us both like a huge ghost outfit, waiting for the entire neighbourhood to descend and throw shoes at me. Alex looked up at me, wide-eyed and lost, as I closed my eyes and tried to think where on earth I could possibly move to when I got summarily ejected from the flat.

Nothing happened. I flopped out from under the curtain and tilted my head like a fox. Not a sound. I pulled Alex out, having wiped most of the dried blood off his face. He stood there dumbly while I tried to silently fix the shower curtain then decided to ignore it and hope it went away by the morning.

Sunday was half over by the time I limped through into the kitchen desperate for fluid. I drank half a pint of milk – YUCK – which was all there was, and steeled myself to go check out the bathroom. It was immaculate, as if we'd never been in. The curtain was back up, the blood was washed away.

I wondered for a second if I'd dreamt it, then shook my head to clear it.

'Ehm, Linda?'

I timidly knocked at her door. She opened it the way women do on *The Bill* when their men are escaping over the back fence.

'Yes?' She peered at me through her thick spectacles.

'I'm . . . sorry about the shower curtain.'

'S'OK.'

'I mean it . . . I'll, buy you another one, or . . . ehm, I'll buy you another one.'

'S'OK.'

I didn't want to get into a staring match with her, so I gradually backed away, feeling creepy, and went back to the bedroom with another glass of milk. Alex was still completely unconscious, and his eye was turning fluorescent.

'Alex,' I hissed, flopping down beside him. 'Alex! Wake up! I'm frightened of my anti-social flatmate! I think she's going to chop me up with an axe! And leave me here, and no one will find me for three weeks!'

'Pfnat.' Alex tried to open his eyes and realized he couldn't, because they'd been punched. He focused on the glass of milk, and his eyes bulged and his skin turned green.

'NO! Don't vomit!' I pulled the glass away. 'Again!'

His eyes slowly closed and he passed out.

'Great,' I thought to myself. 'Caught between the silent psycho and the unconscious phlegm machine.'

I had to get out of the flat. And, of course, I had to find out what had happened to Fran. I thought I'd go round rather than phone; get some fresh air and hangover supplies. Pulling on a pair of jeans and a couple of random jumpers, I wandered out into the frosty afternoon.

* * *

Fran lived in a practically empty bedsit, about half a mile down the road. It was white, immaculate and had absolutely nothing in it. This wasn't really a design statement: she had no imagination, and hated the place, which was why she practically lived around my house – it may have been full of psychos, but at least they were company. I set off manfully, stopping for some emergency Diet Coke infusions before I too vomited from a milk overdose. And a beer overdose, I suppose. The main door of the block was lying open as usual, and I made my way upstairs.

'Yoo hoo!' I yelled outside the door, banging on it loudly.

'Rise and shine, sweetie pie. We have BIG time gossip to do, ESPECIALLY you, Ms Yo-Yo Knickers.'

There were sounds from inside, and I could hear someone moving about.

'Come on!' I yelled impatiently. 'I need to find out about you and that skinny little twerp, and tell you about Angus and Fraser and everything.'

There was more noise on the other side of the door – what sounded like someone trying to pull on a pair of trousers, losing their balance, hopping about a bit then crashing over on to the floor.

It suddenly occurred to me that she may not, in fact, be in there alone. I tried to remember what had happened to Johnny McLachlan when he'd returned to the bar. Shit! He must have left and come back here! Argh! I hoped he hadn't heard me call him a twerp. And she didn't even know he was married! Or – yikes! – we hadn't found out what had happened to Charlie. Maybe she'd gone back on her shag-to-death routine for once. Wow, she'd be annoyed. Oh no, the married man or the prick! *Too* many cocktails.

I leaned into the door.

'Erm . . . d'you want me to go away and come back later . . . ?'

It was too late: Fran had already swung the door open. She stood there, looking exhausted, with a man's shirt on and a towel round her waist. I grimaced.

'I can go away, you know. It's no problem.'

'Hello, Mel,' she said wearily. 'No, I suppose it's OK.'

She drew back her arm from the door, and I entered the fuggy, darkened room – to see, of all people, Angus, looking extremely sheepish indeed, checking the zip on his flies was done up properly.

'!' I expostulated.

We stared at each other. He flushed beetroot, and I tried to recover myself.

'Hi!' I said brightly, shooting a fierce look at Fran.

'Hullo,' said Angus, looking at the floor. He pretended to look at his watch. 'Ehmmm . . . I'd better go . . . I told Fraser I was going to . . . ehm, help him pick a cravat.'

I nodded slowly. We all stood stock-still, until Fran realized it was her cue to take his shirt off. He practically grabbed it, and buttoned it up at lightning speed.

Fran, refusing to look embarrassed, stood poised in her bra. For a moment, I thought she was going to shake him by the hand and thank him very much for coming, as it were.

Angus left, stuttering. I left it a full half-second and turned round.

'WHAT the FUCK was that?!!!??'

'Oh for goodness' sake, Melanie, no need to get so overexcited.'

'Overexcited?? Me?? I'm not the one who managed to shag two people in an eight-hour period.'

'Neither am I, darling. Shall I put the kettle on?'

'Huh? What on earth is up with you?'

Fran walked around the small room pulling up blinds and opening windows, before putting the coffee maker on. I was standing in the middle of the room, wringing my hands in frustration.

'Tell me!' I begged her. 'I thought it was my job to get drunk and misbehave!'

Fran looked dreamily out of the window until I wanted to kill her. She'd always been fairly mercenary in her dealings with the opposite sex, but this was just too bizarre – first Charlie, then Johnny and now Angus, of all people. My new friend Angus, who, I had to admit to myself, I thought had rather liked me, (1), and (2) I had thought was rather noble.

Finally the coffee was ready and she sat down beside me in her 'Frankie Says Relax' T-shirt, which still fitted her.

'Please, Fran,' I said, trying to sound calm, 'just tell me what's going on. Are you on a special mission from space to sleep with everyone we know?'

She patted me gently on the hand. 'It's not what you think.'

'What, there are animals involved as well?'

'No.'

'What then?'

'Well, you know I was being a lioness?'

'Oh yes. So in fact there *are* animals . . .'

'Johnny wasn't quite up to being a lion.'

'I'm not surprised. You practically ripped his head off.'

'That is not true.' She shot me a sharp look. 'We'd gone outside . . .'

'Yeah, to get arrested.'

'. . . for a breath of fresh air . . .'

I snorted.

'. . . and before we'd gone two yards, he burst into tears.'

140

'Honestly, Frannie, that does not surprise me.'

'Mel, does anyone ever tell you that you talk too fucking much?'

'Ehm, yes, actually. Quite a lot. Funny, Alex was saying just the other day that I always talk more when . . . I'm –' I saw her thunderstruck face – 'nervous,' I finished.

Fran harrumphed. 'Anyway. He burst into tears and said he hated his wife and his life and his job and I was the nicest thing that had ever happened to him and how depressing everything was and this was the only party he'd been to for eight years and how I had no idea what it was like teaching geography day in day out to a bunch of illiterate animals.'

She paused, waiting for me to comment, but I wasn't saying anything.

'We ended up in the bar downstairs, with me having the most boring, sober three hours ever, listening to someone else's ghastly life.'

'Why didn't you escape, and come and find me? I was having a great time.'

'Every time I made the slightest move, he started weeping into his pint again and saying I was the best friend he'd ever had.'

'Oh no.'

'Honestly, Mel,' she looked at me haggardly, 'have you any idea how much I know about the amount of paperwork involved in the National Curriculum?'

'Well, it'll come in handy if you ever play Miss Jean Brodie,' I said encouragingly.

'So, finally, I decided I was going to have to leave before I started plunging a fork into my thigh. And then he tried to get off with me!'

'Well, you can understand it from his point of view.'

'Cheeky bastard! If he's going to be a pale and interesting

stranger, that's fine. If he's going to bore the tits off me for three hours about his wife, then he can go piss up a rope, as far as I'm concerned.'

'You are possibly the kindest person I've ever known.'

She sighed. 'I *know*. So, I sent him off with a flea in his ear.'

'Did you hit him?'

'Not that hard. Whining little toad! Then I sat and had a drink or two. And then I came back upstairs again, looking for you.'

'I stayed to the end, so I must have just gone.'

'You had – I saw you from the window, dragging Alex up the road.'

'And you didn't come and help?'

'It was freezing out there.'

'Yes, it was, thanks.'

'And there was almost no one left in the bar except for Angus, who was propping himself up with some double whiskies.'

'I know, I saw him before I left.'

'He looked pretty miserable, so I started talking to him.'

'Did he mention me at all?'

'Ehm, no, not at all.'

'Oh. OK.'

'Why?'

'No reason.'

'Huh.' She gave me another sharp look. 'Anyway, he was pretty drunk, so I let him stay here. And that's the end of it.'

I was extremely relieved.

'So, you didn't sleep with him?'

'Oh well, yes, I slept with him.'

'You are dreadful!'

'I'm dreadful? Who's worse, Angus or Nicholas?'

'That's not the point.'

'That's exactly the point. Anyway, it's hardly serious.'

'You don't even fancy him. You think he looks like a dog.'

'It was you that thought that.'

'Was it?' I couldn't remember thinking that now. Except in the sense of dogs being strong but kind, I suppose. Hang on, dogs didn't have those qualities. What on earth was I thinking about . . . ?

'How's Alex?' asked Fran, sipping her coffee.

'Who? Oh, I think he's OK.' I told her about the shower.

'I hope he's not concussed or anything,' I said suddenly. 'Oh my God! What if he's in a coma for years, all because I didn't take him to the hospital!'

'Then I could perform my special little happy dance,' said Fran. 'Now, drink your coffee and I'll tell you what Angus is like in bed.'

And she did.

I left Fran an hour or so later so she could get some much needed sleep, and walked home, my head spinning.

After buying bacon and eggs, I let myself into the flat quietly. I couldn't hear anything. I was about to tiptoe into the kitchen when there came a sorrowful groan.

'Mel . . . is that you?'

I peeped into my bedroom, which reeked of whisky.

'Alex?'

'Yes . . .' he said weakly.

I sat down next to him on the bed. His eye had gone red and purple and green, but wasn't swollen shut any more.

'How are you feeling?' I asked tenderly.

143

'Like I've been run over by the Death Star.'

'Oh, sweetheart. Can I get you anything?'

'No milk, please,' he said. Then he half smiled. 'Were we awful?'

'You were naughty, and your friend was evil.'

He laughed, and then winced.

'We didn't mean anything. We just went to the rugby and had a few pints . . .'

'And then chaos happened. Amazing that, isn't it?'

He forced a slow grin. 'How awful?'

'You didn't do anything you didn't pay for.'

'I could have had him, you know.'

'Course you could, sweetheart.'

'If I met him again, I'd take him . . .' He reached out for me sleepily, and I let myself be grabbed.

'I'm the most tolerant girlfriend in the world, you know.'

'I know,' he said, asleep. 'I know.'

Nine

I was absolutely desperate for somebody to talk to at work, but the prospects weren't good. Only Cockney Boy, whose name was, inevitably, Steve, bothered to ask me how the stag went.

'It was great,' I said. 'Turned out the stripper was gay and I copped off with her.'

'Yeah?' he grunted, his eyes wide as saucers.

'No.'

'Lezzie cow! Probably couldn't cop off with anyone,' he muttered under his breath.

'Not true, actually. Normally I let the boys watch. But only the ones I like . . . so, tough luck!'

He grimaced at me and went back to his work, which as far as I could tell was mostly colouring in.

'How are you doing, Janie?' I asked her, using the soft, invalid voice I reserved for the troubled of heart.

'Well,' she said bravely, 'he had a ticket for the rugby on Saturday, but came to Ikea instead.'

'See? He loves you. Anyway, I was at this party on Saturday night, right . . .'

'But then he didn't want to go to the Homes and Houses Exhibition at Earls Court . . .' She started to sniffle a bit. 'And he didn't come round until the end of *Football Focus*! When it was too late to go!'

I stared at her. 'Are you bonkers? You can't take him to the Homes and Houses Exhibition after two months. You can't ever take him to the Homes and Houses Exhibition. Jesus! You're going to have to stop reading the bloody *Daily Mail*. Anyway, there was this bloke at the party who I thought quite liked me, right, but he went off with my best mate. And I can't fancy him anyway, because my boyfriend is terrific and I'm completely in love with him. But he's – the first boy, not my boyfriend – trying to sabotage his brother's wedding and he wants me to help him. Apart from which, he's really nice. But, obviously, I'm in love with my boyfriend. But I'm really pissed off that the first bloke slept with my mate. Almost like I was jealous – if I got jealous, which, really, I don't. So, what do you think I should do?'

She stared at me, mouth open.

'Apart from take them both to the Homes and Houses Exhibition and see which one can find the hardest-wearing carpet?'

Unbelievably, she had tears welling up again.

'I only wanted to look at cushions. Cushions aren't too committed, are they?'

Arrgh! This was it. I was going to have to phone the Samaritans and ask them. Although, knowing my luck, they'd only give me lip or be completely distracted. I put on my martyred expression and turned towards Janie in a saintly fashion.

'Ookaay. So, first of all, why wouldn't you let him go

to the rugby? He's a boy. Boys need rugby. Believe me, I know.'

She blinked at me. 'Do you let your boyfriend go?'

'Sure!'

'And it's OK?'

I reflected on this for a bit. I didn't want to say: *Well, apart from the beating and being insulting to strippers and throwing up on yourself and sleeping rough* . . .

'Sure!' I said. God, if he would only hurry up and leave her, so I could talk about my problems for a change.

'You know what you should do, dolls,' said Cockney Boy, who had somehow been managing to colour in and listen to our conversation at the same time. 'You should both learn to play rugby, yeah? Then you birds can run around the pitch yourself, getting all covered in mud and stuff. That way everyone will be happy – the blokes can watch the rugby, and you'd be, roight, playin'' . . .'

We both turned and stared at him.

'You spent an awful long time alone in your bedroom as a teenager, didn't you?' I asked him.

'No,' he pouted. 'No, I didn't.'

'Day after day, just staring at the wall, picking your spots and listening to your Phil Collins albums.'

'Oh, shut up.'

'Dreaming of the day Linda Lusardi comes past and accidentally breaks down in front of your little Cockney house.'

He held up his arms and walked off. 'I don't have to listen to this.'

'Oh, Steve, Steve, thank you for fixing my car . . . what can I, Linda Lusardi, possibly do for you in return?'

He turned at the door and flicked me a V-sign. But he was smiling a little bit. I hoped.

I had three messages. One was from Fran, wanting to know

what to wear to Amanda's hen night. If she thought she was going to that, she had another think coming. In fact, neither was I, given that I liked both my eyes the way they were, thank you.

The second was Alex, who had 'just called to say good morning, pumpkin.' He'd been terribly soppy since Saturday. Which was a good thing, clearly, although slightly unusual. Previously, in fact, unheard of. He sounded practically wimpy!

The third one started oddly. There was a long pause, and it kind of went 'urrr'. Then a throat was cleared noisily, and then apologized for. I realized who it was.

'Angus,' I said into the phone, even though it was only a message. 'Don't worry. It's only me. Yes, I do think you're a plonker, but that's OK. I don't mind.'

'Erm, hullo there, ehm, this is Angus. Umm, Angus McConnald.'

Ah, *that* Angus.

'So, really, Ah just wondered how you were going after Saturday night, and, ehmm, whether you wanted to go to lunch or something to talk about, you know . . . just for a chat . . . I won't talk about the wedding or anything . . .' There was a pause on the answerphone. 'Well, maybe a bit about the wedding . . . They can't . . . Oh God. Well, anyway . . . give me a ring on 555 2127. Sorry, 0171 555 2127. Poncey sodding English codes. Right. Sorry. OK. Bye.'

He wasn't going to let this alone, I could tell. Neither would Fran. I kind of wished they'd leave me out of it, but I hated being left out of things. Also, something in me wanted to see him again. I didn't phone him back right away, but I wrote his number in my address book in ink.

* * *

'We've been invited,' went on Fran, 'so, you know, we turn up and do something. The Hensterminators.'

'That's not even funny.'

'Maybe we could get that stripper to turn up at Quagli's.'

We'd met for a council of war. Or rather, Fran had come over to try and get me to do stuff, and Alex was at the flat anyway. I'd told Fran what Angus had said at the stag night, and she was excited at the potential for devilment, and more convinced than ever that we were in the service of the right by trying to bugger things up, even a bit. I wasn't quite so sure. Alex was reading *The Sunday Times* and couldn't give a toss.

The phone rang. I picked it up, then put my hand over the receiver and popped my head round the living-room door.

'It's Angus!' I hissed to Fran. Two phone calls in two days, I was thinking. I internally hugged myself with glee. I knew I was right. I'd thought maybe he had a little crush on me. Would have to be pretty little, though, for him to have copped off with Fran so quickly. I hated the nineties. A bit of courtly love would not have gone amiss. He should have worshipped me for about ten or fifteen years and then been happy with a mere flower, or something.

Fran shrugged.

'Well,' I said, 'shall I ask him to come over?'

'Why on earth would I mind?'

'I don't know . . . ehm, he's seen you from the inside?'

Alex looked up from the sports pages with his eyebrows raised, but then he'd known Fran for a while.

'Honestly, it's not a big deal,' she said. 'I'd like to see him. He's nice. And he can join in our plan.'

'Hmm.' I wasn't sure how closely I wanted those two working together.

149

'Hey!' I rejoined the phone call with an alacrity which betrayed exactly what I'd been doing.

'Why don't you come over? We're only sitting about drinking wine and being small-minded about people we know.'

'Aye, OK.'

I gave him the address, expecting him to take hours to find it and arrive cursing our poncey southern road system, but he made it in about half an hour, armed with a couple of helpful bottles of wine. Him and Alex smiled fixedly at each other and shook hands, whereupon Alex said, 'I think I'll let you three get on with ripping everyone to shreds,' and returned to his paper.

'Wooo,' said Fran, 'Mr Perfect strikes again.'

'OK, stop nipping at each other, you two.'

Fran shot him a final dirty look then joined us on cushions on the floor.

'So!' said Angus through clenched teeth. He'd obviously been thinking about what to say.

'This isn't at all embarrassing, is it?'

'What isn't?' said Fran.

I kicked her on the ankle. 'No, it's not,' I added. Fran smiled sweetly, leaving Angus looking uncomfortable.

'How's Fraser?' I asked.

'He's fine. Recovered. She's' – there was no mistaking the intonation: it sounded like how people used to talk about Margaret Thatcher – 'making him choose dinner patterns. Then every time he chooses one she tells him it's wrong.'

'I love that game,' I said.

Fran stretched herself out on the floor and turned to face the ceiling, arms behind her head.

'Look, why don't you just tell him. Go up and say, "Fraser, don't marry her, she's a bitch. She's a skinny-rumped, dyed-haired bitch bitch bitch. She's a complete and utter

utter utter bitch. If she was a president, she'd be Bitchaham Lincoln."'

'What's your point?'

'If she was a cowboy, she'd be Bitch Cassidy.'

'Fran, that's a pretty subtle idea. But I think Angus might have already tried it, somehow.'

Angus half tilted his head.

'Kind of. I didn't do the whole bitch song, though.'

'Well, what happened?'

'He looked at me like a mopey dog and said,' – sincere voice – '"Angus, you two just haven't hit it off. Believe me, she's sweet. It's going to be OK."'

'Argh!' said Fran. 'I can't believe there's anything I hate more in the world than women men think are sweet but who are actually complete BITCHES!'

Alex rustled his paper and peered over the top of it. 'Really? What about women who can't stop bitching and shouting all day?'

'Oh yeah? What about men who run off to America and fuck their girlfriends about?'

I froze.

The way I heard Fran – and she always said everything on purpose – well, I suppose I'd assumed, guessed that Alex had been up to all sorts of things when he was away, but, well, I'd never known for sure, and I'd thought . . . I looked at him, already knowing that my eyes were full of tears, the kind that I tried to swallow until it hurt. Fran leaned over, suddenly worried about what she'd said.

'Melanie . . .'

Alex threw down his paper and stormed off. I thought he was just going to leave – forever, probably. My throat felt as if I was being strangled.

Obviously not quite knowing what to do, Alex stormed

back in the room again and nodded for me to follow him, but I was paralysed.

'Come on,' he said sharply. I stood up and walked out with him to the hall. He grabbed me and put his arms tightly around me, then tilted his forehead against mine, trying to regain his cool.

'Your friend really, really hates me, doesn't she?'

'Yes,' I said, biting my lower lip. I almost couldn't ask.

'D-did you?' I quavered.

'Mel, you know I had to discover myself. Try new things. So I could work out where I belonged. Here. With you.'

I dropped his very close gaze and stared fiercely at the ground.

'America . . . it feels like a different life to me now. I did tons of things there I wouldn't do here. Daft, meaningless things. You've got to believe me, pumpkin.'

I wanted to, so much.

'You're so special – I keep telling you that, but you don't believe in yourself. Look, hey, I came all the way back for you, right? You know how messed up my head is. But here I am!'

I looked him in the eye again. He seemed so sincere, so desperate to make it all right. He was nearly in tears himself.

'Please, Mel.'

We stared at each other for a long time.

'It's all right,' I said finally. 'It's all right. It was a long time ago.'

'Do you mean that? Fantastic you?'

'Yes,' I said quietly.

'I thought about you all the time,' he said.

'Really? I didn't think about you at all.' I forced a laugh.

'All that crap is over now, I promise. From now on, it's

just you and me. In fact, if you could only dump that Fran character, it would be absolutely perfect.'

'Lex, she's my best friend.'

'And I'm not?'

'You're my soul mate, remember?'

'Oh, yes.'

I had to ask.

'Do you love me, Alex?'

He smiled and kissed me full on the mouth.

'Ah shags you, don't Ah?' he said in exaggerated Cockney.

'Just tell me.'

'Pet, as much as I love anyone, I love you.'

He left after that. I stood by the door, not wanting to return to the sitting room quite yet. There was a stack of post on a ghastly occasional table. I never bother looking at it usually; bills I let Linda take care of, and everything else she usually flicks under my door. But I leafed through it listlessly, wondering how many animal charities there are in the world. Suddenly I drew out an envelope addressed to Alex, care of me. It was stiff, white card. How bizarre. Underneath, there was one for me too.

It occurred to me immediately what these were – the wedding invites! After all, how many stiff card envelopes did I normally get? (This was my first.) I could put it on the mantelpiece! Except Linda had already covered it with miniature glass kittens.

I walked back into the living room. Angus and Fran were watching me with obvious concern.

'I'm sorry!' Fran yelled immediately, to get it in.

'I'm fine,' I said, sitting down to pour another glass of wine.

'I was only guessing, Mel. I didn't even think . . .' Fran looked absolutely stricken. I patted her on the hand.

'Come on outside. I need to tell you something.'

She followed me.

'Fran, don't worry. If anything, it did more good than harm. He . . .' I felt a bit shy and crap. 'I didn't want to say this in front of Angus, but . . . he said he loves me. For the first time.'

'That weasel?' Fran was immediately scornful again. 'He doesn't love anyone but himself.'

I shot her a look that said she wasn't forgiven.

'OK, OK, I'll stop. I'm pleased for you. I really am.'

'Look, Fran, I mean it: are you going to stop being so horrid whenever he's around?'

Fran groaned.

'Are you? I mean, it's driving him crazy – and me.'

'OK. OK. If that's what you really want, I'll curb my natural instincts towards that creep.'

I gave her a friendly squeeze. 'Fran, I'd love your natural instincts – if only they weren't those of a cornered cougar.'

She snarled at me affectionately. We headed back in.

'Do you two always live in such pitched drama?' asked Angus, who was quietly toying with his wine.

'Hang on – which one of us is trying to sabotage an entire wedding again? Oh, it's you, isn't it?' I reminded him. 'Ooh, which reminds me – look!'

I drew out the envelopes.

'Invitations?' Fran made a grab for them. 'How come you got two separate ones?'

'They can afford it, I suppose,' I said airily, opening mine.

I gazed at the gold-rimmed card in shock.

'That bitch!'

'What?'

'Look!'

Fran took it from me.

'Twenty fucking years! That BITCH!'

Joan and Derek Phillips, the card said, *invite you to the post-reception of the wedding of their daughter Amanda Serena Phillips to Fraser Alasdair McConnald at Pyrford Manor on December 21st. A coach will be available to pick up guests from Central London at 4.30 p.m. Formal dress will not be required.*

Fran and I stared at each other. Then she tore into Alex's. Sure enough, it said: *Joan and Derek Phillips invite you to the wedding of their daughter Amanda Serena Phillips to Fraser Alasdair McConnald at Pyrford village church, noon on December 21st, after which lunch at Le Coq Fantastique, followed by dancing at Pyrford Manor. Morning Dress.*

Enclosed with both of them was a wedding list, placed at Heal's. The cheapest thing on it was three hundred quid.

Fran and I stared at each other.

'OK,' I said to Angus. 'What do we have to do to fuck this wedding up the bum?'

'It's only fair,' added Fran. 'For years and years of all that shit she used to pull at school.'

I winced in remembrance. 'For that time she got the boys to hold us still while she pulled our hair.'

'For that time she insisted on taking our dinner money and giving it to charity,' hissed Fran.

'For that time she wouldn't own up to stealing the teacher's ruler and I took the blame.'

'For that time she told Stacey Norton I wanted to fight with her.'

Angus was watching us, agape.

'For that time she told on you for stealing lipstick from Woolworths!'

'Oh yes!' Fran remembered. 'For that time we were meant to be going to the pictures and she didn't want to go and pretended to be sick until it was too late and we missed it.'

'Aargh!' I said. 'That time she got into that nightclub and I didn't, and she didn't come back for me!'

'That time she got off with Legsy Forters just because you liked him!'

I buried my head under the cushion. 'Legsy! Legsy!' We were getting hysterical.

'Let's do it!' shouted Fran. 'For every mean little thing that bitch has ever done, let's do it.'

I was fired up. 'Yeah!'

We turned to look at Angus, who was backing away with a scared look on his face.

'You know, girruls, we only have to reason with them, not blow them up or anything.'

I opened the third bottle of wine.

'OK, we need a plan.'

'Well, we're going to the hen night,' said Fran.

'No we are not.' I shot her a dangerous look.

'Fine. If you want to stay at home and smooch with the love of your life, so be it. I'm going there for reconnaissance. And I'm going in wired.'

Nobody said anything.

'You're what?'

'You heard. Wire me up. I'll tape what she talks about and, if it's suitably evil, we'll play it back to Fraser. Painful, but effective.'

There was a further pause.

'That is absolutely brilliant!' said Angus.

'Well, I'd better come too then,' I volunteered. 'Um . . . you'd never get in otherwise.'

'Bet I could.'

156

'Stoap it, youse two. I've already got one partnership head-ache on my hands. OK, Francesca, that's an excellent idea.'

I was watching them closely for some hint of sexual tension, but it was as if nothing had ever happened.

'You'll need to wear something baggy, so it doesn't show.'

'I haven't got anything baggy. How do those tarty TV babes do it?'

'Doesn't matter. We'll sort something out.'

'Hang on,' I said. 'What if they aren't sitting together? There's going to be hundreds of people at this bash.'

'Well, you're both just going to have to be really friendly.'

Fran sneered. 'Yeah, given that she didn't even ask us in the first place, that's going to be easy.'

I had a flash of inspiration. 'I know! You could pretend you're completely pished and pass out underneath the table at her feet! Then you'll catch everything.'

Both of them looked at me with surprised faces.

'Maybe you could do that bit,' said Fran. 'Then we wouldn't have to pretend.'

'Ha ha ha,' I said sulkily.

'OK, right, just try and stay close to her and make sure she does a speech,' said Angus excitedly. 'Then we'll play it to Frase and he'll come to his senses!'

'How will he know we haven't taped the Queen's Christmas message? That's what she sounds like,' I said.

'Doesn't matter. Doesn't matter.'

I was pretty excited all week after that. Well, we had a mission now. The following night, Alex and I went out for a very cosy romantic dinner. He thought the plan was on the childish

157

side, but I didn't mind so much about that. And he had an interview for a job, at a record company, which meant things were looking up. He lived rent-free at Charlie's gaffe, though, and got regular influxes of guilt money from both parents, so he was never going to starve. I toyed with my mussels and gazed out the window of Café Rouge – OK, not exactly the Ritz, but it would do for now.

Late-night opening, Fran and I went to find a microphone, which was easier said than done, especially in the high street electrical outlets.

'Have you got a small mike?' I asked the glazed-eyed brat standing next to the door. He looked blankly at the CD shelves and nervously pretended to look for something that clearly wasn't there.

'Eh, um, naow.'

'What's this?' asked Fran, smiling sweetly and picking up a microphone.

'Yeah, it's a mike, yeah.' The boy scratched himself nervously. Where did they grow these morons?

'Have you got any small ones?' Fran continued to encourage him.

'That's, uh, as small as they go, like.' I noticed the damp patches under his arms.

'So . . . what's this, then?' said Fran, picking up a smaller mike. I grimaced at her to stop.

The boy stood there, staring straight ahead in a catatonic state to avoid answering the question. I wondered if he ever got punched.

'Look,' I said to the boy, 'it's simple: we just want a tiny microphone, like they have on TV – you know, TV? – that we can attach to a Walkman to tape something with.'

He focused again, and came out of about-to-be-punched mode. 'I'll . . . I'll check out the back.'

And he disappeared. For ever. Finally, Fran growled at an assistant manager long enough for him to sell us one.

She tried it on in the nearest wine bar, slotting the tape machine inside her jeans and the mike tucked inside her shirt. Then we disappeared into a toilet cubicle together to check whether it was working or not.

'God, you've got noisy tits,' I told her, rather too loudly.

'Shh! For God's sake. Now, hang on.' She wound the tape back and switched it on. And sure enough, there it was, slightly muffled: the boring conversation between two old bankers who'd been sitting next to us. Every word of their interminable discussion about insurance rates was clearly distinguishable. We grinned at each other over the seedy loo.

'Partying again?' said Cockney Boy on Friday morning, clocking my little glittery bag and spare pair of tights. 'You'll be turning into a right alcoholic at this rate.'

'What, you mean I'll feel ill in the mornings? I thought that was just the effect of seeing you.'

'You think you're well funny, don't you?'

'Actually, no. But as long as I'm annoying you, I don't care.'

He went and got himself and Janie a cup of coffee and didn't get me one. Bastard.

I was very worried about the night ahead. What if Amanda hadn't booked for us? What if she wouldn't let us in? What if everything cost £100 and we couldn't afford it? – Fran was permanently skint anyway.

And what on earth did we think we were doing? I mean, she deserved it in principle, but surely our interference wasn't going to make much difference: people would do what they were always going to do, except they'd hate me into the bargain.

I sighed deeply over my copy. Really, I wanted to stop my life for a moment, get off and catch my breath, then start again, instead of dashing on headlong. I tried to do some deep breathing exercises, but after thirty seconds I realized I was bored rigid, and if I stopped to think about everything that was going on I'd probably end up in a catatonic state listening to people pity me as they loaded me into an ambulance. So I phoned Fran and arranged what time I'd meet her.

Ten

Despite the cold, there was a buzz about the West End at eight o'clock on a Friday night. People had a set look on their faces, as if Fun was in serious trouble if they didn't find it. Students on some ghastly rag week spectacular were irritating passers-by, running around with buckets and pints and their legs tied together.

Fran was uncharacteristically nervous. 'This is going to be a laugh, isn't it?'

I didn't want to share my own misgivings. Going into a roomful of strangers predisposed to hating you, trying to ingratiate yourself, then taping the conversation – not my idea of a great night out.

'Course it is,' I said. 'Think of it as a great acting role. Your début in the West End.'

She grinned. 'If anything goes wrong, we leg it, OK?'

'Let's go, Mulder.'

'OK, Scully.'

We pushed open the heavy doors of the restaurant. Stiff napery and mirrors stretched for miles. The light was expensively dim and golden.

'God, not McDonald's again!' I whispered to Fran. She smiled, tilted her head, and with cut-glass drama school English and an imperious gait, walked over to the maître d', and smiled.

'The Phillips party, please.'

'Certainly, madame. Follow me.'

He led us through tables of elegant women and corpulent old gents. Everything tinkled and glistened, and heads turned to look at Fran, who kept her head high and looked as if she owned the place.

Tucked in a banquette in the corner were several manes of straight blonde hair. I stiffened.

'Amanda, darling!' Fran went over and gave her a kiss, careful not to get too close in case Amanda felt the wire, while also trying to avoid Amanda's very elaborate lip gloss.

I studied the pert little face intently. If she was annoyed to see us, she certainly wasn't showing it.

'Hello there, darlings!' Actually, there were some signs of strain. Looking round, I soon realized why.

We were half an hour late — we couldn't bear to walk in on our own — and all along the banquette there were places laid. There must have been thirty, stretching a quarter of the way up the restaurant. However, surrounding Amanda there were five people, all identikit blonde types.

'Where is everyone?' I asked, and immediately wished I hadn't.

Amanda smiled sharply. 'Oh, they'll be joining us later on — most people have so much on in London at the weekend!'

'Oh, well, yes, of course.' I sat down and bit into a breadstick to stop myself biting her.

Fran sat next to Amanda, her brown hair bobbing in a sea of blonde.

'Introduce us to everyone, then.' She was plainly making the effort.

'Well, this is Jacintha, Araminta, Veronica, Larissa, and Mookie.'

'Hello, everyone!' said Fran gracefully.

'Umm . . . hello, Mookie,' I said.

There was an embarrassed silence.

'Right,' said Amanda. 'Din-dins!'

Fran and I shot each other a nervous glance as we picked up the menu. Sure enough, everything inside looked exceptionally complicated and extremely expensive. I found something that looked just about do-able, then realized it was the side vegetables. I hated thinking of all the cool stuff I could have bought instead.

Amanda waved over the waiter professionally.

'Four bottles of Bollinger,' she said crisply. 'For starters. And a bottle of Perrier for me.'

Fran and I shot each other a glance of pure terror at this latest development. Amanda caught it. 'Don't worry, girls, it's all on me,' she announced. 'It's so good to see my real friends.'

Her tone was tinged with disappointment, and I almost felt sorry for her, especially if she was including Fran and I in that analysis. Plus, the other five were so bland and identical-looking they only really counted as one person. So, quite a sad state of affairs really. I looked at the menu with renewed vigour and sampled my newly poured glass of Bollinger. What the heck, I thought. Friends were friends wherever you found them. And champagne was champagne and posh nosh was posh nosh, so I was bloody well about to enjoy myself.

'To Amanda!' I proposed, almost despite myself. 'And her gorgeous hubby-to-be.'

'Lady Amanda Phillips-McConnald,' squawked one of the blondies – Jacintha, I think. 'How absolutely glamorous!'

'Shame about the hubby!' squealed another one, and they all burst out laughing, and tinkled their glasses.

I ordered expensive pâté for starters and some very complex beef thing for the main course. I could also see the pudding trolley and was looking forward to it. Fran went for some extremely rare fish – unique, by the price of it – and young lamb. The other six ordered plain salads with lemon juice.

'Come on, girls!' I said jovially. 'I thought we were celebrating! What are you having to eat?'

They looked at me and giggled like I'd just made the most enormous joke.

'God, you wouldn't believe the size of my thighs in the mirror last week!' said one of them.

'Jesus, I know. I thought I was going to break eight stone!'

They all gasped in unison.

'I'm not eating more than five milligrams of fat a week until the wedding,' insisted Amanda.

'Five milligrams? You'll die!' I said in horror. 'Or you'll look like you're about to. Between you and Frase, you're practically two-dimensional anyway.'

She smiled gracefully at this mention of her life partner and went back to the juicy details of who was and who wasn't throwing their guts up daily in the cause of national celebrity.

'Well, you know she's on TV every day; she has to look thin all the time. I've heard she lives on Diet Coke, Dexedrine and dipsomania!'

The blonde brigade laughed themselves stupid as the waiter put down our starters. Suddenly, I was extremely conscious of my thighs rubbing together, and didn't feel hungry at all. I drank some more champagne. Fran looked at me enquiringly, then plunged in. She had one cooking ring in her bedsit, so didn't get around to cordon bleu that often.

The girls were now looking expectantly at my foie gras; salivating, I was sure of it. Even the cold toast would have been enough for them. To distract myself, I turned to the nearest blonde.

'So, what do you do?'

'Oh, telly, you know.'

I didn't, actually.

'Really, who for?'

'Oh, documentary programming. Terribly dull, really.'

'It doesn't sound dull. What have you worked on?'

'Ectually, I . . . it's more research ectually.'

Amanda nudged me from the other side.

'Araminta finds guests for *Trisha*,' she said, in a stage whisper. 'She doesn't like to talk about it.'

'Ohh. OK.'

Araminta was dabbing at her mouth with a napkin, although she hadn't eaten anything. I think I'd upset her. Still, the distraction was enough to get stuck into my food, which was absolutely glorious.

I obviously had upset her, as she immediately lit up a Marlboro Light and drew on it deeply. As if on cue, the other five did the same. I saw my pâté disappear below a wreath of anxious smoke.

'So,' she shrugged, 'what about you?'

'Oh, I lead Arctic biochemical expeditions.'

'Rally?'

Conversation over, she turned back to the blonde on our other side, and I said 'Fuck!' several times under my breath.

'So, anyway, I was in Gucci,' started one, 'and I told him;

I said, "If Meg Matthews is wearing it, I want nothing to do with it, OK?" That told him.'

'Yah!' nodded all the heads around the table. In amazement I noticed Fran nodding vigorously too. What on earth was she on about?

'I mean, she's like the Antichrist, yah? Just do the opposite of what she does and you'll be all right?'

'And Kate hates her, apparently,' joined in another.

'I think she's fat,' said one.

'Are you kidding? She looks like she's been flayed!' I said.

Silence reigned. However, they were well brought up girls, and tried to be deliberately polite to us shitkickers.

'Oh, you know, I am going to be in a film after all!' yelled one suddenly. Fran's ears pricked up. 'Yah, Daddy stumped up a major stake. He'll never see it again, of course, but the director's so hunky, and apparently Rufus is interested.'

'Put the fork down,' I tried to psychically send to Fran, 'just put it down and no one will get hurt.'

She was coping well, even if she did look a bit strained. I still hadn't had a chance to ask her if she was going to see Angus again. Not that I should care. But she normally told me everything, and she'd hardly talked about this at all. Maybe it was only a drunken fumble that had passed.

Amanda was talking about the floral arrangements for the service, and I could see the caged look in Fran's eyes. Fearing for Amanda's safety, I distracted her.

'So, what's Fraser wearing for the big day then?'

'Oh God, he can't dress himself at all.'

'I like Converse trainers,' Fran interjected.

'Yes, well, some people like lager and some people like champagne, Francesca.'

Fran made clawing motions behind her back.

'Daddy took him to his tailor, so at least he'll look semi-decent.'

'Is he excited?'

'About what? Going to a tailor?'

'About the wedding, stupid.'

Amanda looked contemplatively at her glass.

'I suppose so.'

I shot a completely overt look at Fran, who raised her eyes to heaven and nodded her head. Yes, the tape was on.

I gushed on: 'Gosh, you two are going to be so happy together.'

She fixed me with a stare.

'You know, I'm only telling you this for your own good, but you can be incredibly naïve, Melanie.'

Huh, tell me something I didn't know.

'This . . . I mean, hell, it's a great excuse to have a party, but it's also a bloody practical affair. That castle needs sorting out, and Daddy's happy to put up the loot to do it with.'

My eyes widened. That was proof all right – I assumed. Then something struck me; she was so matter-of-fact about it. Maybe Fraser felt the same way? Maybe this was how tons of people got married. After all, the aristocracy had been doing it for generations. I supposed this was how it all worked. Not helped by the copious champagne, I suddenly felt sad.

'Don't you love him?'

She sniffed. 'He's a nice chap. It's a good situation. It'll be a fabulous wedding.'

'Hyear hyear!' said one of the Sloane clones.

Amanda took a drink and continued: 'You don't believe in all that Hollywood crap, do you? I mean, God, how many times do you have to find out, Melanie? Men are complete bastards. Look at what Alex did to you. That wasn't a terribly Tom Hanks way to behave, was it, darling?

167

This way, everyone wins. We'll have a beautiful home and a beautiful life, and we'll be as happy as any marriage is these days, because we went into it with our eyes open. Fraser is a nice boy and he'll have no objection to us both living our lives.' She turned to the waiter. 'I'm sorry, but I don't know why you waste your time bringing us anything at all if you can't get the lemon juice right.'

I looked at Fran for support, but she was nodding in agreement – presumably to keep Amanda talking, but it didn't feel that way. Suddenly the situation felt dangerous. The blood rushed to my head a bit. I stood up, unsteadily.

'I don't care,' I announced in a trembly voice. The waiter thought I was talking to him and stepped forward, then hopped back again. 'I do believe in all that crap. Well, not all of it. But some of it. The actually being in love with someone stuff. Ehm, yeah. And . . . and I think you lose. Because you've got a lovely bloke like Fraser and you take the piss out of him and you just think of that bloody castle – which I have seen, by the way, and it's a complete heap of shit – and that bloody title and you've absolutely no idea what you've got and how happy he could make you. So, I think you lose.'

I turned and made to walk out of the restaurant. Realizing I didn't have my bag, I made a dignified right turn into the toilets, then leaned over and looked at myself in the low-lit mirror, breathing heavily. My throat felt tight.

What on earth was I doing? If I wanted to start a fight with Amanda, I should have done it a long time ago. And who, exactly, was I defending? But then, if Fraser did have his eyes open – which I doubted – Angus certainly didn't. He had a blind spot for Fraser the size of the chip on his shoulder. Oh God.

Fran came crashing into the bathroom after me with two fresh glasses of champagne. She was absolutely delighted.

'Ohmigod, the look on her face! What on earth were you talking about?'

I sunk my head into my hands.

'Really, I don't know.'

'You went for her.'

'I know. And I don't even know why!'

'Well, she was asking for it,' Fran reflected.

'No she wasn't! She might even be right, for all we know. That probably is the best way to get married: find a nice bloke that you get on with all right and then ignore each other for the next fifty years.'

'Well, I've heard stupider reasons.'

'Like what?'

'Well, you know my brother Brendan?'

'Yeah.'

'He got married because he kept losing his socks.'

'Fuck off!' I looked up briefly.

'It's true. He kept losing his socks, and one day he said, "That's it, I'm fed up of losing all my fucking socks. The next woman I meet I'm going to marry, as long as she can count socks." And he did.'

'How are his socks now?'

'Dreadful. She divorced him for being a sexist pig who talked about socks all day long.'

I giggled. 'Complete socks maniac.'

'Completely.'

We both smiled and sipped our champagne, and I felt better. It helped that the toilets were nicer than my entire flat.

'So, ehm . . .' I toyed with my glass.

'What am I going to do about Angus?'

'Psychic, you!'

She smiled. 'I thought he might come up sooner or later.'

'I thought he already did.'

'Have you got a soft spot for him?'

'No.'

'Lying cow.'

'Fuck off!'

'Well, to set your mind at rest – although, if you will let me be so bold, if you would dump Mr Trevelyan and go out with the dumpy yet delightful Mr McConnald I would be the happiest best friend alive – he phoned me to apologize.'

'To apologize? Why?'

'Because he wasn't going to phone me. To which I said it was quite all right, I didn't mind a bit.'

'No, no, hang on. I don't understand. He phoned you to say he wasn't going to phone you?'

'Yes. So if I was hanging around the phone, I could stop and get on with my life. Which of course I wasn't. So we had a nice little chat and said our goodbyes. An extremely civilized end to a one-night stand, I have to say.'

'That is too weird. I don't know whether it's extremely polite or a damning indictment of today's decadent society.'

Fran checked her make-up in the mirror and I joined her, still wondering.

'What are you going to do now?' she asked.

I winced. 'Oh God. Apologize to Amanda, I suppose. I must be off my head. They're probably all pissing themselves laughing at me.'

'The only way you could make those girls laugh would be to tell them Anthea Turner's put on three stone. Do you want to stay?'

I weighed it up.

'Did you get it on tape?'

'If it works, then yes.'

170

'Well, I suppose there's no reason to stay, then.'

'Not really.'

I thought longingly of the dessert trolley.

'There's always pudding,' said Fran.

I clapped her on the shoulder.

'Will there always be pudding, Fran?' I asked gravely.

'There will always be pudding, Mel. I promise.'

I took a deep breath and walked out there. All the girls were huddled together, obviously talking about us, ignoring their spiky-looking salads. Our main courses were being kept on a hot plate by our faithful waiter.

I walked over and grabbed the back of my chair for support.

'I'm sorry,' I said to Amanda, as sincerely as I could.

'Oof, don't worry about it for a second,' she said, waving me to sit down. I smiled gratefully.

'You've been a little naïve, haven't you, darling? I shouldn't expect it to stop now, just because we're supposed to be grown-up!' She tinkled the patented Amanda laugh. Beside her, I watched Fran bare her teeth.

'Now! More champers all round! I absolutely insist.'

'Rah rah rah!' shouted the other girls, all of one mind. A half-witted one.

The waiter brought main courses for Fran and I, and we tucked in, letting the girls get on with discussing their boyfriends' cars. Suddenly, there was a near hush in the restaurant. Looking up from my trough, I turned round to see what the matter was. Weaving between the tables was one of the most beautiful girls I'd ever seen in real life. Almost six foot tall, her shiny, pure blonde hair glimmered in the lights. She was dressed in pale, slim-fitting, elegant flowing things, and appeared to float rather than walk. The ratio of her legs to the rest of her body was about 2:1.

'That's who I'm going to look like when I'm grown-up,' I whispered to Fran, who nodded violently. Behind her was a gorgeous, gorgeous bloke, wearing an expensive – but not showy – suit. He looked vaguely familiar.

Amanda stood up, wearing an eager expression I didn't often see her use.

'Lili! Darling!' she screeched in her ladylike fashion. It was the most emphatic 'darling' I'd ever heard from her. 'Over here!'

Lili's swan-like neck moved a fraction, and she swept her eyes over our measly group. The empty spaces had been taken up by latecomers, noisy City boys showing off. Her eyes passed over me without even looking; I had obviously fallen below some imaginary bar whereby one became actively invisible.

Her white teeth glistened for a second as she bestowed the merest hint of a radiant smile. Amanda, amazingly, was all nerves and practically pleading.

'You've met Jacintha, of course, from Freud's . . . Araminta from Carlton . . . Please, take a seat. I'll pour you a glass – I see you've brought a friend, ha ha.' I could almost hear her accent crack.

Lili bent down elegantly, her white hands long and tapered. 'Oh, we can't stay, we're off to Philippa's bash. We just popped in to see everyone' – her deep voice sounded pointed – 'and now we're off.' She bestowed fifteen alternate kisses on Amanda's cheeks then turned and floated off in a cloud of rare and precious perfume. The broad shoulders of the man disappeared as he gently guided her elbow across the floor.

I stifled a sudden terrible urge to giggle. Well, just when you thought you were pretty far down in the food chain, you discovered a whole new layer you'd never even dreamt of.

'Who the hell was that?' demanded Fran, chewing the last of her lamb.

'Oh, isn't she great?' said Amanda, her eyes wide.

'Well, from that in-depth and emotional meeting, I'd say she's a bit of a stuck-up cow, actually.'

Amazingly, one of the blondies – I think it was Mookie – giggled independently, then blushed bright red and stared at her carpaccio.

Amanda sniffed. 'Well, you would say that about one of the most important fashion people in London. And she came to my hen night.'

Fran and I looked at each other. 'She didn't come to your hen night!' said Fran in amazement. 'She did a Red Arrows fly-past of your hen night.'

I kicked her on the ankle. But Amanda seemed unperturbed.

'Darling, she *showed*. That's all that matters.'

Fran looked at me, but I simply shrugged. Nothing Amanda did made any sense to me.

As the main excitement of the evening was clearly over, I saw Amanda beckon the waiter. Fran and I eyed the dessert trolley eagerly.

'Nobody wants pudding –' Amanda's voice rang out clearly – 'so, just the bill, please.'

I let my shoulders sag and drank a little more champagne.

'Can we go now?' whispered Fran. I nodded.

'And can you order us a couple of limos?' said Amanda.

Good God, I didn't even know you could do that. And I'd never been in a limo . . .

My eyes cut to Fran. She sighed and looked upwards, then nodded her head.

'OK, everyone?' shouted Amanda brightly. 'Are we ready to party?'

The girls giggled and shrieked, 'Yars!'

'I know the limos are naff, but, hey, it's my hen night! We're gonna go crazy!'

Seven reserved posh girls did their best to look crazy as Amanda signed her name with a flourish and flashed her gold card. Then we manoeuvred through the chairs. Outside, as if by magic, were two absolutely ludicrous jet black limousines.

'Our carriages await! Yanna's, please!' Amanda ordered the drivers.

Yanna's was some desperately exclusive club in Mayfair. Shrugging her shoulders, Fran squeezed into the first of the cars, and I followed her. There was a slight pause outside as we realized that the girls all wanted to go in the second limo with Amanda and not us, but that got sorted out somehow, and the one I'd identified as Mookie slid in gracefully.

I looked around the limo. It was done up in high seventies style, with lots of burgundy leather, and there was a white fur rug on the floor, as well as a phone on a string, a TV, and a little fridge in which – hooray – nestled even more champagne.

'My God, this is a white trash fantasy dream,' sighed Fran as I opened the champagne. 'I wonder how many revolting old men have shagged teenage blonde girls in the back here?'

'Shall we ask the driver?' I said mischievously, pointing to the button that raised the screen.

'Do you really want to know? Yuck!'

'What, if Mick Jagger had fifteen young virgins on the floor? Sure.'

'It probably does one hundred and fifty hen nights a year

174

and two smart functions,' said Fran gloomily. 'Really, it's a bit of a wanker's mobile.'

As if in confirmation, as the car inched its way down Regent Street, some students came up to the blackened window, shook something at us and yelled, 'Rich bastards!'

I looked at Fran in disbelief. 'We're rich bastards!'

'Well, hooray!' said Fran.

'Gosh, how terribly amusing,' said Mookie, looking at the students, although she wasn't smiling. Up till now she'd been sitting silently, and I'd assumed she was disgruntled at not getting into the Princess's limo. 'Did you know those chaps?'

I looked at her. 'Ehm, no. Why, did you?'

She giggled at this. 'No! Me neither!'

This felt almost like a conversation, but not quite.

'OK. Are you having a good time?'

'Why, erm . . . yars, of course.' She looked a bit mystified by the question. 'I mean, the restaurant was in *Vogue* this month, it's almost impossible to get bookings.'

'Really?' said Fran. 'God, we were lucky.'

'How long have you known Amanda?' I was persevering with the small talk, while making my usual subtle nudges to Fran to put the tape on. She glowered at me.

'Well, Jacintha and I are cousins, and we were at school together with Philippa – she's having another party tonight; she doesn't like Amanda . . .' – my eyebrows raised – 'I think she had her eye on Fraser herself. Well, most of the Right Hons are spoken for, or will only go out with models, or are complete poofters, so there's not that many left, rally,' she finished sadly.

Oh.

'Anyway, the Vryker-Lyons are old neighbours of ours from the village, so when Araminta went up, she met Amanda, and that's how it all fits together, rally.'

175

'Right. I see.'

'So,' said Fran, 'are you and Amanda really good friends?'

'Well, I'm going to be one of the bridesmaids.' Mookie was blushing more and more at being bombarded with these questions. I wondered if, underneath it all, she might be rather nice.

'That's lovely,' I said, reassuringly. 'And . . . what do you think of Fraser?'

I expected her to get stroppy, remembering my little outburst earlier, or silent and defensive.

Instead she looked mildly uncomfortable, and blushed again.

'Well,' she said. Fran helpfully refilled her glass.

'Go on, you can tell us,' I said. 'We won't tell anyone.'

Except, you know, Fraser, I thought.

'Scout's honour,' said Fran. With one hand behind her back.

She smiled. 'You won't tell Amanda?'

'Oooh no.'

Slightly drunk, she burped and said, 'You know, rally, I kind of agreed with what you said earlier.'

I nodded encouragement.

'Well, when Fraser first came on the scene, he was rally innocent, you know? He kept getting invited to these parties, and he thought it was because some people he knew from university rally liked him, you know?'

'How stupid can you get?' I said, smiling through gritted teeth.

'Rally! So at first we took the piss a bit, especially with Amanda rally coming on to him like that . . . I mean, she was still seeing that guy from *Les Mis* at the time.'

'Oh yes?'

'Rally — I think she finished it, though. For the wedding and stuff.'

'Well, that was good of her.'

'Anyway, then I got to know him a bit more. And now I think he's rally nice.'

'Oh, he is.'

'And Amanda bosses him about rally horribly. I mean, I know she's dead lovey-dovey in public, but honestly' — she lowered her voice — 'I've heard her be rally nasty to him.'

'There's a surprise,' I said.

Fran tutted. 'For God's sake, let's just kill her,' she said.

Mookie looked down suddenly and giggled. 'Oh, it must be the champagne,' she groaned. 'Please, promise me you won't tell anybody.'

'Ehm . . . we promise.'

'Then, kind of, I agree with you. Rally, I don't think they should get married.'

I was touched.

We stepped out of the ridiculous car. There was a crowd of people queuing on the pavement, but Amanda knew where she was going, and she waved us ahead fiercely. Evidently a lot of people who hadn't quite been able to drag themselves out for dinner were there, and Amanda passed up the line kissing and squealing with laughter. Yet again everyone was about eight foot taller than me, with designer clothes and loud voices. Mookie disappeared into a crowd of flowing blonde hair. The night was full of peacocks and screeching, and more exotic birds than us, and out of the club came the ghastly thumping of mid-eighties rock. All this detective work had made me extremely tired. I looked for Amanda. She was at the front of the queue, and I just overheard her say, 'Well, of course, Lili came.'

'Shall we go?' I said to Fran.

'Thought you'd never ask,' she said, and we finally collapsed into a cab and made our way home.

Neither of us spoke until we were nearly at my house. One after another, we let out huge sighs, for quite different reasons.

'Are you coming in?' I said as I paid the driver. However, she was already halfway up the mildewed stairs.

Eleven

We sat in my sitting room giggling and trying to play the tape. I was terrified about noise, as Linda had put a big sign up on my door that said, 'Please don't make nois!!' [sic], so I felt a bit in the last-chance saloon.

The tape crackled and spat through a lot of rustling – and a fair bit of chewing on Fran's part – and eventually cut into the conversation:

'You know, I'm only telling you this for your own good, but you can be incredibly naïve, Melanie.'

The familiar tinkle. I cringed.

'Why do I let her say this stuff?'

'Because you have no self-esteem,' observed Fran. 'If she said anything nice, you'd think she wasn't good enough for you, and you'd never see her.'

I tried to work this out as the tape ran on, but the tape took over. It was unbearable. By the time it got to my famous 'I do believe in all that crap' speech, I was rolling on the floor in embarrassment – first, at my Estuary tones, and second, at the whole ghastly situation of hearing yourself talk bollocks when pissed, which in most of life is fortunately never repeated.

I leaned over and switched the tape recorder off.

'Well, that's it then,' I said.

'What?' Fran grabbed the recorder back fiercely.

'You're not playing that to Angus. Or Fraser. Or anyone. I'm throwing it out right now.'

'But, Mel,' said Fran innocently, 'I believe!'

'Shut up!'

'No! No, I do now truly believe in the power of love, thanks to your moving words.'

'Fuck off!' I leapt at her to try and grab the tape. She grabbed my arms and we rolled about on the carpet, knocking over a frilly lamp with a paisley shade. It crashed off the coffee table.

'Oh God.' I sat up, while Fran held the tape out of my reach. 'SHH!' From next door there came the almost imperceptible sound of a long sigh. Come on, I beckoned Fran quietly, and we went into my bedroom, which was the other side of the flat at least, and you could shut the door properly.

'You definitely can't play that bit,' I hissed. 'It makes me sound like fucking Barbara Cartland. Fraser will think I'm in love with him.'

Fran wasn't listening, instead gently crooning 'The Power of Love' to herself. I kicked her.

'Wind it on. Wind it on to that bit with Mookie in the limousine.'

Unfortunately, Mookie in the limousine sounded exactly like Bagpuss, only with less distinctive vowel sounds.

'What's she saying?' I leaned close to it. '"I agwee?" What does she agwee with? Jesus, that's dreadful.' The tape filled up with traffic noises.

'This is pointless,' I said.

Fran looked at me. 'It's not pointless. You're only going to have to play the first bit to the boys. So what if they think you're an over-romanticized idiot?'

'I think there are enough people in the world already who think I'm an idiot,' I grumbled sulkily. 'I don't want you to play that stupid tape. Let them get married. I don't care.'

'Fine. I don't care either.'

'Fine.'

'Fine.'

'Oh God.'

Fran's lip curled.

'OK, play the damn thing. Can you tell them it's not me?'

'That's right, it could be almost anyone of a million friends I had at that hen night. With a Woking accent.'

'I've got it! Stop it immediately before that bit. Then you just hear the Amanda being a cow bit and nobody gets to hear my speech.'

Fran pulled the spare mattress from under my bed and put the tape recorder under the pillow.

'But that would be no fun,' she protested.

'Hey, nobody said a detective's life is easy, schweetheart.'

Alex and I met up the next day. He'd been out with some of his pseudo rock-star mates, and looked pretty wasted. I wanted to do some early Christmas shopping, but knew there wouldn't be much point in suggesting it, so we were lazing around in Charlie's house, nursing our hangovers.

I'd told him about the invites, and he'd offered to phone up and get me into the wedding if it meant that much to me, then I'd had to explain that that wasn't the point, then

181

he'd said, well, what was the problem then, and I'd looked at him like he was a moron and he'd shrugged his shoulders and said what did I want him to do, go read *Men Are from Mars and Women Are from Venus*? and I said no, forget it, I was having my period.

But I couldn't stay in a strop, because I had to tell him about the night before – in a highly edited version of course, centring around the idea that I might have some ethical concerns about the whole business. He couldn't believe we'd actually gone so far as to wire ourselves up, and thought it was pretty cool.

'Shall we join the FBI when we grow up?' I asked him dreamily.

'Yes, I think so. Do you think they get a million morons a day asking to join their alien division?'

'I don't know. Let's phone them up, ask to join, and measure how pissed off the person's voice is. Those are the kind of forensic detective skills you need to join.'

Alex nodded sagely. 'So what are you going to do with the tape?'

'I don't know. Fran thinks we should play it to Fraser. I'm not so sure.'

'Why not?'

'Well . . . it's illegal, isn't it?'

'So, you think Fraser might report you to the police?'

'No . . . although I couldn't join the FBI with a record.'

'Or without American citizenship. Come on, do you really think it's criminal?'

'No-o-o . . . I just think it was a bit embarrassing and I kind of wish we hadn't done it now. I mean, what if Fraser just shrugs his shoulders and never talks to us again?'

'Well, you know me, I don't really give a shit about this wedding . . . or any wedding for that matter . . .'

Point taken.

'. . . but if you think it's such a horrendous idea, well, then don't you want to stop it? Like you won't let your friends drive drunk, will you?'

'Oh God, not that damn crocodile again.'

'What?'

'Never mind. I do want to stop it. I just didn't think I'd actually, you know, have to do hard things.'

'That's why people tell other people to mind their own business.'

'I know.'

'But if they insist on interfering, pumpkin . . . they should carry it through. Can I hear it?'

'No.'

'Why not? What does it say on it? Does Amanda renounce Fraser because she's desperate for my body?'

'You wish.'

Alex shrugged.

'Really? Would you really wish?'

'No, my darling, I prefer my women more . . . Rubenesque.'

'Fuck off! I can't believe it. If she walked in here naked right now and offered it to you, would you take it?'

'Are you still here at this point?'

'No. Say I don't even exist.'

'Well, maybe.'

'Maybe?'

He grinned. 'Well, you know . . .'

'But she's evil!'

'So you say.'

'You've seen her be evil!'

'When?'

He was right. I couldn't remember a single occasion. God, she hid it well in front of men.

'You have the morals of a lobster,' I grumbled.

'Oh, come on. You asked.'

'Yes, and you're supposed to say "no". Always. Even if it's like a whole Helena Christensen/Naomi Campbell lesbian-type thing. You're always supposed to say no, you'd prefer me.'

'But you don't exist.'

'Yes, well, apart from that.'

Charlie wandered in. When he saw me, he looked slightly embarrassed. I didn't say anything.

'Hey,' said Alex.

'Hey,' said Charlie. Then he took a deep breath.

'Urm . . . Melanie.'

I looked up, surprised.

'I'm terribly sorry about last week.'

'Oh, I'd forgotten all about it,' I lied.

'Huh. Right-oh. Erm, how's that friend of yours?'

'Which one?' I asked him deliberately.

'Yas, you know, erm . . . Fran.'

I smiled, and decided to embellish it a bit. 'Oh, she's doing absolutely great! Ever since she started seeing Angus . . .'

'She's seeing Angus?' cut in Alex abruptly. 'Since when?'

'Since that night, actually.'

Charlie looked utterly crestfallen. 'Gosh, I rather buggered that up then.'

'What?' said Alex. 'She had her tongue down that other guy's throat when we left.'

'Well, you know Fran. Always up for a bit of adventure.'

Charlie perked up a bit. 'Really?'

'Only with Scottish people though,' I said sympathetically. His crest fell again and he turned and left the room.

'Damn gorgeous totty,' he muttered as he went.

Ooh, it was working.

I studied Alex. 'You looked utterly dumbfounded that Fran might have a boyfriend.'

He made a hangdog face. 'Not really. It's just I'd never have put those two together. Mind you, they're both pretty fierce.'

'No they're not!' I said indignantly. 'OK, Fran is pretty fierce. But Angus is a big pet. He's really sweet.'

'So, it won't last long then. D'ya want tea?' Alex went through to put the kettle on.

Actually, it's already finished, I thought to myself, slightly embarrassed for having fibbed about something so pointless.

'You told them WHAT!?' said Fran.

'I thought it would be funny. Wind Charlie up a bit.'

'I decide when I want to wind Charlie up.'

'Oh yeah, NEW RULE!'

'Oh, forget it. You really have a big mouth, don't you?'

'Yeah, you mentioned that.'

Hurt and annoyed, I slumped back in my chair. We were in a greasy caff in North London waiting for Angus, who had been pestering us to know what had happened to the tape. I fiddled disconsolately with the grubby sauce bottle and drank my slightly suspect tea.

'Angus!' she said in a pleased tone as he popped into our booth, shaking the rain off like a dog.

'Angus!' I mimicked under my breath, then gave up and grinned at him. He grinned back and sat down opposite me and next to Fran, his heavy ribbed grey jumper taking up more than half his side. He pushed back his dark red hair.

'Well?' he said heartily.

I looked at Fran. 'Breakfast first!' she said, and we trooped up and ordered bacon, sausage, mushrooms, tomatoes, beans,

185

eggs, and white bread and butter, with a cholesterol seizure to follow.

'I am honour bound to say,' began Fran, once we were all tucking in, 'Mel doesn't want me to play this tape.'

'Why not?' said Angus, looking at me intently.

'Well, you know, there was this big bunch of free champagne, and Amanda says lots of incriminating things, and I say, you know, lots of moronic things,' I said quickly.

He smiled and his eyes went all crinkly. 'Och, I never say anything stupid when I'm drunk.'

I smiled back. 'Actually, normally I make trenchant political speeches about the European monetary system. I do not know what came over me on Friday.'

'Must have been a bad pint . . . of champagne.'

'OK, you two, have you got a sec?'

'Yes,' said Angus. 'Bravery of the officer noted.'

Fran brought the recorder out. I cringed, and paid very close attention to my sausage. Angus watched me quizzically.

The mannered tones came across clearly:

'You know, I'm only telling you this for your own good, but you can be incredibly naïve, Melanie. This . . . I mean, hell, it's a great excuse to have a party, but it's also a bloody practical affair. That castle needs sorting out, and Daddy's happy to put up the loot to do it with.'

Angus's face went red. 'Bloody cow,' he said vehemently.

'Don't you love him?' That was me, and I winced.

'He's a nice chap. It's a good situation. It'll be a fabulous wedding.'

She went on to talk about Fraser being all right, and someone who would have no objections to her living her life.

'Does Fraser think that?' I whispered to Angus.

'Of course he fucking doesn't.' His fried egg was all but forgotten.

Here came my big set speech.

'I don't care,' I heard myself howl petulantly. 'I do believe in all that crap.' On and on and on. 'So, I think you lose!' My voice cracked at this bit, as I got ready for stomping off. My entire body cringed.

Fran switched the tape off after that.

'Thanks,' I grimaced at her. 'You could have switched it off before.'

'Could I?'

Then we just sat there in silence for a bit. Angus looked cross. 'He's so stupid,' he said. 'I can't believe he's a year older than me but so completely stupid.' Then he looked at me across the grimy table.

'Do you really think all that stuff you said?' he asked suddenly.

I shrugged. 'Maybe. I'm sorry about the castle bit.'

'Well, I don't think it's embarrassing at all. And the castle is complete crap. I think you were quite right,' he said. 'And so does Fraser. That's why we've got to stop him getting into this mess.'

'Are you going to play it to him?' asked Fran.

Angus heaved a sigh.

'I don't know.'

'Gus!' I implored him. 'After what I went through?'

'Oh yes, I only did the taping and wore the wire and sorted it all out and switched it on and off inconspicuously,' huffed Fran.

Angus looked at the remains of his breakfast. 'Oh God, it's just so embarrassing. And so wrong.'

We nodded our heads.

'But I suppose I have to.'

We nodded our heads again.

Fran got up to refill her coffee cup.

187

'Mel,' Angus whispered urgently, 'would you . . . would you come with me when I play the tape?'

I was touched.

'Well, yeah . . . Why did you ask me?'

'Ehm . . . in case it gets a bit messy and he tries to punch me or something. And you and Fran are the only women I know down here.'

'Oh, right. Why don't you ask her?'

'I will if you like. But you know Fraser and . . . and, well, I'd rather have you.'

'Cool. OK.'

'OK what?' said Fran, rejoining us.

'OK, that is definitely the best way to lift scum off a cup of tea,' I said, picking up my cup.

'Fascinating,' said Fran. 'Do you know, I think you two are made for each other.'

We had to pick a night Amanda would be out. Fortunately, that was every night, so it wasn't too difficult. She'd moved Fraser into her little pied-à-terre, after complaining too vehemently about his shared boy-tip in Finsbury Park and the copies of *FHM* left wrinkled up by the toilet for use in emergencies. They were only there temporarily: her father was scouring London for a large townhouse suitable for his noble offspring.

Where they lived at the moment turned out to be a small but immaculate apartment in a mansion block in St John's Wood, next to Regent's Park. Angus and I met up beforehand, to plan, and for moral support. The November wind was freezing as we walked across the park. Angus betrayed his nerves by constantly kicking leaves out of the way.

'Right,' said Angus, 'how are we going to do this?'

'Have you got the tape?'

'OK, let's start a little later than that bit.'

'Ehm . . . really, I think we should just go in and not be nice at all. Just push past him with stern faces and say, "Look Fraser, there's something we have to tell you."'

'In a deep American voice?'

'Yeah.'

I wrapped my arms around me.

'Are you cold?'

'Nervous. And cold.'

He clapped his arm round me briefly, which did the trick, as I blushed incredibly red and got warm almost immediately.

'We're nearly there.'

'We have to be brutal about this, Gus. We've got to walk in, just tell him, put the tape on and get out of there. He'll forgive you in – oh, four or five years.'

Angus didn't say anything.

'What? Are you wishing you had brought Fran after all?'

'No . . . I was just thinking.'

'What?'

He looked around.

'That it's a nice night for a walk. It feels such a shame that we're going to, well, you know . . .'

'Do a nasty thing.'

'Yes.'

We walked on.

'Actually, it's a freezing cold and miserable night for a walk,' I said.

'Yes. I suppose it is.'

'Shall we go and do a nasty thing then?'

'Yeah, all right.'

*   *   *

My mysterious and stone-faced FBI persona lasted about ten seconds after Fraser answered the door.

'Hi! Come in, great to see you! Hello, Mel dear.' He kissed me on the cheek. Every time I saw him, I remembered how lovely he was.

This was not going to be easy.

'Did you survive the hen night all right? 'manda told me it was amazing.'

'Yeah, yeah, it was.'

'Hello, Gustard.' He playfully punched Angus on the stomach. Angus was doing better than me, and gave a quiet half-smile.

'Come in, come in. What do you want? Beer, wine . . . ?'

He split off into the kitchen and we trooped into the tiny but tasteful living room. The carpet and the sofas were white, which made me extremely nervous. There was a leopardskin bean bag in the corner and some expensive-looking candlesticks dotted around. Fraser had put out little bowls of peanuts and crisps, obviously in anticipation of our visit. They gazed at me pitifully, so I ate a few for luck.

'Amanda doesn't like people coming round usually – she worries about the carpet,' said Fraser, emerging from the kitchen with three glasses and an open bottle of red wine. I gulped.

'Really? Where is she tonight then?' I asked.

Angus shot me a dirty look and I realized this was not the time for small talk.

Fraser motioned for us to sit down and make ourselves comfortable. The sofa was squashier than it looked and, as I sank into it, a dribble from the wine glass made its way over the side. Fortunately, it dropped on to my trousers. Angus stayed standing up.

190

'Oh, God knows. She's always disappearing to some do or other.' He laughed. 'I can't keep up.'

'Don't you go?'

'No chance. Totally BORING.'

I nodded, and took some more crisps. 'Actually, the hen night . . .'

Angus cleared his throat overdramatically and we both looked up at him. He pulled the tape recorder out and sat down next to me. I covered my glass with my hand.

'Fraser,' he said seriously, 'Melanie and I . . .'

Fraser smiled at the sombreness of the tone, but leaned forward to hear.

'We have something to say to you about your wedding.'

We did? I didn't remember agreeing this.

'Well, really, I'm more here for moral support . . .' I said.

Angus ignored me, continuing: 'Fraser, Ah hate to have to tell you this, but . . . Ah don't think you should marry Amanda.'

Fraser sighed and gulped his wine. 'I don't believe it. I mean, you have actually told me that before. In fact, nearly every day since I met her. Please don't say that's what you came here for. God, and I thought you were coming round to visit me.'

'Aye, well. And Mel agrees with me.'

Fraser looked at me, wounded.

'But I thought . . .'

I gazed back at his stricken face, feeling horribly guilty and embarrassed.

Angus ploughed on regardless: 'And we've got some proof . . . I'm sorry.' He put the tape recorder down on the table. One of the wrought-iron candlesticks fell over.

191

'What's going on?' asked Fraser. 'Are you forming some Moonie-type cult which aims to outlaw marriage for brothers?'

'No.'

'Then why the fuck don't you just keep your nose out of it?'

'Because your ma brother, for fuck's sake.'

'What's on that tape?'

'Melanie talked to her. She doesn't love you, you idiot. She just wants to have some kind of title and swank about and get in *Hello!* magazine and have posh people for friends because she's actually a completely shallow cow.'

Fraser looked at the tape as if it was a snake.

'Is that what she says?' he asked me.

'Not exactly,' I whispered. My voice sounded shaky. I felt absolutely terrible.

He stalked to the other side of the room – which, given the size of it, took two seconds – grabbed the sill and stared out of the sash windows.

'Play the damn thing then.'

Angus was looking at me, but I couldn't look back. This was much much worse than I ever thought it would be. I'd had visions of him even thanking us. Angus leaned over and clicked the switch, and there it came again:

'You're so naïve, Melanie.'

It echoed in my brain like a special effect.

'You're so naïve, Melanie.'

Of course I was, otherwise what was I doing in this tiny, pristine, overheated room, betraying one friend and losing another?

'You're so naïve, Melanie.'

Who did I think I was, Mystic Meg? What had I done this for? Silently, I began to cry. This lovely, gorgeous bloke was still going to get married, and he was going to hate me into the bargain.

Fraser stood stock-still, looking out into the rain and the heavy traffic. Fortunately, Angus managed to stop the tape before my big speech, so at least we were spared that.

Nobody spoke for what seemed like a long time. I was trying to dry my tears without anyone noticing. Unfortunately, to maintain the silence, I had to let some snot drop out of my nose so I didn't have to sniff. It plopped quietly on to the white rug, and I rubbed it with my foot.

Finally, Fraser turned round.

'So, actually, she didn't say any of those things you mentioned, about the title and the magazines and all that shit.'

I could feel Angus looking at me, but I couldn't return his gaze. Fraser's voice was furious.

'In fact, she spoke for ten seconds about keeping her individuality after she gets married and having thought the damn thing through beforehand, and you take that as proof that she's some kind of social-climbing bitch. Like you know anything about my wedding, or about my girlfriend or my own fucking life. Not only that, you manage to draft some of my friends into this idiotic scheme . . . Melanie, are you crying?'

'Nooo,' I whimpered.

He came and stood beside me and patted me on the arm — which of course made it worse — without stopping talking.

'I mean, Gus, what the fuck do you want? What do you really want? Do you want the damn title? Because you're making so much bloody fuss about it, you might as well have it. It doesn't matter to me, but it looks like it matters to you.'

'Of course it doesn't matter to me,' growled Angus, who looked sullen and red.

'Well, what then? What the hell is it? Why won't you leave this damn thing alone? You're trying to sabotage this whole thing, and I don't even know why.'

His face was a mixture of anger and misery, and genuine miscomprehension.

Angus bowed his head low. 'I'm sorry we came.'

'I'm sorry you came. And why are you dragging Melanie into it, for God's sake?'

I snuffled.

'I'm sorry I did that too,' said Angus. 'I meant well. I'm sorry.'

'Please,' said Fraser. 'Please, just . . . leave it alone. You're like a dog with something between its teeth, Gus. Always have been. You won't let things fucking well alone.'

'I'd better be going.'

'You better had.'

I stood up awkwardly to follow him.

Fraser took my arm and looked at me with some concern. 'Are you going to be OK?'

'Do you hate me?' I choked.

He smiled sadly. 'No, of course not. Gus, are you going to take her home?'

Angus nodded. Fraser turned away from us.

'Bye then.' It was a dismissal.

We trooped through the corridor. As we got to the door, Angus turned round and went back to the sitting room. Blindly, I followed him.

'Do you . . .' he began, as he stepped through the door.

Fraser was sitting there, staring at the tape recorder in his hands. He looked up at his brother, his eyes damp.

'What?' he growled, caught off guard.

Angus blushed furiously. 'Nothin'. Just wondering about cabs. Bye.'

That time we left for good.

Angus strode fiercely through the park, the rain blowing back his hair and coat, all mention of a cab apparently forgotten. I trotted along beside him, ashamed of myself, and terrified of what he was going to say. I felt like such a stupid girl. He didn't speak for what seemed like miles. I was tempted to slip quietly behind him and go the other way, but I didn't dare. Suddenly, in the dark, I tripped over something or other and let out a strangled yell. Angus whipped back and immediately his stony face softened.

'Are you OK?' he yelled across the wind.

'I'm . . . fine,' I croaked, although I didn't feel fine at all. I tried to stand up, and it was agonizing. Angus caught me keeling over.

'What've you done?'

'I . . . I think I've twisted my ankle.' I leaned on him heavily, feeling a bit green.

'Are you going to be sick?'

'I wouldn't . . .' I tried to take a step forward, 'rule it out as a possibility.'

'Great,' he said gloomily, supporting my elbow. 'Is this the best evening out you've ever had?'

I managed another step, wincing. 'Well, it's the best freezing cold family feud twisted ankle evening out I've ever had.'

'That's something, I suppose.'

He indicated a park bench, but I could see the lights of Camden in the distance and pointed to them.

'Can you make it?'

'Can you carry me?'

'I could try.'

I giggled. 'Only kidding. I'd kill you. Just let me lean on you for a bit.'

The next ten minutes were agony, but finally we collapsed in the first pub we came to. It was so good to be out of the cold and the wet, I felt better already. The pub was quiet and old-fashioned. It actually had a fire lit in the grate, and we sat beside it to dry off.

Angus got up to fetch me a whisky. I'd rather have had a glass of white wine, but I stuck to his judgement in situations like this.

Angus returned with two large glasses. 'Thank God for civilization,' he said.

'Can I have some ice in mine?'

'No, you bloody well can't.'

'That's not very civilized, telling people what to do.'

We both stared into the fire for a bit.

'What do you think will happen?' I ventured finally. Angus heaved a sigh.

'I wish I knew,' he said. 'I felt like such a bloody fool. Tell me it had to be done, Mel.'

I thought of Fraser's face – so pained and miserable.

'Ehm . . . I suppose so.'

Angus rubbed his eyes. 'It's the rest of his life. Every day, having to wake up next to someone who thinks he's an idiot. Oh God, I don't know. I just hate her so much. And, you know, I've only got one brother. Since Dad died . . . we've been really close. Well, I thought we were.'

'Have you fallen out before?'

'Not like this. Apart from the whole *Star Wars* figures thing. But that was a long time ago. Normally, when I speak to him about the wedding he treats it as a joke . . . but it's getting so close.'

'God, yes . . . it's soon, isn't it?'

'Three weeks' time. Pyrford village church. Good Protestant vicar and four hundred guests to a five-course meal.'

'Not for me.'

'Oh, I'm sorry . . .'

'Nope, I don't care.'

'You may not have to. Did you see the way he was holding that tape recorder?'

'Yes, because he was so pissed off with you.'

'Did you think so? I thought he was pissed off with her.'

I sipped my drink.

'Hmm,' he said. 'Mel, can I ask you a question?'

I hate it when someone says that. What they usually mean is: *Mel, can I insult you and get away with it, having warned you in advance?*

'Uh-huh?'

'Why did you start crying?'

'That's, umm, a very good question.'

'Sorry. I don't mean to intrude.'

'It's OK. I'm really sorry, actually. I got upset about things – it seemed so rotten. Why can't everyone just be nice and end up with nice people? . . . That sounds pathetic.'

'No, it doesn't,' he said gently. 'Do you include yourself in "everyone"?'

'That's the standard definition, isn't it? I'm sorry. About all of it.'

'Oh, it's my fault. Don't worry, I'm sure we'll recover. We are brothers, after all. Blood and stuff. I think I'll give him a wee ring in the morning, once it's all blown over a bit.'

Phew, at least I didn't have to do that. I finished my whisky and suddenly felt enormously sleepy.

'How are you going to get home?' asked Angus.

I realized to my surprise that, actually, I didn't want to go home; I wanted to curl up in front of this big fire and put my head on his shoulder. But I didn't say that.

'I can't get a cab; it'll cost a fortune,' I said. 'I think I'll phone Alex. He can drive Charlie's car and come and pick me up.'

Angus lent me his phone.

'Does this work in underwater pipes?' I asked, picking up the big thing with a huge fluorescent stripe down it.

'Maybe,' he grinned.

Charlie answered.

'Is Alex there?'

'Erhm – what?'

'Charlie, it's Mel.' Brain of dough. 'Is Alex there?'

'Ehrr, um, I've just got in . . . Ehm, I'll go and check.'

I shot Angus a look. 'That boy gets more moronic every day.'

'It's the inbreeding.'

I nodded. There was a lot of scuffling in the background, and some whispering going on.

'Hello?' asked Alex doubtfully.

'Alex? Hi, it's me.'

'Oh, hello, pumpkin. I, ehm, thought you were out tonight.'

'I am. Was. Look, I've twisted my ankle, pretty badly. Do you think you could come and pick me up?'

'Ehm . . . where are you?'

'Camden.'

'Camden. Jesus, that's miles away! Can't you get a cab?'

'If I made twice the salary I do now, I would get a cab. Look, I'd rather not, I don't feel well and I've really hurt myself.' I started to get upset again. 'Can't you come and get me?'

'Look, Mel, sweetheart, I'm kind of in the middle of something right now.'

'What? What the hell is it? Why do I have to plead with you to come and pick me up?'

'Ehm, some of the lads are round and I've really had too much to drink to drive.'

'I don't believe you. I think you just don't want to come and get me.'

'Pumpkin, I would if I could, honest. Trust me, it's just impossible. Why don't you just take a cab home and I'll see you tomorrow?'

There was a pause. I didn't know what to say, so I hung up the phone.

Angus looked away, embarrassed. I waited till the urge to cry had passed and swallowed hard.

'Bastard,' I said.

'Sounds like one,' said Angus. 'I'd carry you home.'

I looked at him. 'You would too.'

'Damsel in distress. My speciality.'

I laughed. 'I'm tempted.'

'Be tempted.' His voice suddenly turned serious. He looked at me face on, with that direct gaze of his, and my heart started beating extremely fast. We looked at each other for what seemed like a long time. Our faces began to come a little closer. Then I moved slightly, and jarred my ankle really, really hard against the chair.

'AAAYICK!' I yelled, bending over. The whole sleepy bar looked over to see who was being murdered. I put my hands on my ankle, trying to make it better, but it was agony. Shockwaves of pain careered up my legs.

'Ow! Ow! Ow ow ow ow ow.'

'Oh, you poor thing.' Angus got up with me, as I started hopping about on one leg.

'Ow ow ow. God, my fucking ankle! It really fucking hurts.'

199

'Do you want to lean on me? Go to Casualty?'

'No, no no. Jesus! This has happened before. Ehm, the best thing I could do really is just go home and take some aspirin. Arsing hell.'

A look passed between us. The moment when whatever might have happened was going to happen had gone.

Angus went to the bar and called a cab. I was escorted out by him and the barman, and an hour later I was safely tucked up in bed with four Nurofen and the comfort of a guaranteed sickie in the morning.

Twelve

Unfortunately, my ankle felt practically fine in the morning. Well, stiff, and it hurt if I really put my weight on it, but not quite enough to justify sickie status. And as I felt, overall, that my morality rating wasn't at its highest, I got ready to go in.

My mind felt like scrambled eggs, so I decided to make some for breakfast.

'Linda, do you want some scrambled eggs?'

She emerged, fully dressed but looking sleepy, from her bedroom. The look on her face plainly told me how amazed she was at this whole me-cooking thing. However, surprisingly, she took me up on it. Well, there was food involved, I supposed.

There would be no point, I surmised, in asking for her advice. So I asked her about the bank instead.

'What bank?'

'Ehm, don't you work in a bank?'

'No.'

Actually, I could pull my own teeth out just fine, thank you.

'So, where do you work, again?'

'Brimley's.'

'Brimley's . . . ?'

'Insurance.'

'Right! Right . . . So, how's it going?'

'Fine.'

I sipped my tea. It was going to be a long day.

'I need the weekend,' she said suddenly.

I thought she might be asking me to give back something I'd borrowed off her, and I racked my brains to remember, but couldn't.

'The what?'

'The weekend,' she said, enunciating very slowly as I was clearly such an idiot.

'Right . . . the weekend,' I said. This was turning into some sort of perpetual conversational nightmare.

'Before Christmas. I need the flat for the weekend.'

'Oh, right. You want me to get out?'

She nodded. There didn't seem to be much room for argument.

'Fine, OK,' I said without thinking. 'That shouldn't be a problem. Which one?'

'All of it.'

'Which weekend?'

'The one before Christmas,' she explained patiently.

Oh. Speak in sentences, you dozy cow.

'OK. OK, fine.'

That was the weekend of the wedding, so I supposed we'd be away anyway, somehow or other. But what on earth was Linda up to? Her actually doing something threatened the stability of my already fragile view of the universe.

'What are you up to?' I asked her.

She stared at me, stood up abruptly from the table and walked out. Great.

I couldn't face washing up the scrambled egg pan, so I left it and limped into work.

'Ey up, snoots.' I bumped into Steve coming in. 'You been in the wars, then?'

I groaned. 'You should see the other guy. And he was a Cockney.'

'Yeah, right. You'd be dead.'

'Actually, now I think about it, that's true. I'd rather kill myself than have physical contact with a Cockney.'

I walked into the office, and got a huge sense of *déjà vu*. Sitting on my desk was another cheap bouquet; and there was another crying jag from my next-door neighbour.

'What's the matter now?' I said brusquely, dumping the flowers in the bin.

'I thought they were for me.'

'Do you want them?' I looked at them in the bin, now covered in banana skin and old plastic coffee cups.

'No. Aren't you even going to read the card?'

'I can predict the card.' Nonetheless, I took a quick peek. 'Sorry about your ankle, pumpkin. Can I see you tonight? I'll pick you up,' it said.

'Fuck off,' I said sourly, and plumped myself down on the stool. The phone rang.

'Fuck off,' I said again, and picked up all the unopened post that was spilling over my in-tray.

The phone rang fourteen times that morning. Each time I swore at it and concentrated on what I was doing instead. Finally, Janie leaned over and said quietly, 'You know, you could put that on voice mail, then you wouldn't even have to hear it ring.'

It pissed me off that that was such an eminently reasonable suggestion, so I just said 'huh,' and went back to being in a big sulk.

At lunch time the receptionist put her head round the open-plan office door.

'Melanie Pepper!' she shrieked.

I tentatively put my hand up.

'You're not answering your phone!'

Stop shrieking at me! I stood up carefully.

'There's someone here to see you in reception.'

Jesus. 'Is it a man?'

'It sure is.'

'Can you . . . tell him I'm on a business trip?'

'You ain't on no business trip!'

'No, but could you tell him that?'

'You can come right upstairs and tell him yourself.'

'How can I . . . ? Oh, forget it, never mind.'

The receptionist had already retreated up the stairs. I followed slowly, trying to figure out a strategy. The bastard. He was going to pay, the selfish bastard.

Fraser stood nervously at the top of the stairs, pretending to admire our annual report. He looked tense. If it were an earlier age, he'd have been playing with his top hat and gloves.

I stood looking at him for a second, then crept up behind him.

'Don't tell me: you're a masochist,' I said suddenly. Startled, he turned round, then smiled shyly.

'Hullo.'

'What are you doing here?'

'Well, Angus gave me your work address . . .'

'You spoke to Angus? What did he say?'

'I'll tell you in a minute. Would you like to go to lunch? I work quite near here. Anyway, there's a little Italian around the corner . . .'

'I know it,' I said. 'Yes, please.'

Steve was crossing the reception area.

'Hey, Steve, can you tell Flavi I've gone out for lunch?'

'Blow it out your arse.'

'Thanks.'

Fraser looked quizzical. 'One of those informal offices?'

'Something like that.'

The Italian was busy and smelled wonderful. I remembered that I hadn't had any dinner the night before, and the scrambled eggs were a few hours away, so I ordered spaghetti carbonara. And some garlic bread. With cheese. And minestrone soup. And a glass of wine.

'How's the ankle? Angus told me.'

'Much better, thanks. So, what happened between you two? Tell me everything.'

Fraser eyed me munching my way through the garlic bread. 'Well, you seem in good shape.'

I grimaced. 'Did you come over to see if I was still a snivelling wretch or not?'

'Something like that. Angus asked me to pop in and see if you were OK. He was worried about you, and he knew I worked nearby – you know the Xyler building?'

'The big pinky-coloured one? Yes, I know it, that's just across the road. Huh! And I thought you'd flown in to whisk me off to some glamorous lunch.'

'This isn't glamorous?'

We heard two of the waiters having a loud disagreement

205

in Italian through the multicoloured plastic strips of door covering.

'Well, you know, for those of us more used to the delights of Quagli's . . .'

'Ha ha.'

He took some bread and mopped up the remnants of my soup with it.

'So, tell me,' I said, agog to know how they'd managed to make it up.

'Really, it was nothing. The Gustard and I fight all the time.'

'That's not what he said.'

'Oh yes, sure, *Star Wars* figures and, you know, all the usual stuff.'

'Girls?' I asked him mischievously.

He grinned.

'You're feeling better, all right. No, we don't usually fight about girls.'

'Except this one.'

He misunderstood.

'Who, you?'

'Ehm, no . . . Amanda.'

'Oh, right, I see what you mean.'

Momentarily embarrassed, we looked around in a flurry for our waiter.

A steaming plate of pasta was put in front of me, and I inhaled greedily.

'So, what did you say?' I urged.

'We made up. You're never going to eat all that.'

'Watch me, skinny boy.'

'He came round late last night after you'd gone, and apologized. Actually, I think he was more worried about you than me.'

'That was just a cover. Boy thing.'

'Hmm. Anyway, he took it all back, blah blah blah, promised not to mention the wedding any more, etcetera, etcetera.'

'Right.' I felt perversely disappointed.

'You're pissed off with him, aren't you?'

'No.'

'It's OK, you know.' He smiled. 'I don't mind if you don't want me to get married.'

'It's not that,' I protested, lying. 'I just don't want you to get married to her.'

'Ah, so you admit it.'

'Of course I admit it. I'm sorry. Please don't hate me.'

'I don't hate you. I told you already. And, anyway, I listened to the rest of the tape.'

'Oh shit, did you?'

'Don't worry, I forgive you for what you said about my castle.'

'Your big pile of rocks.'

'Whatever.'

I toyed with my pasta.

'Don't marry her, Frase. It's only money.'

I realized I'd said the wrong thing again, but he took it all right.

'God, if it's not one thing it's the other with you two. Now suddenly, I'm the bastard. She's fine and I'm a money-grabbing bastard, marrying for the wrong reasons.'

'I'm sorry! I always say the wrong thing.'

'Forget it. I'm boring myself to death with this damn wedding business. Mel, please, we've been friends for a long time. Can you promise to stop going on at me, like Angus did?'

I thought about it. 'What, just because it's none of my business?'

He nodded.

'OK. Seeing as it's you. And we've been friends for such a long time. Apart from the five years in the middle when we lost touch.'

He held out his hands. 'You vanished. One moment you were being a bit pissed at Graduation, next thing you phone up out of the blue five years later.'

I never had been able to say goodbye.

'OK then. I promise.'

Having finished his lasagne, he launched into my spaghetti.

'Don't you get fed at home?'

'Not really. Less than five milligrams of fat a week until the wedding.'

'See, you started it! Less than two seconds that lasted! Wedding, wedding, wedding. Here, help yourself.'

He smiled sadly, and I felt awful. I mean, what did we think we were playing at, with tape recorders and all that shit? This was someone's life we were fucking around with.

Whenever I get into one of those arguments about nature over nurture – which isn't that often, to be honest, as I don't seem to see my genetical ethicist biology friends so much these days – I always bring up my overwhelming desire to feed people I feel a bit sorry for, despite my absolute lack of culinary ability, and think about my mother.

'Do you want to come round to dinner?' I asked him. Damn genes.

Fraser of course has known me for a while and looked up from my plate, where he was gulping down pasta.

'Are you feeling sorry for me?'

'No, definitely not. Definitely, definitely not. In fact, I've been planning it for ages.'

'Really? Who were you thinking of inviting?'

208

'Well . . .' – fuck! – 'you're guest of honour, you choose.'

'God. How amazing. You're having a big dinner party?'

'YES!'

'With all of us?'

'Who's us?'

'You, me, Amanda and Angus.'

'I'm not sure about that definition of "us". But yes, why not?'

'Oh, can I bring Nash? He'll be down. McLachlan . . . kind of resigned as my best man, so I'm asking him instead.'

'Wow. Yes, sure.'

'And Amanda will want to bring one of her bridesmaids.'

'Don't push it.'

'I'm sorry, I thought you were doing a big thing.'

'I am. Ehm, can you make it be Mookie then?'

'I cannot for the life of me tell them apart. Why that one?'

'No reason.'

'Is she the one on the end of the tape who sounds like Bagpuss?'

'Maybe.'

'I thought so.'

He looked at me and smiled.

'Are you sure you want to put yourself to all this trouble?'

'What, just shopping, cooking, serving and washing up for six? How hard can it be? I made scrambled eggs this morning.'

'Well – what a nice surprise! Thank you. It's really kind.'

I beamed.

'Ehm, can I ask you something?'

Uh oh. Not another one of those.

'Just out of interest . . .' he leaned over the table, 'what exactly is going on between you and my wee brother?'

I was genuinely shocked.

'Nothing!'

'That's what he says. Which means one of you must be lying.'

'Thank you, Socrates.'

'Aw, go on. Tell me.'

'There's precisely nothing going on. I'm seeing someone.'

'Angus says he's a bastard.'

'Angus seems to think he has the last word on everyone's relationships around here.'

Fraser smiled. 'Well, yes. But do you like him?'

'Your wee brother?'

'Yes.'

'Why, what's he said?'

'Nothing.'

'Fine. I'm not saying anything either.'

'So you do.'

'Piss off, piss off, piss off!'

'Oh my God. You really like him.'

'Look, shut up,' I said. 'Truthfully, I don't know who or what I like at the moment. Everything is so fucked up. Everyone goes out with the wrong people. Everything's so mixed up at the moment. Alex is driving me crazy, but what's the difference between that and your brother driving me crazy? So, maybe you were right just now when you said that maybe we should all keep our heads in our own affairs.'

I must have sounded more serious than I'd intended, because Fraser dipped his head and slowly nodded.

'Yikes. Yes, ma'am.'

'Yes ma'am, indeed. Can you buy me lunch, given that you're nearly loaded?'

'You should buy me lunch for trying to ruin my wedding.'

'You should buy me lunch for turning up unannounced.'

'You should buy me lunch for ambushing me in my own house.'

'You should buy me lunch for asking inappropriate personal questions about your brother.'

He laughed.

'Ha! You should buy me lunch for giving me inappropriate diktats about my fiancée, don't you think?'

The waiter returned, holding the bill.

'Actually,' I said quietly. 'You should buy me lunch because I left my wallet in the office.'

He laughed. 'Minx! But it would be a pleasure.'

'I'll get it next time. Also, I want to see whether you write "laird" on your Switch card.'

'What, in case anyone around here doesn't already think I'm a wanker?'

We headed back up the road, through the crowds of people wandering their lunch times away aimlessly.

'Thanks for taking me out to lunch,' I said.

'Thank Angus – he suggested it. Angus and Mel, up a tree, K-I-S-S-I-N –'

'Shut it.'

'How much abuse can one man take?'

'You're about to find out for the next forty years of your life. Now, scram.'

And I waved him off, much lighter in my heart than I had been just an hour before.

I had a record-breaking twelve voice-mail messages, a mixture of fawning from Alex and offence from the receptionist. And one from Fran. Immediately I heard it I thought, 'Oh my God, Fran!' I'd completely forgotten her for my dinner plan.

But now we had a six, plus Alex, I supposed. Plus I probably had to invite Linda as she wouldn't be out . . . and I only had five chairs as it was . . . maybe I'd just not tell her. That was an alien thought to me. Normally I couldn't put my socks on without phoning her up a couple of times. I wrestled with my conscience slightly – I was going to have to invite Linda, because she'd be there anyway, and wasn't known for her ability to enhance the ambience . . . maybe I could persuade Amanda not to bring Mookie . . .

Suddenly it dawned on me what I'd let myself in for. God, what had I got myself into? I didn't have a pot big enough to scramble eggs for eight people. I didn't mind fiddling about in the kitchen when I had hours and it was just me, and Alex who would eat tadpoles if there was nothing else available, but this was bad. I wished I wasn't such a show-off, and so desperate to make it up to Fraser.

I decided to phone Angus. What was he up to anyway, backing down like that? It wasn't very Braveheart of him. He was busy, unfortunately. He'd been asked to stay longer in London, so at least his job was going well.

I took the voice mail off in case he rang. Which it immediately did. My heart leapt – God, he'd got back to me quickly. However, it was Alex.

'I'm sorry,' he said. 'Please, for God's sake. We were a bit pissed round the flat, and it got out of hand. I should have sent a cab for you.'

'You creep. You completely embarrassed me in front of my friends.'

'Who?'

Suddenly, I wasn't sure I wanted him to know I'd been out with Angus on my own.

'Just Angus and Fran – we went over to Fraser's.'

'Fran?'

'Yes, why?'

'Ehm, no reason, I thought I saw her on the tube last night.'

Bugger it, what a stupid lie.

'Ehm, I didn't mean Fran, I meant Holly.' I named another friend I scarcely saw these days.

'Right.'

There was a pause, and I was sure he knew I was lying. But he obviously decided to ignore it.

'Do you forgive me, pumpkin?'

I sighed.

'Why do I feel like I spend the whole of my life forgiving you? I'm getting sick of this.'

'What do you mean?'

I became very conscious of Janie and Steve on either side of me, ears on poles.

'Well, you know, I'm just . . .' I heard myself saying it: 'I'm not sure I want to put up with this kind of behaviour any more.'

There was a silence. Suddenly I felt very, very cold inside. Where had this come from?

'Look, I . . .' I could hear Alex run his fingers through his hair, like he did when something irritated him. He took a deep breath. 'Can we talk about this?'

'Not now.'

'Fine. Any time. Can I meet you from work? We'll go for a drink, maybe. I think . . . we need to talk.'

My heart was in my throat. Was this it? I mean, it was all so sudden. One minute I'd been planning to give him a hard time about being so selfish, and the next I seemed to have inadvertently started the chain which would eventually lead to the break-up process. It always started with 'we need to

213

talk', always. Unless of course they simply left the country. God, I wasn't sure about this at all.

'Sure, whatever,' I managed to say, casually. Stage two, agreeing to the need to talk.

He named a place, and trembling, I wrote it down, put the phone down and stared into space in disbelief.

Janie was agog. 'Oh my God, did he just dump you?'

'No,' I said crossly. 'I nearly dumped him, as a matter of fact. He's currently pleading for his life.'

Her eyes widened. 'Why would you dump him?'

'Because he's a selfish son of a bitch who only pleases himself?'

Her expression didn't change.

'Have you ever dumped anyone?' I asked. She shook her head mutely.

'What do you think might be grounds for dumping someone?'

Still silent, she shrugged. I managed a half-smile.

'Don't worry. I've got a substitute.'

Her eyebrows nearly reached her hairline.

Cockney Steve was deliberately ignoring all this girlie chat – or had been, from the moment he found out I wasn't on the receiving end.

'Have you ever been dumped, Steve?'

'Course not.' He flushed to the roots of his over-gelled hair.

'Have you ever had a girlfriend, Steve?'

'Fuck off!'

'Are you sure you're not gay? Lots of people who work in marketing are, you know. Look at the colour of the walls.'

He fingered his gold chains and muttered at me.

It made me feel better, but didn't solve the problem. What

in the hell was going on? This was beginning to feel like a very fucked up time in my life.

God, I'd spent months drooling over Alex, waiting for him to come back to me. Which he had. And now, well, I didn't know what I was doing at all, or even how I felt. I loved him, but he was driving me crazy. More than anything, I wanted someone to come along and point me in one direction and say, *This way. This is the way to go to be happy. Go this way.*

I didn't think that was going to happen. But I phoned Fran anyway.

'I'm thinking of finishing it with Alex,' I said to her as soon as she picked up.

She gasped. 'Why?'

'What do you mean, "why"? You think he's a good-for-nothing cocksucker. Isn't that a good enough reason?'

'No, I mean, why now?'

'Oh, like about a billion little things. Like last night, I really hurt my ankle and he wouldn't even come and get me. He said he was in with some mates, but I don't believe him. I think he was just being a lazy bastard. I mean, he really doesn't care about me at all.'

'I think he does, you know.'

'What the hell is this, the Alex Appreciation Society?'

'Well, OK then. You know what I think. Chuck him immediately and go out with one of those nice McConnald boys.'

'What do you mean, one of those nice McConnald boys? Only one of them's free, you know.'

'So you'll take whatever's available?'

'Shut up! You're not helping.'

'Yes I am. Chuck Alex immediately and go out with some-one nice. What better help could I give you than that?'

'But Fran . . . you know, it's Alex.'

'Alex who you were madly in love with. I know. But now he's behaving like a prat, you're not in love with him any more. So, who gives a bison's bum? Move on!'

'But I'm a great big yellow cowardy custard!'

'All the more reason to do it now, while you're cross at him.'

'I don't know what I'm going to do. I don't think I'll know until I see him. I'll phone you later. God, I feel sick.'

'Fine, good, be sick, whatever. But please make sure you DITCH that sucker once and for all.'

'Hnnn,' I said.

The day wore on for about thirty-four hours. I tried to concentrate, but it wasn't easy. My heart was beating fast and I couldn't sit still. All the time, the mantra ran through my head: Life without Alex. Life without Alex. It had been so long since I'd considered the possibility – in fact, I never had.

I remembered the look on his face the day we'd planned the taping, when he'd said he loved me, and my gut wrenched. But, if he loved me, why couldn't he behave like it? Not just do what he wanted, all the time, then send apologies afterwards.

I wished there was some space to pace up and down in. That might have helped.

'Cheer up, might never happen,' winked Steve.

'I know that. But if that is the case, should I move on now? Or should I stick at it and work on something that might have just started to build?'

'You've gone bonkers, you 'ave,' he said moodily.

*   *   *

At last I was free. I ran out of the building at top speed, even for me. I was meeting Alex in a trendy bar just down the road in Covent Garden, and when I reached it, I saw he was already there. Sitting with his back to me, the figure, in his leather jacket, looked sad and despairing, nursing a beer and staring into space. My heart sank. I wanted to run up to him and put my arms round him, pull him back to me.

He turned round to check the door and saw me standing in it, gazing at him. Without a word, he got up and ran to me, pulling me to him. I felt his strong body against me and closed my eyes. Tears ran out.

'Please don't break up with me,' he said.

'You have got to stop doing things like this!'

His face looked grey and haggard.

'I know, I know.'

'We can't go on having these bloody conversations! That's all we ever do! You behave like a prick and I forgive you!'

'Shh. Come on. Sit down.'

We sat down at the table.

'Can I get you a drink?'

I had a coffee. I stared into space while he fetched it, trying to figure out what to say.

He came back and sat facing me, and there was a silence.

Finally, I swallowed, and said it. I needed to hear him deny it. I needed to hear him tell me that he needed me.

'Alex, I think we should maybe stop seeing each other for a while.'

He sat very calmly. Finally, and to my intense relief, he said, 'I know. Please don't do this, Mel. Please.'

'Give me one good reason why not. Really, since you got back, it's . . . it's been one slap in the face after another for me.'

'You can't finish this because I was too drunk to pick you up.'

'I'm not finishing it because of that. I'm finishing it because you turn up pished, you insult my friends, you fight with my friends, you let me down, and you won't commit. Is that a long enough list?'

Still calm, he reached out and took my hand, then looked to the ceiling as if trying to collect his thoughts.

'Mel, there's something I have to tell you . . .' Then he reconsidered. 'I mean, I can't tell you. But honestly, if you knew, it would change everything.'

'Tell me. Or it's not going to.'

'OK. Look, Mel, I didn't get that job. The one at the record company. That bloke who was going to help me . . . he won't return my calls, or see me or anything.'

He looked wretched.

'I don't think I'm ever going to get into the business. I mean, I'm twenty-nine now, and apparently they only want sixteen-year-olds these days.'

I waited for him to go on.

'I don't know what I'm going to do for a living; I've never done anything much. In fact, my life, really, is a complete piece of shit.'

'Thanks . . .'

'Except for you,' he shushed me. 'I've been thinking about this – trying to use some of the techniques I picked up, you know, when I was in India. Trying to figure everything out. And I think what's happening, subconsciously, is that I don't think I'm good enough for you. I'm trying to push you away, to make you prove you love me by misbehaving.'

'That's a big piece of crap! And the worst excuse I've ever heard.'

'I'm sorry you think it's crap,' he said calmly. 'I'm sorry

that you think that the state my life is in is just a piece of crap.' He stared at his empty glass.

'I don't,' I said. 'I just don't see why your being miserable means you get to be nasty to me.'

'I know. It doesn't. It's inexcusable. That's why I'm trying to explain it, to work it out in my own head. You're the last person on earth I want to hurt. But I'm doing it, nearly every day. I think . . . I mean, you know, you're doing really well, you've got a good job.'

'I've got a pissy job!'

'And you're quite together.'

'I'm . . . scrambled eggs!'

He looked at me curiously. 'Anyway, you've got your life going on one track, and you don't need me. I think I'm just trying to get your attention. And trying to warn you off from such a fuck-up as me. Which, really, I don't want to do.' He paused. 'I want you.'

'You never think about me. You didn't think about me last night when I was in Camden, and miles from home, and hurt.'

'Believe me, I did. I thought about you all night. That's when I really started to work out why our relationship is the way it is.'

'It's the way it is because you're a big selfish pig.'

'No, Mel. It's the way it is because I'm scared . . . scared of how much I feel for you.'

He shook his hair out of his eyes fiercely.

'Honestly. And I want to believe in myself enough to be with you.'

I narrowed my eyes.

'So, I'm not going to be frightened any more,' he continued.

'You're not.'

219

He fiddled intensely with his coffee cup.

'No. I'm going to stick to my guns for once in my life. Mel, I thought –' he looked up at me briefly, then back at the table. 'Well . . . if you'll still have me . . . still want me . . . well, if you don't absolutely hate me like I hate myself at the moment, I thought we might – if you could forgive me, if you were willing to give it one last shot, we could maybe, hem, try and move in together? For a bit. See if we could take it to the next stage. After Christmas, ehm, I thought maybe we could find a room or a flat somewhere?'

I was as surprised as Wile E. Coyote is when he chases Road Runner off a mountain and realizes he's running in mid-air.

'I don't think we've been communicating since I got back,' Alex went on. 'We're always busy, and we're so concerned with other people's business, I think we've neglected our own.'

He looked up at me hopefully.

'Since I moved to Fulham, I hardly get to see you.'

'You moved out,' I pointed out. 'Four hundred miles away.'

'Yes, but I was just back. Trying to establish myself. Get myself straightened out. I told you, I didn't want to rush anything. But now I've thought it through. And I reckon you were right all along. We *are* meant to be together.'

I'd forgotten this was my idea to begin with.

'We should set up shop. Give it a shot. What do you think?'

He stared at me, still calm, I thought. Then I glanced downwards, and noticed his foot jiggling like it was auditioning for *Riverdance*. Suddenly, I felt a big wave of affection towards him.

'I don't know what to say,' I said. 'Have I been going out with your evil twin all this time?'

He took my hand. 'Well, in a funny way, you have.'

I moved my hand away. 'OK, you're scaring me now.'

'Sorry. I was up late last night thinking about a lot of this stuff.'

'Right.' I stared at the tablecloth, ears burning. This wasn't what I was used to at all. In my world, 'let's meet for a chat' meant being told that something or other was not working out and therefore it was all over on the job/love/friendship front. I wondered gloomily how Lili, Amanda's glamorous friend, coped with things like this. She probably got asked about fifteen times a day. She probably got them to buy her a flat first, then turned them down and kept the flat.

'You don't have to decide anything now,' said Alex, caring sharing hippy king.

'Don't I?'

'No, of course not, I don't want to pressure you.' He grinned an old-fashioned Alex grin. 'Although, obviously, you are driving me absolutely crazy, pumpkin.'

This sounded more characteristic. 'Am I driving you mental?' I asked.

'I am at one with despair, until I get your answer.'

'Good. Serves you right, for a change.' I sat back and folded my arms.

He stood up and, without a word, went and got us a couple more coffees. I watched his broad back at the bar in wonder.

Suddenly, a tiny spark of excitement lit up inside me. Living together! Long lazy Sundays in bed, proper cooking, shopping for things, talking all night, taking baths together. No more trekking home on my own, no more empty house. Well, it was never empty, but it might as well have been for all the sparks of warmth there were. Dinner parties and coupley invitations. God, it was bourgeois, and God, it was boring, but . . . oh, I liked the idea.

Alex was still at the bar, his fingers tapping the top with nerves. My heart softened. How much had it taken him to ask this? He must have agonized for hours. Oh, and he'd have to tell Charlie. Hooray! And I'd get to tell Amanda, who had always made it perfectly clear that she didn't think I was good enough for him. And, oh my God, I'd get to meet his parents. My imagination was filled with the image of couples in furniture adverts who are always having pillow fights for some reason. That would be us. And where would we go? Alex was sure to get a bunch of money from his parents at Christmas time, so we'd be able to lay down a deposit on something quite nice. They might even pay all the rent, if we got lucky . . .

I'd started choosing the curtain material by the time he came back with two more cappuccinos.

He sat down. 'Tell me you're mentally choosing curtain material.'

'Don't be daft. I'm trying to think this whole thing through sensibly.'

'What's there to think? It's not like we're getting married or anything.'

'No, I suppose not.'

'C'mon, pumpkin, say yes. It'll be a laugh. I promise I'll be good. No Charlie, no rugby, just twenty-four-hour devotion to you.'

'You're a lying hound,' I said.

'I'm just a soul whose intentions are good,' he pointed out. 'Oh Lord, please don't let me be misunderstood.'

I looked at him.

'Oh my God, what am I letting myself in for this time?'

'You said yes! She said yes!' he called out to the entire bar. Being English and not American, they didn't immediately burst out into spontaneous applause but looked at us as if we were a pair of loud-mouthed idiots.

We spent the rest of the evening in excited chatter, planning where, how, when. We compromised on somewhere nice and up and coming in North London. There was a fair chance his parents would pay the rent, which would be fabulous. I'd give Linda two months' notice and we'd start flat-hunting after Christmas. Flat-hunting! I was so excited. Then we went home and made love all night, to commemorate the beginning of something new.

'You'd better stay this way,' I said to him fiercely, as we were lying with our arms round each other. 'This is absolutely and utterly your last chance.'

'I know,' he said sleepily. 'And thank God I got it.'

Thirteen

Fran was furious. Absolutely fucking doing-her-nut furious. She was almost unspeakably angry, and enquired why I didn't just sell myself off to white slave traders now, if that's what I wanted to do with my life. I knew her feelings on the matter, but it still hurt, and she was really overreacting.

'You know why,' she said, nastily, when she'd exhausted all other modes of persuasion.

'Charlie doesn't want him there any more.'

'How the hell would you know?'

'Charlie and I have an . . . understanding,' she said.

'Have you seen him?'

'Maybe.'

'But! But . . . you can't! It's the rule!'

'Well, maybe the rules changed.'

'Shit! So you've been round there? Did you see Alex the other night?'

'For God's sake, I do not give a flying fuck about Alex.'

'And do you know what? I don't give a flying fuck about Charlie. You could shag Stephen Hawking for all I care, and I wouldn't get all pissy about it. Why can't you just let me be happy for once?'

She sighed. 'Look, can we not talk about this? We're only going to fall out.'

'As opposed to what we're doing at the moment?'

'Look, let's leave it. I'll be around to pick up the pieces, as usual, in about six months' time.'

'You always have to have the last word, don't you, Fran?'

'No, only when you cock up your life with a big FREAK.'

I put the phone down.

Angus had rung and left a message, but I didn't respond. I didn't want to think too much about that night. We'd perhaps been getting too close for comfort, and I was going to stick to my new policy of non-interference. The decision was made: I had one relationship to concentrate on now, and I was going to stick to it. His voice on the answerphone over the next couple of days grew increasingly confused, then he stopped calling altogether.

I didn't have time to miss him. Alex and I lunched together, spent every night together, at the cinema, out with his mates or just lazing around, looking at apartments to rent, planning what kind of thing we'd go see. We always went to my house. Paranoically, I did ask him about Charlie, but he dismissed it out of hand as nothing – I was the one who had to get up for work in the morning, and he was on twenty-four-hour devotion watch.

And I handed in my notice to Linda. She received it with the biggest, broadest smile I had ever seen, and said that would be absolutely fine. The light positively glinted off her spectacles. I wasn't sure if that was good or bad.

So everything seemed to be – at last – settling into place.

Life was, suddenly, a lot less hectic. Almost quiet. Until Amanda phoned again . . .

'Darling, so kind of you to be putting this dinner on for us.'

What dinner? Oh my God, I'd completely forgotten.

'It is this weekend, isn't it?'

Was it this weekend? Jesus, I hadn't the foggiest.

'Ehmm . . .'

'I've invited Mookie . . . I'm amazed you two got on so well. Although she's always been a little on the eccentric side . . . And of course Nash is coming down from Glasgow a week early just to make it. Let me see . . . do you know, Fraser hardly mentioned it! God, he can be slow, that boy, wasn't even sure we should . . . whoops! I'm sorry! Almost forgot – can't slag off the hubby in front of Melanie. Ha ha ha! Anyway, I've got the address somewhere. Are you sure you want Angus there? You know what a drag he can be, especially if he's in one of his moods, which he is all the time. Why not ask that nice Charlie instead? He's great fun. Did you know his father owns a racing stable? Anyway, are you sure you can cope with all of us, darling? I mean, forgive me, but cooking's never been quite your strong point, has it? Unless, of course, it's a cheese-on-toast dinner party! Ha ha ha! Now, listen, is it formal? I assumed not, obviously, but just let me know if you want us to make the effort . . .'

'Ehm, can you hang on for just one second?'

'Of course, darling, no problem at all, lots to do, yah? We'll see you on Saturday. I'll assume it's eight for eight thirty – that's how people normally do dinner parties, darling. Ciao!'

I sat back, stupefied. Oh, Jesus. I'd forgotten all about it; events had rather overtaken things.

I couldn't see how I could have seven people round, a fair proportion of whom hated each other, one who thought making voodoo dolls of me and sticking pins in them had succeeded in driving me out of her dwelling, one whom I'd considered . . . gulp, well, whatever, and now wasn't returning the phone calls of, and two I didn't actually know.

Alex thought it was a great idea. Get everyone together, announce the fact that we were moving in – not that it was an announcement as such, I just hadn't seen anyone apart from him – drink and relax with our friends. He even promised to help me cook, which made me stare hard at him and wonder if the *X Files* was true and he was being brainwashed by the government through his asthma inhaler. Of course I couldn't tell him why I didn't want Angus to come.

I even managed to ask Linda. She gave me that look she had, which always went on too long without blinking.

'On Saturday night?'

'Yes, just dinner, a few friends, a couple of drinks . . . nothing wild.'

'But next weekend you'll be away?'

'Yes, I promise, next weekend I'll be away.'

The following weekend was the wedding – at last, the great occasion – and we had decided to book a bed and breakfast. I would have stayed with my parents, but post-wedding didn't seem the most auspicious time to introduce my new living-in-sin partner to them, and the wedding was actually being held in a beautiful little village called Pyrford, the nearest place to rural English gorgeousness you got in the Woking area.

She pondered it pudgily.

'OK.'

'Fantastic! Great!' I said, trying to imply how much we would be enriched by her company. When I got in later, it was

written in pink letters on her kittens diary. 'Dinner. Saturday
– 8 for 8.30 p.m.' I wondered how she would possibly manage
to slot it in.

Friday night Fran phoned. I hadn't spoken to her all week.
I was avoiding her. She knew it.

'Hey,' she said cheerfully, and nervously which meant she
was worried. If she'd thought everything was normal, she'd
have been grouchy.

'What are you up to this weekend?'

'Oh, ehm . . . seeing Alex, you know, usual boring old
stuff.'

'Right, right. So you're not having a dinner party or
anything?'

My heart sank. Of course I should have known it would get
back to her. I tried to think of an exit strategy that wouldn't
make me look bad, but there wasn't one.

'Do you want to come?' I said quietly, waiting for the
cutting put-down.

There was a pause.

'Yes!' she said tremulously. There was another pause. Then
we both started, stupidly, to laugh. We laughed at nothing,
we laughed because we were friends, and I laughed because
I managed to persuade her to come early to help me with the
cooking.

'Now we're going to be nine,' I mused. 'Aren't these things
supposed to be balanced?'

'You could always invite Charlie . . .' she started.

'No way!' I said. 'Not you as well. But you are coming to
this on the sole grounds that (1) you talk to Angus, because
he thinks I hate him; and (2) you tell me EVERYTHING
about Charlie – and I mean everything.'

'OK,' she said. 'You can ignore Angus all night while I talk to him, and that will prove you don't hate him?'

'Yes.'

'And I will talk to you about someone I hardly know and rarely see.'

'I don't believe you.'

'Huh. I'll see you tomorrow.'

'What are you up to tonight?'

'It's a secret. Bye!'

There was no doubt about it. Alex and I had to go shopping. In our new-found status as full-time couple, shopping was going to be something we were going to be doing a lot of, so we might as well get it off with a test run.

We had to buy dinner and wine for nine, as well as candles and flowers and all that crap — although how that would distract from the fact that all the chairs were of various hues, some from next door, some with floral tie-backs and one nasty seventies high stool which would make whoever ended up with it have to watch over the proceedings like a judge, I didn't know. All plumped round two tables of different heights put together and covered with an old plastic tablecloth. We also had to get a wedding present for Amanda and Fraser, plus a hat for me, plus a new tie and some new pants for Alex, whose pants had suddenly decided to spontaneously revolt all at once and make a break for freedom. (We never saw them again.)

Neither of us could face the hell that is central London on a Saturday close to Christmas, so we headed to the nearest South London equivalent: the Elephant and Castle Shopping Centre, a fearsome bright pink monstrosity that looked like a robot vomiting a strawberry milkshake. It sold lots of cheap international phone calls, but very few things that you could truly classify as a wedding present.

We stared dolefully at mops for an hour, avoided the manic Santa Claus, and had a quick look at the everything-for-99-pence shop, all without inspiration. Alex was obviously crazed with boredom but trying his hardest not to show it, even inviting me to try on the kind of hats that give you a start if you see one lying on the ground accidentally, because you think it's a mutated insect.

By two o'clock (we'd had a long, lazy lie-in, which had been wonderful, but tightened the schedule somewhat, particularly since I was planning on making lasagne), I'd started to panic slightly.

'If only they had a shop called "Everything You Need for a Run-Down Castle",' I lamented, picking up some eight foot imitation sunflowers for the fourth time.

'Well, what do they need?'

'Nothing! Absolutely nothing! Amanda has a Dualit toaster, a Philippe Starck lemon squeezer and every other bit of tat that's ever turned up in a magazine ever, plus an account at Heal's and an interior designer. And I've seen the wedding list and, I'm sorry, but I am just not ready to start selling my internal organs to rich Americans.'

'OK, pumpkin, calm down. What would Fraser like, then?'

I thought for a moment. 'Ehm, a Gameboy, probably.'

Alex clapped his hands together. 'Perfect. We'll get him one of those.'

'A Gameboy?'

'How many Gameboys do you think they're going to get?'

'Hmm. Well, none, I suppose.'

'There you go, then. Perfect.'

Two minutes later in Woolworths, it was done. Carry bag, extra games, the works. I paid, but then they were my friends.

'Piece of cake,' said Alex airily. 'And look –' he pointed to a shop which on first sight sold lots of different sizes of basins, but on closer inspection also sold CDs, teapots, pants and various other random items.

'Eight pairs of boxers for a fiver!' he exclaimed triumphantly.

'Oh, feel their bristling electrical quality.'

'I don't care. Maybe my other pants will get jealous of their new, inferior replacements and come home.'

'Good point.'

We were two points up now. Plus Alex had decided to wear his old school tie, which pissed me off, but only slightly, and almost put us ahead of the game. I'd given up on the hat.

Tesco's was a different matter altogether. Alex said the squalor and the crowds reminded him of India, but I ignored him in my search for an unbroken packet of spinach lasagne. Meanwhile, he loaded the trolley up with cheap red wine and a bottle of gin.

'That's a lot of wine,' I pointed out dubiously.

'There's a lot of people coming.'

I sighed. 'We'd better get on. I don't know how I'm going to cope with nine.'

'Nine? I thought you said eight.'

'Yeah, I know. Fran phoned and I felt really guilty, so I invited her too. It won't matter if it's uneven.'

Alex looked cross.

'Yes it will. God, Mel, she'll ruin it. Can't you phone her up and tell her not to come?'

'No! For God's sake, you two are dreadful. I already had

a word with her about not being so rude to you. She'll be fine. I'll put her beside Angus or someone.'

'I still think it's too many. You could phone her. She'll understand.'

'Alex, isn't this a little early for us to stand about bickering in supermarkets? She's coming, OK? She's making up for Linda, who doesn't have a personality, and Mookie, who only has half of one. And she'll shut Amanda up if she's getting too mouthy.'

'Yeah, right. Only Fran's allowed to be mouthy. For Britain.'

'Stop this.' We were in the queue, finally, but it was a humdinger. A baby in a backpack in front of me hit me on the head with a rattle covered in biscuit and scum.

'It's sorted, OK?'

Alex looked a bit sulky for a moment, then wandered off.

'Hey,' I said. 'Aren't you going to help me out with this?'

'I want to,' he said, 'but I'm a bit short . . . Can you get this one and I'll get the next one?'

'But you put a hundred bottles of wine in!'

'Oh, don't cause a scene. Do you want me to take some of them back?'

'No, forget it. Just leave them. We'll drink them some other time if we don't drink them tonight.'

'Right, pumpkin – we'll never finish them tonight.'

'Oh God! I wish I'd never volunteered to do this.'

He put his arm round me. 'Don't worry. It'll be fine. It'll be great. You'll be a sparkling hostess, and everyone will love you, and we'll all be friends again. Chill out.'

I tried to chill out while signing the enormous Visa bill, but it wasn't easy. We got all the boxes back home around four and I dumped them on the kitchen table gratefully.

Immediately Alex tried to drag me towards the bedroom for a little bit of afternoon messing. This, however, was not the day for it.

'Alex, I have four hours to cook a bunch of stuff that I don't know how to. Make yourself useful and chop something.'

'OK.' He kissed me playfully on the neck. 'I'll just go check out the football results.'

'You will not!'

'Ten minutes, pumpkin!'

He vanished, then reappeared two seconds later, confiscating one of the bottles, a glass and a bottle opener.

'And don't you dare get pissed!' I yelled. I followed him in to where he was cosily resting his feet up on the sofa. Linda was mutely removing her tape of *The English Patient* from the machine. I noticed it had been joined by *Titanic*. Interesting.

'I'll take that,' I said, smiling, and swiped the bottle of wine back. 'You know what happened last time.'

'Actually, I remember very little of it.' He zapped the remote control to the footie.

'My point exactly. Linda, do you want a glass of wine?'

She looked shocked at the hour. 'No . . . but perhaps a sherry.'

'Sherry, huh?' Linda had a fully stocked drinks cabinet, which was odd, as she scarcely ever drank. Occasionally, I helped her out with it.

'Go on, be daring.' I handed it to her. She turned a dull red and rushed back to her bedroom.

To even things up I poured myself a glass before I recorked the bottle. There was a long enough night ahead. I picked up the chopping knife and sighed to myself.

*   *   *

234

Two hours later, a big pot of mince, which I hadn't even wanted to touch, stood bubbling on the stove in a faintly impressive way. I was stirring it casually, feeling pretty hot, as it had only taken this long, plus of course the four attempts at a non evil and lumpy white sauce. The kitchen looked like one of those nasty splatter films, all bits of meat and tomato red. When I'd gone in to fetch Alex for chopping the fruit salad, he'd been asleep – extremely asleep, actually, as he didn't wake up even when I deliberately sat on him. Linda was nowhere to be seen. I guessed she was eating lots of chocolate so she wouldn't embarrass herself by going completely feral at the meal and ripping into the garlic bread.

At six the doorbell screeched, startling me out of my wits as usual, and I panicked until I remembered that Fran was coming over to help.

She came in, dark eyes sparkling and flushed from the cold – it had finally turned frosty and bitter outside, and was threatening to snow, which I reckoned it would next week, just in time for the big day. Amanda's dad had probably ordered it wholesale. She was armed with two bottles of wine and a quarter bottle of gin.

'Why on earth have you brought so much booze?' I asked in disbelief. The kitchen was turning into a wine cellar, and I'd already poured half a bottle into the lasagne.

She looked at me like I was a moron.

'Oh, no reason. Can I have a glass, please?'

I poured us both one, reminding myself to pace it. Alex suddenly appeared, looking thoroughly refreshed. He and Fran nodded at each other distantly as I refilled his glass, then he disappeared again, saying something cheery along the lines of 'too many cooks'.

Fran raised her eyes to heaven, then leaned her long body on the kitchen unit and proceeded to chat to me

235

while I tried to cut equal-sized slices out of a kiwi fruit without meditating too long on the pointlessness of it all.

'Why don't you tell me all about Charlie now?' I interrupted her diatribe against the snotty cow who'd served her in the off-licence, once I'd ascertained that the girl didn't actually have to attend Casualty.

She sighed. 'Do I have to?'

'If you want to eat tonight, you do.' I removed the expensive pistachio nuts she was working her way through.

She refilled her glass. It was nearly seven.

'Really, he's a complete twat.'

'Really.'

'Everything went as normal: he was completely miserable and followed me around like a lost dog. So, I kind of . . . saw him again.'

'What!? You never do that!'

'I know. I've no idea what was the matter with me.'

'You LIKE him.'

'I do not. He's a loud-mouth piss bism.'

'You like that kind of thing. Oh my God, Fran's in love, Fran's in love!'

'Can you hand me that chopping knife, please?'

I'd passed it over without thinking before I realized my fatal mistake.

'OK, OK, I'll stop!'

'Sure?'

'Yes!'

Fran slowly lowered the knife to the table and I risked taking it back to chop up the rest of the kiwi fruit in silence.

Alex wandered into the kitchen in search of the expensive nuts.

'It's suspiciously quiet in here . . . who have you two just been massacring – I mean, talking about?'

'No one,' I said stoutly.

'Ah. So, it was either me or –' he shot a look at Fran, so he must have known – 'Charlie.'

'It was Charlie,' I said, desperate for him not to think that I was discussing him with my friends all day long.

'Oh. Shame,' he said. He tried to pick up the nuts in passing. Fran, without thinking about it, slapped him on the back of the hand, which he ignored, retreating, with nuts, to the TV, which had reached *Blind Date* stage.

'How's Alex?' asked Fran ruefully. From the sitting room I could hear him howling and whooping like a dog as the less blessed single women came on.

'Oh, usual responsible grown-up old Alex,' I said.

'I'm sorry I was so pissed off.'

'That's OK.'

'Arf arf arf,' came from next door.

'Can you give me a hand to put these salmon roulades together?'

Fran looked doubtful, and removed her cardigan. Underneath, she was wearing some beautiful ethereal dark blue thirties-style dress which looked almost see-through but actually wasn't, if you looked closely.

'Oh my God! No, don't worry,' I said heartily. 'That's a gorgeous dress. You look fantastic.'

'Thanks very much: I half-inched it from Madam Elizabeth.'

'No!'

Fran had a couple of days' work as an extra in a high-budget thirties melodrama. No wonder the dress fitted her so well: it'd been made for her. She twirled round slowly. It was slim and diaphanous and beautiful. I wished with all my heart that I could wear a dress like that, in a way that wouldn't make

237

me look like a chunky five-year-old ballerina, and rolled up the salmon and cream cheese mush in approximately attractive ways.

'Do you think we've got enough food?' I wondered gloomily.

'Tons! Amanda and Mookie don't eat, remember.'

'Oh, yes.' I breathed a sigh of relief. 'It's just the boys and us then, really, isn't it?'

Fran indicated Linda's bedroom.

'Bugger it. Listen, would you nip across the road and get me another French stick?'

'But I'll get mugged and killed,' she complained.

'I'll send Alex with you.'

'Why don't you send Alex by himself?'

'Because he'll come back in three days with a fish supper and a new fishing rod. Alex!'

He appeared. Even he looked taken aback by the sight of Fran in her beautiful dress.

'Can you walk Fran across the road to get some bread . . . coffee – real coffee – and . . .' I tried to work out what else I'd forgotten. 'Oh, and some more candles.' I was sticking them in old wine bottles, just like real students do.

'I can go by myself,' said Fran, disgruntledly.

'And if you got mugged and killed, I'd hate it. It'd be rubbish,' I said, pushing both of them out the door. It slammed behind them and I heard them walking off in silence. Oh God, if they'd only get on, everything would be fine. Here I was, part of a couple, hostessing and actually cooking things. I felt uniquely proud of myself. Alex and I would have dinner parties all the time. Hey – we'd get on a dinner party circuit. It would be fantastic. Humming, I went in to lay the tables.

*   *   *

Half an hour later, stepping back to admire my handiwork, I was quite proud of myself. With all the lights out and candles everywhere, the dining room looked less Laura Ashley and more a state of gothic horror – the bows and frills everywhere took on sinister undertones and it looked like a ghostly bride's boudoir. I artistically placed some bowls of nuts around the place. The kitchen might look like a nuclear explosion, but in here was pretty good, particularly after I'd used some of Linda's Celine Dion CDs (she didn't have any books) to prop up the table legs so they almost matched. I toyed with the idea of placecards, then realized two things: (1) I was turning into an idiot, and (2) where the hell were Alex and Fran? The shop was only five minutes up the road. Maybe it hadn't had any bread and they'd had to go elsewhere.

This practical explanation wasn't enough for me, however. What if one of them had been run down and had to go to hospital? What if they'd been mugged? I started to panic. What if they'd had another big fight and Fran had given him a kicking and he was in intensive care and she was being held by the police? Oh God, that would be awful. I was so fascinated by this idea that I almost didn't hear the doorbell ring, despite its closeness to a submarine honk.

Thank God. I dashed to the door to demand where they'd got to. But it wasn't them. It was Angus, with Nash. We stood on either side of the open door, look- ing at each other, as I became more and more aware of the fact that not only were they three-quarters of an hour early, but I was still dressed in my cooking gear – which, as I didn't have any cooking gear, was in fact my pyjamas covered by Linda's apron, which had some pussy cats on it. And I hadn't brushed my hair – because I was cooking – and I was covered in gruesome stains. And I hadn't had a bath. Or cut my toenails, and my feet were bare.

Fucking hell. Both of them had suits on, and Nash was even taller than Angus, gangly and handsome, so they just looked far too good to be here.

Nash looked worriedly at Angus.

'Are you sure it's tonight?' he whispered.

With that, I regained my composure.

'Nash! Angus!' I yelled, in a carefree manner. 'You're VERY, VERY early!'

'Sorry about that,' said Angus, 'we misjudged it. Do you want us to go out to the pub and come back?'

'Man, it's freezing out there,' said Nash. He caught sight of my scary wide-eyed Harpy look. 'But, you know, no problem . . .'

'NO! No, come in, come in. Sorry, you've caught me off guard, you know.'

I didn't know what to do first, particularly when they started taking off their coats and scarves and handing them to me. I held on to them.

'Come through, come through,' I said, and led them through to the sitting room, wondering if I'd remembered to put any pants on.

The two tables filled up every square inch of the space, I noticed.

'Do you want us to sit at the table?' said Angus.

'No! No!' I indicated the sofa, which had been pushed flat up against the variety of chairs.

'Sit here!'

The boys moved over carefully, and crammed themselves in.

'I just need to change, and, well, you know, get ready.'

'Actually,' said Angus, 'I really like that spoon in your hair.'

I clapped my hand to my head, and found a teaspoon

covered in tomato puree peeping out of one of my more unruly curls. I made a grab for it, but dropped one of the coats instead. Nash stood up again.

'Would you like a hand?'

'No, no, I'm fine,' I screeched, trying to reach down to the floor without exposing my breasts over the top of my baggy pyjamas. Despite being practically hysterical by this time, I remembered what came next in the good hostess book of gracious living.

'Would you like a drink?'

The boys muttered that that would be lovely, and started to bring out bottles of wine they'd brought. Angus had also brought a bottle of whisky. They handed them to me, although I already had my arms full of coats. Not knowing what to do, I indicated that they should pile the bottles on top of the coats. As they didn't know what to do either, they did so, and I staggered into the kitchen. Or tried to; I didn't quite make it, and everything fell on the floor. The boys dashed in looking worried when they heard the noise, but fortunately nothing had smashed, so my luck was in.

'Are you OK?' Angus lent me a hand and I scrambled up, blushing fiercely.

'Calm down,' he said, gently, not letting go of my hand. 'It's only us. Me, remember, who's nice, and Nash, who's a bit mad.'

'Aye, right enough,' said Nash.

'I'm sure dinner will be lovely, no one else will be here for ages, so why don't you let us get ourselves a drink, then you can disappear and get changed and beautify yourself, then re-emerge like a butterfly.'

'Will you pretend I'm somebody else?'

'If you like. Just leave those coats there, we'll sort everything out. Now, off you go.'

I escaped to the shower, and was in and out in double quick time. I shoved the grey silk dress on again and bunged on some slap. Twenty-five minutes later, I was just about presentable. Still no Fran and Alex.

I walked back into the sitting room, where the boys applauded sweetly. They were intrigued when I explained my dilemma.

'Do you think I should call the police?' I asked them.

'Naw, they dinnae file until forty-eight hoors,' said Nash.

'What?'

'He means they won't listen unless they've been away for a couple of days,' Angus explained. 'Up until then it's assumed they're out on the razz somewhere.'

That didn't make me feel any better.

'Do you think they're up to anything?' asked Nash, as if the thought had just occurred to him. Angus frowned.

'No, they hate each other,' I explained. 'That's why I'm so worried.'

I got up and pottered around the kitchen, bringing in a bottle of wine.

'They've probably just gone for a pint somewhere to get out of helping you,' said Angus.

Relief that this was obviously the case was tempered with annoyance.

'You're right. They're like a pair of spoilt twins sometimes, those two.' And I stopped stuffing my mouth with pistachio nuts like they were going out of fashion.

The doorbell rang again.

'Christ, what was that?' said Nash.

'I'll get it.' I hoped it was them and I could give them a bollocking. On the other side of the door, however, stood Mookie, looking skinny, blonde and absolutely freezing.

'Hello! Come in!' I said.

'Thank you. Rally! South London. Well, you know, I have some friends in Chelsea, but I never normally get down this far!'

'That is fascinating,' I said, taking her Barbour jacket.

She snorted with laughter. 'I'm more used to Kensington than Kennington!' she said hilariously.

I laughed along merrily. 'You know, Mookie, you are really funny,' I said.

She stopped immediately.

'Do you rally think so?'

'No!' I said, and she laughed herself silly, even though I was being honest. I beckoned her through to the dining room. Angus and Nash were out of sight behind the table.

'Oh God, am I first? That's *so* embarrassing. I'm so mortified. I thought quarter past eight would be fine, but I've obviously completely messed it up. Oh God. This was always happening in Switzerland.'

'Mookie,' I said gently, 'it's fine.'

The boys stuck their arms out from behind the table and waved vigorously.

'What would you like to drink?' I asked.

'Vodka martini, please.'

Ahh. Linda's drinks cabinet was pretty wide, but we'd drunk all the vodka, and it didn't stoop to martini.

'Aha! Look at your face, it's rally funny,' said Mookie. I was regretting asking her already. She'd seemed quite nice in the taxi.

'Here you are, darling!' And she drew out an enormous bottle of Absolut Vodka, some brand of martini I'd never heard of, and a jar of olives.

'I came prepared. Have you got some lemonade, darling? And some ice?'

I nodded, stunned at such largesse. I began to like her again.

'Would anyone else like one?' The boys nodded their assent, and I headed back to the kitchen with the bottles. Mookie tapped in behind me. 'Oh, let me make them,' she cooed. 'I'm very particular.'

So I left her to it and went and rejoined the boys. I was chain-munching pistachios again, which obviously meant I was getting tense. And sure enough, when Mookie brought back the delicious martinis, we sat perched in between the table legs in a not entirely comfortable silence. I sensed Angus giving me faintly wounded looks for not returning his calls.

'So what do you do, Nash?' asked Mookie.

'I work on the rigs, ken.'

'The oil rigs?'

'No, the Runrigs,' he said, guffawing heartily to himself. I didn't have a clue what he was on about.

'The Runrigs? Rally?' asked Mookie. 'What does one do there?'

Nash took pity on her. 'Don't worry,' he said. 'I meant the oil rigs. Hey, Angus, did you hear Runrig are doing a Stones tribute cover?'

'No,' said Angus, smiling.

'Yes, it's called "Hey, McLeod, get off of my ewe"!'

They cracked up at this, although I didn't quite get it. Neither did Mookie, judging by the way she was staring into the middle distance.

'Gosh, my daddy owns one of those,' she beamed. 'But I thought you said . . .'

Fortunately then the doorbell rang again. The draught swirled in with Amanda and Fraser, filling the air with glamorous perfume and a sprinkling of snow from their heavy coats.

'It's snowing!' I exclaimed. 'Fantastic!'

'Revolting, more like. Hello, darling. How are you?' said Amanda, giving me an air kiss.

Traitorous, I wanted to say, but didn't.

Fraser gave me a hug. 'Sorry to put you to all this trouble,' he whispered.

'Oh no! My fault! My fault entirely,' I said cheerily, when of course I should have said, *Not at all*.

'Come in, come in.'

'Well, I've never been to your humble abode, darling.' Amanda had divested herself of her coat and was prowling around.

'Yes, because the last time you were invited you didn't come,' I said. 'For my birthday.'

Amanda pretended she hadn't heard and made an entrance. She was wearing a beautiful champagne-coloured dress, not too fancy and not too plain. It set off her golden hair wonderfully.

Nash and Angus stood up to greet her. She nodded regally at them, and kissed Mookie, who toddled off to make some more martinis, bless her.

'Is this everyone?' asked Amanda.

'Umm . . . no. We're missing Alex and Fran . . .'

She turned to face me. 'Where are they?'

'Well, they went out for a loaf of bread about two hours ago and haven't returned. I'm very worried about them.'

'Worried? God, they've probably gone to America, darling. Now, where is there to sit? Or are we at table already?'

'Umm, no,' I said, controlling the urge to slap her. 'I'm afraid there's not much room, so if you wouldn't mind sitting on the sofa . . .' Nash bunched up, leaving a very small space between him and Angus, which she regarded disdainfully '. . . as soon as we're all here, we can eat.'

'I think I'll stand, darling. This dress creases terribly, you know.'

She accepted a drink from Mookie without saying thank you. And of course, everyone else then had to stand up too. So we leaned on the table, Nash nearly knocked over a candle, and Amanda geared herself up for the latest round of 'What's going on with the wedding?' I noticed she cast very significant glances at Fraser as she prattled on about flower arrangements, and he was nodding politely a fraction of a second too late.

And where the hell were those two? I bet they were in some fucking pub. Slagging me off, most like. They were probably having a Why-Melanie-is-so-awful competition. I was furious.

I decided to start dishing up the first course, as I'd eaten all the pistachio nuts, so I slipped surreptitiously away as Amanda lurched into a detailed hymnal repertoire.

Angus followed me into the kitchen.

'Look, Melanie . . . I . . . Have I done anything to upset you?'

'No!' I said. 'No, definitely not.'

'Well, you know, I thought we were friends, but you didn't return my phone calls or anything . . .'

'I'm sorry,' I said. 'It's been absolutely hectic.' And I explained to him about moving in with Alex. He was amazed.

'I thought . . . I mean, he's a right bastard, isn't he? Sorry.'

'No, that's OK. He's not really. He just gets . . . well, mixed up in things, and he's going through a really tough time at the moment.'

'And you're not,' he said gently.

I hadn't thought I was, but before I had the chance to ask him, he'd picked up a bottle of wine and was heading for the living-room door.

'I'm sorry to have bothered you,' he said.

'You never bother me.'

He smiled ruefully and sweetly. As he opened the door, I involuntarily said, 'Angus!'

He turned and faced me, but I hadn't a clue what to say.

'I . . . er . . .'

There was a long pause.

'You sound like you're waiting for the doorbell to ring, as a useful interruption,' he said, smiling.

I tilted my head towards the door for a second. Just as I was on the point of giving up, it actually did ring.

'Yes!' I said, punching the air.

He smiled one more time and headed back to the others. I felt ashamed of myself.

'Where the hell have you two been?'

Covered in snow, pink-cheeked and giggling, Alex and Fran stood at the door like a couple of children.

Alex leaned forward and kissed me on the nose.

'We've been making up!' he announced. 'We thought you'd be pleased.'

'I'd have been more pleased if you hadn't disappeared into the pitch-black freezing cold in the middle of the night when you were meant to be gone for five minutes!'

'It's only quarter to nine, pumpkin. It's hardly the middle of the night.'

It felt like it.

'What have you two been doing?' I asked again incredulously.

Fran smiled shyly. I had never seen her do this in my entire life.

'We've decided to stop fighting. For you, Mel.'

This smelled fishy.

'You don't fight, you snipe,' I protested.

'Well, now we're moving in together . . .' Alex stepped inside and put his arm round my shoulders, 'Fran and I had a talk and decided that we would try and get on.'

'So we can all be friends,' added Fran.

I stared at them. Moonie Cult! Moonie Cult!

'Are you sure you're not zombies?' I asked them. 'Or vampires, that you have to ask over the threshold before they can eat you?'

'Vampires don't eat you,' said Alex. 'They have metaphorical sex with you. In fact, in many ancient cultures . . .'

'BORING!' Fran and I shouted simultaneously. And I relaxed, took their coats, and went to see how everyone was getting on next door.

Everyone was getting on very poorly next door, and I immediately felt hollow, both as a hostess and as a person.

Amanda was resting delicately on the edge of the sofa, nose to nose with Mookie, whom she looked to be telling off in some way. Angus and Nash were muttering quietly next to them. And Fraser was sitting on his own, staring off into space.

'The fugitives have returned!' I announced loudly, in an effort to break the tension. Everyone looked up like they were exhausted, and said hello briefly without any great warmth. Oh God, this was awful.

'Mookie!' I squealed. This was all getting a bit *Abigail's Party*.

'Could you possibly make us another round of those delicious martinis? And if everyone wants to take a seat, we can start.'

There was a general rumbling from the boys, who were clearly starving to death. As soon as I got them seated, they launched into the bread like ravenous kestrels.

'Did you get the extra bread?' I whispered to Fran.

'No.'

Amanda sat at the head of the table. Fraser was on her right, and Mookie was to his right. Amanda was leaning right across him in order to talk to her. He sat there stoically.

I put Alex on one side of me and Nash on the other, with Fran and Angus joining up to Mookie. And, finally, I brought out the salmon roulades, which almost looked like the snail shapes they were supposed to. Not quite though.

I poured some of the white wine, and we all sat down at last, although some of us were at different heights than others.

'To the chef!' Angus proposed, and everyone else joined in. Finally, the ice was starting to break and I could relax. Alex began gabbing to Nash and Angus about the music business, and they were listening politely. Fran was listening to Amanda with a glint in her eye and a glass in her hand, which could, I suspected, cause problems later.

'I'll just go check on the lasagne,' I announced as everyone tucked in, except Amanda and Mookie who had politely declined — well, not that politely, actually. Amanda had announced:

'It's quite clear you eat dairy products, Melanie, but some of us want to keep our figures,' and rudely handed back the two plates. I wasn't sure Mookie didn't want hers, but she wasn't getting much of a chance.

'Are you going to eat that?' Amanda said sharply to Fraser.

Fraser nodded dully. There was silence as everyone waited to see what she was going to do. However she simply made a martyr face and returned to ignoring him.

Two shocks awaited me in the kitchen. Number one was the lasagne that I had made up ready to go in the oven but hadn't actually got round to putting in there. In fact, the oven wasn't actually on.

'Fucking hell,' I moaned, looking at it in all its dark red and freezing glory.

The second was Linda, who was unobtrusively attempting to pour herself a glass of sherry.

'Fucking hell!' I yelled again. 'Squared! Linda! Why aren't you next door?' I blamed her instantly.

She stared at the floor and shrugged.

'Come on! Let me make you a vodka martini, then I'll take you next door to meet everyone.'

'Maybe I shouldn't come.'

I felt like a complete heel as I jammed the lasagne into the cold oven, turned the heat up, made her a vodka martini and tried to smile ingratiatingly all at the same time.

'Of course you should,' I said. 'Come on, they're dying to meet you,' I lied.

Shuffling and looking at her feet, Linda followed me into the sitting room.

'Ehm, everyone, this is . . . Linda,' I announced. I'd even forgotten to set her a place, so I plonked her down in my seat, although I'd already taken a bite out of the roulade. Then I poured her a large glass of wine and made eye signals to Fran to talk to her, which she studiously ignored.

Back I trailed to the kitchen, to drag in the extra-high stool I had thought I wouldn't have to use. I checked the lasagne in the flaming oven, but it was still so cold as to be solid. This night was not going to be easy. Sighing heavily, I dragged myself back into the sitting room with another couple of bottles of red wine.

'That was lovely,' said Angus, and there were mutters of agreement and a sniff from Amanda. 'What's next?'

'Ah,' I said. 'Well, there's a funny story about that . . . While I was in the kitchen, the lasagne went through a mystery freezing process which reversed its cooked status and took it back to a rudimentary uncooked state. I'm not sure whether it's a time slip or a cryogenic disorder, but the FBI are on their way over. In the meantime' – I put the wine on the table – 'we're just going to have to get drunk.'

There was a pause, then Alex started to uncork the bottles.

'Those aliens are pesky things,' he said. 'We'd better fight them off with this magic elixir.'

'How long have we got, Captain?' asked Fraser, perking up momentarily.

'I've reversed the polarity of the neutron flow,' I announced gravely. 'We can expect to see reconstituted lasagne in about forty-five minutes.'

'God, they're so childish,' I could hear Amanda whisper to Mookie. And I was at the other end of the room.

'Have you got any more bread?' asked Nash.

'Sorry. I've got some salad.'

He stared at his empty plate mournfully.

'Real Scots don't eat salad.'

Strangely, the lack of foodstuffs seemed to break the ice. No one was going anywhere for a while and eventually a beautiful, warming smell of lasagne began to seep through into the room, the candles burnt on, and we found Nash a tin of cold beans in the fridge. Everyone else made do with increasing quantities of red wine, and the chatter level grew commensurably.

Only Fraser sat quietly amongst the kerfuffle. And Linda, of course, but I was less worried about her. I stuck my tongue out at him. He stuck his back, so I felt that he wasn't suicidal quite yet. On the other side, Amanda was trying to make small talk about castle furnishings, and Fran was pretending to listen and making increasingly sarky comments that Amanda was oblivious to. Nash and Alex were having a conversation about rugby versus football (I wasn't sure who was on which side) which looked like it may degenerate into bodily harm, and on my other side Angus was chatting quietly to Linda behind Nash. Linda was staring terrified at her place, but occasionally nodding along. Suddenly Alex shouted out, 'Game! Game!'

Everyone stopped talking.

'What game?' said Fran.

'I don't know. Let's play a game. Something. Ehm, Truth or Forfeit.'

Everyone groaned.

'If only we were all fifteen,' said Fran, 'that would be a great idea.'

'No, come on, guys . . . just for a laugh.'

Fran passed him an empty bottle. 'Hey, maybe then we can spin this!'

'Fine, OK.' Alex hated losing his cool like that. 'I don't give a toss. Just thought it might add a bit of spark, given that we're sitting here starving to death.'

'Thanks very much,' I flared up from the top of my high chair. Then I remembered that they were my guests and I was starving them to death, so I shut up again.

'Rally, I don't mind, but why don't you ask the first

252

question and we'll see if we want to play or not?' said Mookie quietly. The girl was a born compromiser.

Alex still looked a bit sulky. Then he took another drink of wine and sat back.

'OK then.' There was a general groaning around the table, but the wine was going down easy and we couldn't talk football for ever. I looked at Angus, and he seemed relieved that his nursemaiding duties would be over for a bit.

'Here we go,' said Alex. 'Who's —'

'Wait a wee minute,' said Nash. 'Whit's the forfeit?'

'You'll find out.' Alex showed his teeth.

'Och, that's no fair, ken. You cannae just make up the rules.'

'For God's sake, you two!' said Fran. 'Jesus, you can't let boys anywhere near each other when it comes to games.'

Nash sat back in his chair.

Alex decided to start with Mookie, across the table.

'OK, Mookie, who's the most embarrassing person you've ever fancied?'

'Hang on,' I said, 'famous or not famous?'

'Famous. Unless everyone else knows them.'

'Fine.'

Mookie thought for a minute.

'Well, we did have this very dishy stable hand, but I don't suppose that counts.'

'Boy or girl?' asked Alex curiously. I threw my napkin at him.

'Oh, rally,' said Mookie, blushing. 'No, I suppose it would have to be . . . Adam Ant.'

'Adam Ant's not embarrassing!' said Fran and I practically simultaneously. The boys howled with laughter.

'Oh God, what turned you on most?' asked Alex, laughing. 'The highwayman or the pirate?'

'Shut up! At the time, it was not embarrassing!'

'Erm, actually, I fancy him now,' said Mookie, going red.

'Ohhh.' That put a different slant on things.

'Who is he now?' I asked.

'I don't know. Still a highwayman, probably,' she said dreamily. My mouth dropped open as Fran and I looked at each other in horror.

'Definitely straight into the lead there,' said Alex.

'I thought this was Truth or Forfeit?' said Nash. 'How come there's points?'

'There's points for the most embarrassing truth,' said Alex.

'Oh, right. New rule,' said Nash. Everyone else yelled at him to shut up.

'OK, you next,' said Alex.

'I'm no going if Ah don't know what the forfeit is.'

Alex looked exasperated. 'Melanie,' he yelled at me unexpectedly, 'even though we're moving in together, we're never having kids in case they end up like him, OK?'

I nodded understandingly.

'The forfeit is, if you don't answer the question, I hang you out of the window by your ankles for two minutes.'

'That's no a forfeit for me, that's a forfeit for you.'

'Believe me, it's a forfeit for you.'

Nash thought about it for a moment.

'Aye, all right then.'

'So, who's the most embarrassing person you've ever fancied?'

Nash looked shyly at his hands for a moment, then smiled to himself.

'Gail Tilsley.'

It took us a moment to figure out who this character was, before remembering *Coronation Street*.

'No!'

'When?'

'How?'

'Well, ken, I just felt sorry for her, and it kind of went from that, really.'

'Felt sorry for her how?' asked Fran. 'Because she still uses curling tongs on only half her hair?'

Nash still couldn't help himself grinning with embarrassment.

'No, like, after Brian died and that.'

I laughed merrily to myself. This was working out well after all.

'That's pretty good,' said Alex.

'Do Ah get more points?'

'No, I'm afraid a twenty-year attachment to a man named after an insect is worth more than a passing sympathy fuck for a fictional character.'

Amanda was next.

'This is a stupid game,' she said.

'Oh my God – not the pony!' yelled Fran. Everyone burst out into guffaws. Definitely, there was a bit too much wine floating about for this early in the evening.

'Don't be ridiculous, Francesca.' Amanda's face resumed its habitual snotty look.

'Forfeit! Forfeit! Forfeit!' Angus and Nash took up the chanting.

'Oh, for goodness' sake!' she looked furious.

'Forfeit! Forfeit! Forfeit!' Alex had started banging his cutlery on the table.

'Oh, bloody hell. OK, then: bloody Gerry Adams. Now, fuck off.'

Instantly there was silence. Fran clapped a hand over her mouth.

'No!'

'Ha, so, now you don't believe me!'

'No, but just . . .'

'Don't say it. He's a politician, that's all.'

'He's not a politician! He's a . . .'

Amanda shot Fran a very dangerous look. Fran grinned and edged away slightly.

'You don't . . . know him, do you?'

'No, of course not. Right, can we move on now, please? I've done mine.'

Alex raised his eyebrows. 'I'm afraid dodgy Irish type beats dandy highwayman. Sorry, Mooks.'

Amanda looked cool as a cucumber, but as the attention moved to Fraser, I saw her take a huge swig of wine. Well, bloody hell. Maybe there were some depths to this woman, after all. Or maybe she just liked beards and a sense of danger. That must be it.

Fraser was pondering. 'I suppose I should say Amanda,' he said. Nobody laughed. 'Only kidding,' he said. Still, nobody laughed, although we did try to look encouraging.

'God, I don't know,' he sighed.

'I do,' said Angus, looking evil.

'Who?' said Fraser.

'You know.'

'No, I don't. Remind me.'

Immediately, Angus got up and started stroking and fondling imaginary long hair.

'Don't push too far . . .' he sang. 'Your dreams are/China in your hand . . .'

Fraser's smile widened. 'No way!'

'Don't wish too hard/Because they may come true.'

'That red-headed midget from T'pau . . . ?'

'. . . And you can't help them/Don't push too far . . .'

'Jesus, I can't even remember her name!'

256

'China in your hand . . .' finished Angus, managing to mime a huge pair of tits and look coy at the same time. 'I love you, Fraser McConnald.'

We gave him as much of a storm of applause as eight people could muster – seven, if you discounted Amanda, who was looking furious.

Fraser laughed heartily. 'So I did. I thought she was gorgeous, then I looked at her one day and thought she was absolutely awful.'

'She was awful,' I agreed, nodding my head vigorously.

'I know. Well, there you go. How do I do on the points-ometer, Alex?'

'Not too well, actually, old chap.'

'Why not?'

'Ha!' said Nash.

'Erm, no reason,' said Alex, blushing.

'Did you –' I started with delight. Fran coughed up her red wine until it came out her nose.

'Carol Decker!' she spluttered, getting red wine everywhere. 'That was her name!'

I was helpless with laughter watching Fran spit everywhere.

'But she was four foot one!' I yelled. 'She made Kylie Minogue look like a heifer!'

'Kylie Minogue only has the brains of a heifer,' said Fran.

'Ehm, Kylie was going to be mine, actually,' said Angus. 'I don't need to have a go now.'

'No!' I yelled. 'I can't believe what a THING you boys all have for fucking skinny midgets! Sorry, Amanda.'

I realized suddenly that I had put an apology in where there should never have been one.

Foot, mouth, and easy insertion instructions.

Amanda sniffed imperiously, and looked at her watch.

'Is this game finished? Because, Fraser, it's time we were going.'

'Amanda, it's only ten o'clock and we haven't eaten yet.'

'Well, I'm tired and I want to go home. Take me home, please.'

Fraser looked at her straightforwardly. 'I'm not ready to go yet. It would be rude, and I'm hungry and I want to stay here and chat to my friends.'

'Oh, for God's sake, Fraser! Do you want me to go by myself?'

'I don't mind.'

There was a silence.

'OK then, I will.' Her face went very tight. 'In fact, I think I'll just go out on my own.'

'I thought you were tired.'

'Shut the fuck up!'

Shakily, she stabbed at her mobile.

'Jacintha? Hi, darling, it's Amanda.'

'Yes . . . no, just at this really dull dinner party. Thought I might come over. Where are you? . . . Oh, Blinski's – great. I'll hop in a cab and see you there in half an hour. Ciao, darling.'

She hung up, then stalked imperiously out of the room.

'I'll get my own coat, thank you,' she shouted as she heard me get up.

'Mookie, are you coming?' we heard from the hallway.

Mookie looked at us, terrified. Fran shook her head vehemently. 'You don't have to go,' she whispered. Mookie took a deep breath.

'Ahem . . . no,' she said quietly. We could hear Amanda pausing outside.

'Say hello to Gerry for us!' hollered Fran.

Then the door slammed and she was gone.

258

Fourteen

Silence fell. Everyone gazed at their plates. Finally Fraser heaved a sigh.

'I'm sorry, everyone.'

'What, for your wife? Might as well get used to that,' Fran said.

'Shh,' I said to Fran. 'Don't worry about it, Frase. She must just be really tense.'

'Tense,' he said. We watched him with bated breath, but he didn't say any more.

'Rigid, more like,' said Alex, and Nash sniggered.

'Can we get on with the game, please?' Alex poured himself another glass of wine.

'Thanks, Mr Sensitivity,' I said snidely.

'God, it's the all-in couples fun match night tonight,' pointed out Fran. Alex grimaced at her and she shut up.

Out of the corner of my eye, I saw Nash risk a very small piece of salad.

'Oh my God! The lasagne!'

I dashed into the kitchen, followed closely by Angus. As I opened the oven and smoke poured out, he knelt down next to me with a serious look on his face.

'I think we should get Fraser NOW,' he whispered urgently.

'For God's sake, how many times do I have to tell you not to talk seriously to me while I'm holding burnt lasagne?'

He grinned. 'You know what I mean. I'll tell Mookie – she's on our side –'

'I don't have a side any more.'

'Och, come on. Yes, you do.'

'No, I don't.'

He ignored me.

'Then we'll get him pissed and talk him out of the wedding.'

I dumped the lasagne on the kitchen unit. It was black and hard round the edges. I started to file those bits away with a knife.

'What do you think this is, *Mission: Impossible*?'

'Come on. Look at the way she behaved. Bet you he's having second thoughts.'

'Gustard, no one ever has an idea of what's going on inside other people's relationships. We just don't know. I think we should leave them alone. He seems fine to me.'

'What seems fine to you?' said Alex, coming in to get some more wine. He lost his grip on the doorway temporarily, but caught it again.

'Ehm, I always refer to my lasagnes as he's. Makes them, er, rise better.'

Alex stared hard at the blackened mass before him. 'Looks like fucking terminal cancer to me.'

'Yes, well, never mind about that. Go back in and sit down.'

Grabbing another bottle, he stumbled back into the living room, where I heard a whoop of laughter from Fran and Mookie. Must have been telling them about my lasagne, the bastard.

I stood back and prodded my handiwork with a knife.

'Maybe if I just feed Nash and get some pizza in for everyone else . . .'

'That would be great,' said Angus sweetly.

'I spent all day making this lasagne.'

'I know.'

'I put nutmeg in it and everything.'

'Don't worry.'

I walked back into the living room and cleared my throat. Fraser was still staring unhappily at his glass of wine, and downing it at an extraordinary rate, while Nash patted him companionably on the arm. Alex had moved to sit between Mookie and Fran, who were laughing around him like a couple of starlets, and he was interrogating Linda, whose face was a dreadful colour.

'Come on, pet,' he was insisting, 'just tell us who it is.'

Linda's face looked like it might explode.

'Yes, come on, do tell us,' encouraged Mookie. Everyone seemed to have forgotten Linda's name.

Finally, she gritted her teeth. 'Ralph Fiennes,' she said, almost inaudibly.

Fran waved her glass in the air. 'No, Linda, it's got to be someone embarrassing as opposed to someone rich and handsome and gorgeous and lovely and . . .'

'Four foot nine,' finished Alex snidely.

Linda looked up at him, eyes burning.

'You'd never understand!' she shouted. I'd never heard her

261

shout. 'None of you could ever understand what he means to me!' And she stomped off to her bedroom, slamming the door behind her.

There was a silence.

'Two down,' said Alex, not very helpfully.

'Would you like me to go and see to her?' Mookie offered gravely.

'Thanks,' I said, 'but, well . . .'

'I'll go,' said Angus.

I turned round gratefully. 'Would you?'

He nodded. 'That means I'm not here when you tell them about the lasagne.'

'What about the lasagne?' said Nash, stricken.

'Ah.'

Half an hour later, everything was much improved. The pizzas had arrived and even Nash had had enough, although he insisted on picking every piece of vegetable matter off them first. Linda had gone to sleep, and Angus assured us she was OK. Well, not suicidal. We'd cleared the stupid, mismatched tables out of the room and the seven of us sat bunched around the sofa or kicking our heels on the floor, trying not to knock over the candles, which had stayed with us. Van Morrison was playing, but very, very quietly.

'You haven't gone,' said Alex to Fran.

'Oh, go away, I don't want to go.'

He started poking her in the side.

'You've got to! Forfeit, remember?'

Fran rolled over and lay on her stomach.

'I'm refusing to answer. I'll take the forfeit.'

'Wooo,' we said. 'Forfeit! Forfeit!'

'What, though?'

Alex grinned. 'You could show us your tits.'

I kicked him. 'Don't be disgusting.'

Fran sighed. 'Yes, and everyone's seen them.'

'I haven't!' said Mookie.

Everyone looked at her.

'Later,' said Fran.

Angus was leaning against the sofa.

'I know what you could do, Francesca,' he said softly.

The room turned to listen to him.

'You're an actress. Why don't you do some acting for us? Do a piece. What are you auditioning for at the moment?'

There was a chorus of 'good idea'. Fran looked embarrassed but shrugged.

'I'm auditioning for *Much Ado*,' she said. 'To tour schools with. I'm trying out for Beatrice.'

'OK, give us a bit of that then.'

We shifted around to give her some room. For about a second she pretended not to be absolutely thrilled to be asked, then just got on with it.

'Beatrice has just been asked if she's going to get married,' she said, then began:

'Not till God make men of some other metal than
earth. Would it not grieve a woman to be
overmastered with a pierce of valiant dust?'

'Valiant dust?' whispered Alex loudly. 'Woo . . . scary.'

'Shhh,' I said.

'. . . to make
an account of her life to a clod of wayward marl?
No, uncle, I'll none: Adam's sons are my brethren;

263

and, truly, I hold it a sin to match in my kindred.'

She was extremely good; her voice was strong, and the
words rang out with perfect clarity.

'The fault will be in the music, cousin, if you be
not wooed in good time: if the prince be too
important, tell him there is measure in every thing
and so dance out the answer.'

'Not another man-hater,' said Alex. Truly he was extremely
drunk, and I pinched him hard on the thigh.

'. . . For, hear me, Hero:
wooing, wedding, and repenting, is as a Scotch jig,
a measure, and a cinque pace: the first suit is hot
and hasty, like a Scotch jig, and full as
fantastical; the wedding, mannerly-modest, as a
measure, full of state and ancientry; and then comes
repentance and, with his bad legs, falls into the
cinque pace faster and faster, till he sink into his
    grave.'

Everyone clapped; then suddenly Fraser leaned forward and
clasped his head.
'God!' he said. 'It's just so much! It's just such a huge
thing to do!'
We fussed around him and told him not to worry.
'I'm not sure I want to dance the boring dances,' he sighed,
holding his glass. 'Not yet.'
'You're right,' said Angus. 'Listen to your instinct. Don't
do it. In fact, let's take a vote on it. Hands up all those who
think Fraser shouldn't get married.'

'Please, don't do this, guys,' Fraser said, but too late. Angus's hand was already in the air, as was Fran's. Alex put his up, 'but only because all marriage is a bunch of crap.' As he was sitting on the floor, he lost his balance and tipped over backwards, then decided not to get up again. Once we'd ascertained he hadn't set his hair on fire, we left him there. 'I'll second that,' said Nash. Mookie, once she'd realized that everyone else had, put her own hand up tentatively.

Fraser looked straight at me. 'What about you, Mel? Are you conscientiously objecting? Has some doubt crept into your mind after my fiancée's delightful behaviour this evening?'

I realized I'd forgotten to put my own hand up.

'Oh, no, I, ehm, got momentarily distracted.'

'But you're still putting your hand up?'

I put my hand up and stared back at him resolutely.

'Yes. Definitely.'

'Just checking.'

'Are you putting yours up?' said Angus to Fraser.

Fraser laughed hollowly. 'What, you mean I'm allowed to have an opinion after you lot?'

'Yeah, go on, Fraser, what's your vote?' said Fran.

'Tell me what he does,' said Alex.

Fraser looked at his glass and laughed. 'I don't think I have a vote.'

'Of course you do,' said Angus. 'Make your own fucking decisions, man.'

Fraser got to his feet, wobbling. 'Against the might of the wedding industry, Pyrford Parish Church, Earthworks flower company, *Hello!* magazine, the PR industry, Charlotte Coleman Bridal Designs, Gieves & Hawkes the tailors, Sloane Caterers Inc, Asprey's, Moët & Chandon, Heal's furniture shops, the Phillipses, the McConnalds, and my great auntie Margaret, who is eighty-two and flying in from Australia,' he declaimed dramatically, 'I am afraid I have no vote,' he bowed from the waist. 'No vote at all.'

We all looked at him for a bit.

'That,' he said, 'would have been a great moment to depart. If I wanted to go, and not sit here and drink my little brother's whisky. As long as you promise to shut up about the fucking wedding.'

And so it was only once he'd gone to the loo that Mookie could come out with her idea about the bomb.

Alex sat bolt upright when he heard about the bomb.

'Whaaa . . .' he coughed. 'What bomb.'

Mookie was blushing, as usual, at being the centre of attention.

'Well, rally, I suppose, it was an awful prank at school.'

'What was?' Alex demanded.

'When we wanted to ride our ponies and not go to assembly.'

'Oh God, yes, we did that too, didn't we, Mel?' I shot Fran a Woking look.

'Anyway, we set off all these smoke bombs – oh, the mess of it, rally – and that set off the fire alarms, and by the time they'd sorted everything out it was far too late to do anything at all. And of course with weddings, they're one after another, rally, aren't they? It's like Heathrow. If you miss your slot, you're there for ever.'

We stared at each other, stunned by the criminal genius.

'Nash,' said Angus, taking command, 'go distract Fraser.'

'Hey, I'm the best man, ken. If I'm going to choke to death, I want to hear about it, OK?'

'Fair enough. Alex, could you do it?'

'Wha', walk into a toilet with your brother? He'll think I'm a fuggin' botty burglar.'

'Go on, Alex,' I said. 'You don't care anyway. Just distract him. Do a tap dance or something.'

'Tap dance. Yeah. Right. Tap dance.' He staggered to his feet. 'Fucking tap dance.'

Next thing we heard was the bathroom door opening and the sound of copious vomiting. Fraser's voice could be heard, enquiring as to whether he was all right.

'What a stroke of genius,' said Angus.

'What a fucking piss-head, more like,' I said, crossly.

'OK,' said Angus. 'This is a brilliant plan.'

'Like the last brilliant plan?' I added.

'But have we got the balls to carry it out?' Angus continued.

We looked at each other. Having come up with the idea, Mookie had retreated again and was staring at the floor.

Noticing our silence, Angus continued:

'Where do you get the bombs, Mookie?'

'Ehm, well, one of my cousins, he's pretty high up in the Met.'

'You're joking – we'd steal them off the police?'

'Not stealing, rally – he keeps a few around his house.'

Nash whistled through his teeth.

'Then we'd need a couple of people to check the fire alarm – and a couple of people to make sure all the grannies get out and stuff.'

'Maybe we could keep the grannies out of the church all together?' someone said.

'Hang on!' I said. 'What if there's a mass stampede and hundreds of people are run over and killed? What if Amanda has a hysterical fit and commits suicide? What if Fraser never speaks to any of us again? What if you all get arrested?' God, I nearly wished I was going.

'It could be a sign,' said Angus. 'A beacon across the land to those in danger of wedlock.'

'Oh no! Dangerous David Koresh visionary thing!' I said, getting agitated. Off stage, the vomiting seemed to be quieting down. I hoped he wasn't going to use my tooth-brush.

'For people to think more carefully about why they're getting married and who to. We'll only set off a little one. We'll make sure nobody panics. Then we'll run for it. Think of it in the slightly naughty rather than the deranged criminal stakes.'

'Well, I'm up for it,' said Fran.

'Of course you're up for it: it's got an element of chaos!' I said.

'Huh! Well, if that's what you think . . .'

'I know where to place the bombs for, you know . . . well, the best places for them to go off, rally,' said Mookie shyly.

'Great, great,' said Angus. 'And Nash, you'll be at the front, so you're on granny duty. Fraser will help you.'

'I doubt this will sound so good when we wake up in the morning,' I said sourly.

'And I'll do the fire alarms.'

'As well as being the criminal master mind,' I said. 'This is a terrible idea.'

'We don't really need you,' said Fran.

Great. My own house, and I didn't even get to feel needed. I mumbled something about putting the coffee on and wandered off.

Alex was drinking water at the sink in the kitchen.

'I feel great!' he said. 'Much better.'

'You look green.'

'But I feel . . . great!' He bounced back into the sitting room. 'More ale, mistresses.' There was laughter.

Fraser was still standing there beside the sink, trying to make himself useful. We smiled ruefully at each other.

'Thanks for doing all this, Mel,' he said sweetly. 'I did say you didn't have to.'

'I know. I never listen to sensible people.'

'Ah yes. Me, Fraser Sensible, Esq.'

'What will you say to Amanda?'

'I was planning on blaming it all on you . . . Is that all right?' His tone of voice was gentle, but quite serious.

'Don't you dare!'

'OK. Really, it has been lovely.'

'It's been ghastly.'

'All dinner parties are ghastly. This was better than most.'

There was another gale of laughter from next door.

'See? They're having a great time.'

'You don't want to know what they're laughing about,' I said.

'Oh, I think I already do.'

He handed me a fresh glass of water. I took it.

'I'm sorry you've got mixed up in all this,' he said suddenly.

'That's OK,' I said cheerily. 'I'd never have met your brother otherwise.'

'Ah, yes . . . ehm, he's a nice chap.'

'Yes, he is — Oh, look!' I ran over to the window. 'The snow's lying!'

'So it is.' Fraser crossed over beside me to see. 'I love snow.'

'Me too. We should go out and make angels.'

He looked at me, smiling. 'OK, then.'

269

I looked at him. 'Is that a dare?'

'Might be. Are you up for it?'

I hesitated for only a second. 'Yes!' And we tiptoed to the door, shushing each other so as not to let people in on what we were up to. We crept outside, left the door on the latch, then bounded down the stairs, killing ourselves laughing.

The road outside was completely deserted, only the tall, crumbling Victorian buildings standing blankly all around. I launched myself first, then Fraser lay with his head touching my head, so we could make symmetrical angels. The snow wasn't very deep, and we were soon scraping gravel, lying there, soaking and freezing, laughing our heads off and looking at the cold, cold stars.

'It's all shit, isn't it, Mel?' yelled the voice from above my head.

'It's like the snow,' I yelled back, metaphysically. 'Looks gorgeous, but there's nothing but dog-poo and gravel underneath.'

He laughed. 'And once you're in it, it's cold and damp.'

'But if you weren't in it . . .'

'You wouldn't get any angels!' we chorused.

And we lay there for a while, till we knew we'd be missed, and realized we couldn't feel our extremities, and decided we'd better go in before we died in a tragic accident.

In one of my ludicrously small jumpers, Fraser helped me assemble the coffee cups and we took everything through. Only Angus bothered to look up; everyone else was far too pissed to notice the passage of time. The tone had changed completely, and people had started to espouse their personal theories of the world in drunk but desperately sincere tones, and finally I started to relax.

Drinking Angus's whisky, I let everything turn hazy and mused fitfully on things, occasionally dragged in to answer questions or provide opposition support when Alex finally did get round to suggesting a game of Spin the Bottle. Occasionally, I'd hear someone mention something to do with the wedding, or smoke, which would make everyone else go 'shhh!' and start to giggle. And finally, finally, Nash looked at his watch, and announced:

'Christ, I can't see what this watch says, ken. Which means it's time to go home.'

He heaved himself up to go phone a cab, and in a flurry of time I didn't notice swimming along, I waved, and kissed goodbye. Angus clapped his hands round me warmly. Fraser tried to refuse the piles of pizza which Alex insisted on passing him to take to his fiancée, as she hadn't eaten, but gave in in the end. The freezing cold air shot in briefly from outside as I touched his hand and said goodbye. His curly hair was still damp from the snow.

I wandered back into the living room and surveyed the carnage. Ashtrays and empty bottles littered the place; we seemed to have drunk everything in sight. Dreamily, I wandered into the kitchen to start hauling things away.

My first shock was this: I didn't walk into the kitchen, I walked into the airing cupboard.

Two: I must have been pissed, because I had no idea we had an airing cupboard.

Three: Alex and Fran were kissing in it.

Fifteen

I staggered backwards, grabbing for the wall. Alex didn't see me, but Fran did. Her dark eyes widened in horror, and she pushed at Alex's shoulder.

'Whaa?' he said, nuzzling her.

She indicated me, and he looked round.

Everyone looked at each other for a bit. I was frozen stiff; an icy waterfall seemed to be running through me, tightening up my throat and my heart, and chilling my stomach. I kept backing away. I knew I had to say something, but I couldn't get hold of what. All that went through my mind was the old cartoon strip of the husband coming home early and the lover hiding in the wardrobe. This wasn't funny though.

Finally, in a high-pitched squeak which didn't sound like me at all, I said, 'Go home!'

Alex lurched forward, jarred into sobriety.

'Yes, Fran, I think you should go. Melanie . . .' he hurtled towards me, arms outstretched.

'Melanie, what can I say? I'm . . . I can't believe . . . never happened before . . . too much wine . . .'

I couldn't even hear what he was saying.

'Go home!' came the terrible squeak again. 'Go away! Both of you! Go away! Go away!'

And I turned and ran from them into my room, and pitched forward on to the bed. I had intended to cry myself to sleep, or at least consider the situation, but the wine and the shock had a stronger hold than that, and I practically passed out on the bed.

I woke up at five o'clock in the morning, shivering uncontrollably. I was lying on top of the bed and, I dimly noticed, two coats. Instantly it came back to me, falling over me like a sheet of dark cloud. I crawled into bed and tried to get warm, but realized that my teeth were chattering for a different reason. I tried to think about it, but realized I didn't want to. All I could think of was them disappearing for two hours . . . they must have been laughing their heads off at me. I looked down on the bed. Still, I'd managed to make them leave without their coats. Thinking about this, I started to cry. And I didn't stop.

I cried all through the next day, while managing to forcibly prevent Linda from doing the washing-up. There appeared to be bits of burnt lasagne stuck to the ceiling. That would have made me laugh, if I hadn't been crying my heart out. I cried emptying the ashtrays, I cried taking the bottles to the bottle bank. Even pretending breaking the bottles was breaking their skulls didn't help. I cried every time the phone rang and I couldn't pick it up, and Linda took the thank you messages – none from Fran, though. I cried when I thought of the wedding, I cried when I thought of the flat we were going to have, I cried when I thought of the little bed and breakfast we'd booked for next week, I cried when I realized that I still had to get out of the flat for Linda's mystery reason and had nowhere to go, I cried when I thought of all the fucking money I'd spent so Alex could get pissed enough to make a pass at my best friend.

Alex showed up about noon. The bastard, couldn't even sleep outside my door all night. I threatened to call the police if he didn't stop ringing the ear-splitting doorbell.

'At least give me my coat,' he cried piteously.

'I've burnt it.'

'Please, Mel. Please.'

'Go round to Fran's. I'm sure she'll keep you warm.'

'Oh well, at least we're talking.'

I stomped off and ignored him. This bit, the bit where I got to shout at him, in some strange way, wasn't too bad. It was the bit that would come, the bit without him, which was going to be really difficult to bear.

He sat outside my door for four hours. He was wearing two rugby shirts one over another, but he didn't have a flask with him.

Eventually, when it was clear that I wasn't coming anywhere near him, I heard him stand up to go.

'I'm going,' he yelled.

'That assumes I care.'

'If you don't want to talk about it like an adult . . .'

'You snog your girlfriend's friend – ex-friend – in an airing cupboard, then want to get into a maturity competition?'

'At least hear my side of it.'

'You have no side of it. You ask me to move in with you

and six days later go after someone else. End of story. Change the fucking record, Alex.'

There was a big sigh on the other side of the door. Then he leaned down to the letter box and said gently, 'Just because I got pissed doesn't mean we can't move in together.'

'On the contrary; I think the European Court of Human Rights says that it does.'

'For God's sake, Melanie, have you no understanding at all? My way of behaving, it was all a reaction to the big step we're taking. It shows how much I love you – how scared I am; how much I'm willing to sacrifice. It was a spur-of-the-moment thing and, I swear to you, it will never ever happen again.'

'Yes, it will,' I yelled. 'But not to me. Now go fuck yourself.'

'Phone me,' he said. 'Phone me when you're ready to make the commitment. I think your over-reaction shows you're as scared as I am.'

I leaned over and slammed the letter box on his fingers. He yelped, and I felt better. He turned to go, paused for a second, then really did go.

I collapsed back into my bedroom. For all my bravado, I still felt hollowed out. The rain had come and driven away the snow and so everything outside nicely reflected my mood.

'What to do now?' I thought to myself. I really had no idea. There were no conscious thoughts in my head. I felt the urge to go somewhere, but I couldn't bring myself to move. I wanted to talk to someone, but there was no one on earth I wanted to talk to. I wanted to distract myself, but everything distracting would be full of images of happy, excited people, doing happy exciting things, and I wasn't. Wasn't wasn't wasn't. Single again. Single in December. At least I should have held on for a Christmas present. Although Alex thought they were bourgeois. Oh, God, what a twat.

I lay back, wishing I had a teddy bear or something equally crap to cling to in my hour of need. I wondered if I should phone the Samaritans. Although it wasn't like I was picking up the knives. I thought the Samaritans were only for really sad people. Not like me or anything. God, I missed him. No I didn't. Yes I did. No I didn't. Ticking like a mantra in my head, I started to cry again, even though I had absolutely nothing left to cry with and it came out dry. Finally, rocking myself back and forward, I sank right forward and finally got to sleep. And that was my weekend.

Having fallen asleep so early, I woke up on time the next day. My options being another day crying in bed or going to work, I decided to go to work. Big fat tears ran down my cheeks as I pulled my tights on. I looked in the mirror. I looked like one of those people they use to advertise the dangers of heroin. Gleh. Bleagh. Bleagh.

I walked into the office expecting everyone to instantly fall to their knees in sorrow as they caught a glimpse of me and my obviously huge tragedy, but, annoyingly enough, they all behaved exactly as usual.

'Hey, mate, another rough weekend for you, yeah? You look like a tart's backside,' said Steve as I dragged myself in, looking, I thought, like Mary Magdalene.

'I feel like one,' I replied despondently. 'Only less hairy.'

He eyed me strangely. 'What's the matter wiv you, like?'

'Oh, everything. I ditched my boyfriend.'

'Why? Don't tell me, he copped off with someone else and you had to save face by dumping him?'

'Jesus, Steve, when are you going to evolve frontal lobes? Piss off, I don't want to talk about it.'

Silently, Janie passed over her box of king-sized Kleenex. I took it gratefully, having decided just to let the tears drip down when they came rather than give myself a migraine pretending they weren't there.

'How's James?' I asked her, to relish the irony. They were probably getting married too.

'Oh God,' she began, grabbing the box of tissues back. 'We were at a party on Saturday and his ex-girlfriend was there.'

'That's legal.'

'So, of course I walked out immediately. Then he didn't want to come with me!'

'Where was the party?'

'Kent.'

'You came all the way back from Kent because his ex was at a party?'

'Well, for God's sake! It was so insensitive!'

'Did he know she was going to be there?'

'Well, he says no, but I don't know whether I believe him. It was at university, you see.' As if that explained everything.

'Ohh. What kind of party was it?'

'Oh, some college reunion . . .' Suddenly her face fell.

I looked at her. This woman was clearly bonkers.

'So, surely she might be expected to be there . . . ?'

'I didn't think,' she said, ashen.

'That's because you're a moron.'

'Oh my God, poor James. How could I?'

'Because you're a moron. Can I borrow the tissues again, please?'

'He's really going to dump me this time!' Her voice rose hysterically. She held on to the tissues for grim life.

'Jesus!' said Steve. 'That's it. I am putting in for a transfer before my periods start to fall into synch with you two mad bitches.'

That lunch time, I ate my sandwich disconsolately, remembering the time Fraser had come and picked me up unexpectedly. I could do with that now. If I didn't get it out of my system soon, I was going to explode. Then I remembered that he had problems enough of his own in six days, and the last thing he wanted was to be poured upon by a dumb Harpy like me.

I thought of Angus too, but that was more difficult. Everything was so complicated.

I managed to raise my only smile that day by thinking about the smoke bombs. If they were going to carry it out . . . It was nuts, but, God, it might be funny. It might even work. Probably not though. I was sure the vicar could do the service anywhere these days. He could pop next door and do it in the pub.

I definitely wasn't going to go to the reception. There'd probably be armed guards on the door keeping me away, anyhow. And I couldn't feel less like a wedding. Fran would probably turn up. That girl had front enough for anything.

Fran. I hadn't even started to grieve for her yet. I was too busy splitting myself over Alex. Telling myself she was just a big slut didn't help. I'd known her all my life. And now . . . that was over, as if she'd died. She hadn't even phoned me. Too ashamed, I presumed. Maybe she didn't even care. That idea filled me with sadness. Maybe they were together even now. Alex was deciding he'd made a big mistake all along hanging out with me. Why would he want to – Fran was so gorgeous and skinny. She'd probably help him get a job with his pop-star mates, just by being thin and disdainful and glamorous. I had the horrible thought that he was trading up. And another equally horrible thought was on the bus right behind it: that I'd always known he would. I supposed I'd been waiting for it to happen. I didn't think I was good enough for that low-down piece of shit, which made me a gnat on the underside of the low-down piece of shit. I wept again. I just hadn't thought he'd go so close to home, that was all.

No flowers this time. He knew it wouldn't work any more. Probably too busy at home with Fran. They'd be laughing at something moronic I'd said. 'Oh God, it feels so good to be FREE!' Alex would be saying. 'Yeah, you nearly got trapped big time,' Fran would be saying. Maybe she didn't really hate him after all. Maybe all that time she'd been calling him a cocksucker because she was really in love with him, the way she used to push boys she liked off the wall at school. Maybe she'd just been getting his attention.

Well, she had it now, I thought grimly, and tried to concentrate on something, anything else.

Suddenly, as if summoned psychically by me, a conga-line of people threaded its way into the office, going: 'De-ner de der der deh deh . . . De-ner de der der deh deh,' with party hats on and streamers. A tape recorder was loudly playing Christmas hits. I was so surprised I nearly stopped crying for a second.

'What's going on?' I asked Steve, as one particularly rotund woman knocked my stapler off my desk.

'Christmas party tonight, innit? Just getting in the mood. Gonna be dragging me under the mistletoe then, sweetheart?'

'I'd rather learn to kiss my own arse. Jeez, who has a party on a Monday night, anyway?'

'Every night's party night when I'm around,' leered Steve. 'You coming?'

And he grabbed my arm and forced me to join the conga line. It was then, prancing around trying to look dignified while doing a conga, devoid of friends, career and lover, that I realized I'd reached my nadir. Until ten seconds later, when the music changed to 'Do They Know it's Christmas?' and I realized I'd reached it again.

'This is sick,' I said to Steve. 'I'm not dancing to music about starving people! Let me out!'

Janie looked on impassively.

'Are you coming to the party tonight?' she asked.

'No way,' I said.

'Oh, go on. You have to stay for a bit. The drinks are free till seven.'

'They could buy me a house and I still wouldn't stay for this party. I am going home to eat crisps and feel sorry for myself. Is James coming? And don't cry, whatever the answer is.'

Her lip wobbled. 'He's got training.'

'Oh . . . brushing up on his running skills is he?'

She looked at me wonderingly. 'Yes . . . how did you know?'

'Lucky hunch.'

'Please stay for a bit,' she said. 'I . . . think I should stay for my career. Networking is very important.'

'Steve will look after you,' I said. Steve re-entered the room. His cheap silky tie was loosened and he was carrying an enormous balloon that was the shape of a penis. Janie looked at me.

'Please. Just stay for a bit.'

God knows why I agreed. To take my mind off things, I supposed. The day dragged on and on. Nobody even rang me to see if I was OK. Nobody cared. At five, Flavi clapped her hands together and made a little Christmas speech about what FUN the marketing department had been that year and how much FUN we were all going to have next year, working together as one big fluid copywriting machine. I stood at the back, making baa-ing noises when everyone else clapped.

Then cheap – very cheap, and my tastes weren't particularly rarefied – vino was passed round in plastic cups and we all stood self-consciously talking about work, like we would do anyway.

'Well, this is fun!' Flavi said to no one in particular. Her concept of fun was most peculiar. Steve tapped me on the shoulder.

'Come on,' he said, 'we're off to crash the accountants' party. It's always miles better.'

'I find that simultaneously easy and difficult to believe.'

Steve appropriated two bottles of the vino and the three of us set off to the other end of the building. You could hear the accountants' party a mile off. People were screaming and they already had the photocopier going. Inside, there were accountants jiving – always a sight to see – running around, leapfrogging each other; one chap was lying on the floor having wine poured into his mouth from a great height.

'Wow, who'd have thought being an accountant would be so much fun?' I remarked.

'Nah, it's only once a year,' said Steve. 'They spend the petty cash and they just go crraaazy.' An older businessman waltzed past, with a temp clinging on with her legs round his waist. 'They start at ten o'clock in the morning.'

'No kidding?' After the weekend, I was in no mood to get drunk, but I accepted a small glass of champagne and congratulated myself on my good distracting techniques. Every time I relaxed my grip, the howling precipice opened up beneath my feet, so I reminded myself yet again not to get drunk, and tried to focus on being a detached observer, even when someone pulled up my skirt accidentally and I whirled round ready to beat them to death.

Over in the corner, one of the accountants had just finished explaining why he wasn't really an accountant after all, he should really have been a drummer, and how he had once had an audition for Motorhead. He then proceeded to demonstrate this by taking two rulers and beating the hell out of everything, occasionally hitting the touch-tone phone keys for all-round percussionist setting. The cacophony churned round and round my head, and I suddenly realized I needed to get away. I dashed out of the room and opened the window in the empty corridor, taking deep breaths of the chilly air. The accountants' office was twelve storeys up, and I could see all the other buildings around. Over the rooftops, I identified Fraser's. I knew it was the funny old redbrick one with the carved birds around the eaves.

Suddenly, I just had to talk to him. I had to talk to someone, and it was him. Otherwise I was going to go bonkers, plain and simple. It wasn't that late, he wouldn't even have finished yet. I'd just pretend to be casually walking by and bump into him, then we could go for a quick coffee somewhere.

Although he probably had a million things to do. He probably had to go home and check out the fifteen bridesmaids dresses or something. Put the corsages together. Lick madam's boots.

I changed my mind half a dozen times in a second, then realized I was going to go anyway, so I might as well get a move on. Even to say hello would be enough.

Inside the accountants' party pit, things seemed to be getting wilder. I picked up my bag, then turned round to say goodbye to Steve and Janie. To my amazement, they were grappling with each other on the filing cabinet.

283

Janie looked to have her dress down below her shoulders. Good Lord. Well, good for her. I was going to creep out without saying anything, but she caught sight of me over his shoulder, gave me a huge thumbs-up sign and threw her head back laughing. Well, well, well. I hope this cured her. She certainly looked happier than I'd ever seen her. Although why it had to be Steve . . .

Feeling slightly more optimistic, I bounced out of the building into the frosty night air.

I hovered outside Fraser's office for twenty minutes, trying to look casual and as if I was just walking past. I was absolutely freezing, and I'd lost any feeling in my nose. Finally, at about half-past six, he emerged, bent down against the wind. Oh God, this was a stupid idea. I didn't know how to walk past casually. I was going to look such a fool. I turned away to make a run for it.

'Were you waiting for me?' the Scottish tones said gently.

I looked round. 'No! Well, in fact, yes.'

He smiled. 'Is it serious?'

'Why, do you have to go somewhere? It's nothing really, I'm sorry, you know, I was just passing, but I have to be going . . .'

Fortunately for me, he pulled me into a nearby patisserie, the kind that sold overpriced coffee to lawyers and tourists.

'Come on. You look freezing.'

'No, not at all, just passing.' I calmed down.

'Etcetera,' I said.

'I phoned you on Sunday to say thanks, but you weren't in.'

'I was in. I just wasn't really in the mood to talk to anyone.'

'Not because of Amanda, surely?'

'No . . .'

And I told him everything. I told him about moving in, and I told him about the airing cupboard, and I told him about America, and I told him about Charlie, and I told him about Fran. With embarrassing pauses while the waitress brought us coffee and cakes – she could obviously tell we were having a big dramatic conversation and tried overly hard not to draw attention to herself, thus drawing lots of attention to herself – I let it all spill out, at last.

More tears – where on earth did they come from? – plopped on to my vanilla slice. I tried to smile and change the subject before I went to pieces completely.

'I see you're eating cakes again,' I said.

Fraser grinned. 'I decided that cakes were more important than looking two-dimensional at the wedding.'

'You're still going through with it, then?'

'I've come this far. Anyway, we're talking about you. What are you going to do?'

I sighed. 'I don't think I can do anything. I mean, I never want to see him again . . . It's almost like it's Fran I'm going to miss, really.'

He nodded his head sympathetically.

'I think you'll forgive her,' he said.

'Of course I can't forgive her! I can never forgive her!'

'You're being melodramatic. She got carried away. I mean, you've been best friends for years and she's always been a complete floozie, from what I can work out. I'm only surprised it hasn't happened before. You'll get over it.'

I thought about that for a bit.

'Ditch Alex,' he went on. 'He's a total loser. I could tell from the moment I met him. Total, utter, wanky loser. Run for it. But, you know, Fran just cocked up. She can't look at a bloke without mentally taking his pants off. She just chose the wrong one. I bet she's totally humiliated now, and can't even bring herself to ring you.'

'Or round at Alex's having a wonderful time.'

'Neh.' He loosened his tie. 'How's your cake?'

'Are you trying to distract me?'

'Yes.'

'Am I being boring?'

He sighed. 'No, don't be silly. I just think you should take your mind off it for a bit. Otherwise – I don't know, but I get into a loop of thinking about things and I just lie awake all night and worry about them. Don't do that.'

'What do you worry about?'

He thought for a moment.

'Ehm . . . what kind of cake is the best. What type are you eating?'

I gave up. 'Vanilla slice.'

'Is it the best?'

'Possibly . . . sometimes it runs a close thing with French cake. And birthday cake. And strawberry tarts.'

'See? It never ends.'

And gently, we drifted into normal talk – not emotional, not coy, just talking quietly – even giggling occasionally. The cake shop was empty and waiting to close up, but outside the darkness was all around and here, in this little pool of light, we were safe and comfortable and we didn't want to leave. There were enough things outside to make us cold.

I arrived home later, feeling more at peace. Linda was in the sitting room watching *Titanic*. Tears were dripping off her pudgy nose. Wordlessly, I went and sat beside her on the sofa. A complete first, she put out her hand. I took it, and moved closer. Finally, as the ship went down, I rested my head on her shoulder.

'But you still have to go away this weekend,' she said stiffly.

I'd forgotten that. Damn. Where the hell was I going to go? My parents, I supposed. I wasn't looking forward to answering the question, 'So, how's your love life, darling?'

'You don't need to go till Saturday morning.'

I thanked her for her magnanimity and sloped off to bed, where I lay for several hours plotting scenes of deadly revenge on Alex and Fran before finally sinking into an exhausted sleep.

No one was at work. Some people had left for early Christmas breaks, and quite a few more — mostly connected with financial services, I was unsurprised to hear — were recovering from the party.

Neither Janie nor Steve had made it in, but Steve left a message on my voice mail saying, 'Tell Flavi we're not coming in because we're too busy SHAGGING.' And I could hear Janie screaming with laughter in the background, shouting, 'And if James rings, tell him to FUCK OFF!'

Poor James has been through quite enough already, I thought. Mad pair of bastards! I did miss them, though, in an odd way. The less people around, the more time I had to dwell on the situation, and that was no fun.

Neither Fran nor Alex had rung me. Alex must have finally got the message it was over. He'd given up awfully quickly, though. Not, I sternly told myself, that that made any difference. I might never see the two of them again. Not too soon for me.

I'd phoned my mother, who of course knew that it was

the big day on Saturday (the whole town did, this was the closest Woking got to society – unless you counted Paul Weller, who was born there and spent the rest of his life making disparaging remarks about the place), and couldn't understand why I wasn't going. I hadn't told her the whole truth, naturally. I told her we'd fallen out, in a kind of equal opportunities way.

'Oh, remember when you lost your purse and you all fell out about who had it? The three of you made that up in the blink of an eye.'

'Mum, Amanda took that purse and said if we didn't make friends with her again she'd have one of Year Seven beat us up.'

She ignored me. 'I'm sure you'll sort it out, whatever it is. Oh, Amanda's going to be such a lovely bride. Always was so pretty, and so tiny.'

'And a witch.'

'What's that, darling? Oh, do come home, we're dying to see you. You can tell us all your news . . . How's your exciting new job going? Come and stay with us. But do go to the wedding – you'll regret it if you don't. Derek Phillips certainly knows how to splash out when he wants to!'

'Thanks, Mum. I'm not going to go, and that's that. But I'll see you about lunch time, Saturday?'

'Fine, fine, we'll see you then.'

And she tutted sorrowfully that I would dare to miss such a glorious occasion.

Sixteen

I woke up extremely early on Saturday with a sore head and a deep sense of foreboding. As consciousness returned, I realized what day it was, and my heart dropped like a stone. I hugged my duvet and told myself not to be so bloody silly. It was just a normal day, I would get up, go home and be nice to my mum for a change, instead of a bit sulky. Maybe do some shopping and watch a bit of TV. No problem.

Really, I wanted to lie face-down on the floor and kick and scream and have the mother of all tantrums. But no. I would get up, wash, and dress demurely, then go out and face the world with calm and ease. Alex and Fran might well turn up to the wedding together. Well, that would be lovely for them. I hoped they'd all have a lovely day. Even when the smoke alarms went off, I'm sure that would not stop things too much – and how they would all laugh about it in the years to come, one great big circle of friends. Perhaps Alex and Fran and Amanda and Fraser's children would all play together. They'd probably go on holiday too. How lovely lovely lovely.

Next door, I could hear the sound of shifting furniture. What on earth was Linda doing in there? I yawned, and shook my head to wake myself.

BRRRRRINNG! The doorbell went off with its usual soul-jerking intensity. BRRING! BRRIING! BRRING! That didn't sound like the fat postman. It better not be Alex. Grimly, I pulled on my pyjamas and got up to answer it. Linda poked her shiny face round the living-room door, obviously concerned that I might be disobeying her mandate. I waved at her and peered through the letter box. It was Angus.

'What is it?' I yelled.

'Can I come in?'

I pondered it for a bit.

'Why?'

'Let me in and I'll tell you!'

'What if it's a double-bluff?'

'What on earth are you talking about?'

I didn't know, so I opened the door and let him in. His mischievous smile left his face when he saw me.

'Jings, what's the matter with you? You look like you've been up a wall crying for a week.'

'How intuitive. What are you doing here? Haven't you got a wedding to attend?' I turned cold. 'Have they called it off?'

'Not as far as I know.'

'Oh.' I looked at him hazily.

'Have you just woken up?'

'Ehm, yes. Sorry. Nice kilt. Would you like a coffee?'

He looked at his watch. 'OK. Hi, Linda!'

Linda squeaked like a cross mouse and disappeared.

'I'm not supposed to be here,' I whispered. 'I told her I'd clear out today.'

'Because you're going to the wedding.'

'Of course I'm not going to the fucking wedding.'

He followed me into the kitchen. 'Oh, yes, hum, yes, in fact you are. Fraser told me everything. That's why I'm here. To pick you up. You have to come with me.'

I put the kettle on and turned to face him.

'Sorry. Much as I'd like to help you out on your bob-a-job week, (1) I'm definitely not coming, and (2) I'm not even invited.'

Angus ignored me, and got the cups down while I put the kettle on. In fact, he whistled a happy tune. Finally, we sat down. The kitchen table had disappeared. I ignored this fact, given that my world was already odd enough and I was having breakfast with a man in a skirt.

Angus sat down and continued whistling quietly until it became intensely irritating.

'Stop it,' I announced. 'I am *so* not coming to this wedding, it doesn't matter how much you whistle.'

He kept on whistling. 'I need to take a guest.'

'Take Kylie Minogue.'

He resumed whistling.

'I bet Alex won't be there,' he said between bars and contemplative sips of his coffee.

'I don't care.'

'Or Fran.' The melody had changed to 'Over the Sea to Skye'.

'I double don't care.'

'Come on. Get changed. I've hired a car, so it won't take that long to get down there.'

'No, it won't take you long at all. When you leave, now, and leave me alone.' I crossed my hands over my chest protectively. 'And stop whistling.'

He stopped obediently, and just sat there, waiting.

'Why do you want me to come, anyway? I'm not letting off any of your bloody smoke bombs.'

He shrugged. 'I want you to. And I think you should. So, you should come with me.'

My heart quickened a little. 'It'll be awful. Everyone there will know that my boyfriend's having it off with my best friend.'

'No they won't. And if they do, they won't care.'

'Amanda will be killing herself laughing.'

'I think Amanda's got enough on her mind, don't you?'

'S'pose . . . Oh, I can't, Angus. I can't go and watch two people pledge their troths or whatever the hell it is they're doing, and have the happiest fucking day of their lives while I'm in absolute hell. I'll just be sitting there weeping my head off. And I can do that on my own, thank you. I'd probably snort just when they got to their "I do"s and snotter all over the wedding cake.'

'That would fit in nicely,' said Angus.

'Don't tease me. I'm not coming and that's that. I am going to my mother's to talk about baking cakes and then eat some, hopefully.'

He nodded. 'You're coming.'

'What are you going to do, kidnap me?'

'You have to come. For two reasons. One, to hold your head high, and to say, fine, all this crap is finished with, look at me, I have survived, blah blah blah. You have to. You'll get a kick out of yourself. You'll be proud of it for years afterwards.'

Hmm. 'What's the other reason?'

He looked at me.

'I really, really want you to. And I really, really want you to come with me. Which you knew. But which you still asked. Which proves that you're teasing me. Which proves that you're not too depressed to leave the house. Which means you're coming.'

We stared at each other for a long time. I dropped my eyes first. His intense blue gaze didn't falter. My heart beat faster and faster.

'I . . . er . . .' I cleared my throat. 'I don't think I've anything to wear.'

He grinned broadly at my capitulation. 'Come in your pyjamas, I won't care.'

'Yes, but you're wearing a skirt.'

'Wear whatever you like. Doesn't matter to me. I think you're pretty anyway.'

He thinks I'm pretty! I thought to myself, suddenly jubilant. Then: *As if I'm little girl enough to fall for that one*. Then: *What the hell?*

'Ehm, OK, I'll . . . go and see what I can find.'

He nodded, as if he'd known all along, which he probably had.

'Fine. I'll put the kettle on again. Linda, would you like some tea? We'll be gone soon.'

'No thank you,' came the muffled reply, closely followed by some hammering. What was she doing in there?

In my room, I sat down on my futon and thought long and hard. I was incredibly excited. The urge . . . to do something, to have something happen . . . rose so strongly in me it was like a tidal wave. My stomach rumbled with anxiety.

I had been lying when I said I didn't have anything to wear. I had an old brocade dress in a deep mulberry colour, which I'd got cleaned the week before when Alex and I were busy preparing for things − ha. I slipped into it, and put on some twenties button-style shoes. No hat, but I had a matching ribbon to keep my curls out of the way. Dressing, I took a quick glance in the mirror. I did look pretty, for once.

Good. My cheeks were flushed and my eyes sparkled. I was so excited I kept missing the buttons on the sleeve, but, finally, I was ready.

Angus was waiting for me. 'God, you look gorgeous,' he said.

'Thank you very much. So do you,' I replied, and he did cut a very handsome and sturdy figure in his kilt.

'Do you want me to phone your mother and tell her you're not coming?'

God, I'd nearly forgotten all about her.

'Ehm, unless you want the Spanish Inquisition as to who on earth you are and why are you kidnapping my youngest, then I'd say you probably shouldn't.'

I phoned her. She'd bought lots of baking materials, but sounded much happier that I was going to the wedding and that we'd all made up at last.

'Who knows – maybe you'll meet a nice man there,' she said.

I looked at Angus washing up the coffee cups.

'Who knows,' I said.

He turned as I got off the phone.

'Time to go?' he asked, proffering me his arm.

'Let's do it,' I said nervously, taking it.

'Bye, Linda!'

There was a snuffling noise, and we left her to it.

On the drive to the village, neither of us could say very much. There was too much going on. I was too nervous. My fingers tapped out a beat on my knee. Gently, Angus squeezed my hand in his. His hand was much larger than mine.

'Don't worry,' he said. 'Just keep your head up. We'll show 'em.'

294

Something occurred to me.

'You're not still going to do that smoke bomb thing, are you?'

'Ehm, I don't know. Mookie's not sure she can get them, and we've lost a foot soldier in that damned Francesca. So, it might not work.'

'But you still want to try?'

'If we have to.'

I nodded and stared straight ahead.

'You know it won't stop them?'

'No. But it'll annoy them.'

I turned to look at him. His eyes were crinkled up from smiling. I smiled too.

'Count me in.'

'Really?'

'Sure. If he's so stupid as to marry her after all this, a dose of smoke to the brain isn't going to hurt him anyway.'

'Exactly. You're on back granny watch.'

I laughed, and my nerves increased. I felt ready for anything; ready to do anything. Ready to break free, to leave everything behind. To have an adventure.

'I'm feeling very adventurous,' I announced.

'Really?' He looked intrigued.

'Just a warning.'

'OK.'

There was a watery sun in the air, which didn't look very committed. Small clouds were scudding around, as if they were scouting for the big clouds who were coming along later. The church, however, looked breathtaking. It was a picture-perfect little Victorian place. Holly was strewn everywhere, all round the kissing gate and over the church doors, with hawthorn and ivy and mistletoe. That all seemed a bit pagan to me, but it looked very pretty.

Scores of people were hovering about outside in that embarrassed way people do before weddings, looking off into the distance, or mentally preparing themselves for the long hours of small talk with strangers to come. There were couples who had driven long distances and obviously got lost, and who were now too cross with each other to speak, and an elderly relative contingent, who would grab anyone walking past and force them to reveal lots of personal details.

I noticed a real difference between what were clearly the two sides. Amanda's lot were loud and expensively dressed – lots of young women and rugby-playing men who were something in the City, or wanted you to think they were by their cufflinks. There were a fair number of open-topped sports cars dotted around – despite the fact that it was four degrees above freezing – and quite a few top hats and morning coats, which, despite myself, I rather liked.

Fraser's side, on the other hand, just looked . . . well, normal, apart from the predominance of skirts amongst the men. I saw their mother, and it was her that Angus took me over to meet first. She smiled at me in a slightly knowing fashion, but was charming and warm. Some of the lads from the stag night were hanging around too, and it was nice to say hello to them again. Then I caught sight of Nash, who was standing by himself under a tree. I waved him over.

'Hey there, how's it going?'

He looked green.

'Aye, no bad, ken.'

'Are you nervous?'

'Aye, you could . . . aye, yes, well, a bit, aye.'

'How's your best-man speech?'

He turned even more green and started patting himself up and down. 'Ehm, it's here somewhere, right enough . . .'

'Don't worry, you'll be fine. But, listen, I thought Fraser was supposed to be here with you? Surely that's your job, to get him to the church on time. Where is he?'

Nash looked positively nauseous. 'Aye, well, he said he'd see me there, like.'

Several other people had wandered over, enquiring over the whereabouts of the groom. People started to make crass jokes and asides. I looked at Angus, who shrugged his shoulders emphatically.

It was ten to twelve, and the ceremony was due to begin at twelve. This was cutting it pretty fine. I scanned the roads for a wedding car, but I didn't see one. More and more guests were arriving, and the news that the groom hadn't shown up yet was beginning to filter through the crowd. A photographer was clicking away furiously and approached us, consulting a list in his hand.

'So,' he said to Angus, 'you're the second laird?'

Angus looked at him, mystified, waving away the camera. 'Who are you?'

'Jof de Beauvoir. Photographer, *Hello!* magazine. And my mother's the daughter of the Earl of Suffolk.'

'Oh, in that case –' said Angus and strode past him rudely, grabbing me with him.

Over by the church gate stood a gaggle of bridesmaids – six full-sized blondes, two tiny. The little ones were tugging at their cream sashes, sticking their bottom lips out and kicking each other when they thought no one was looking. I felt a bit like that myself. None of the elder bridesmaids were paying the children any attention; they were too busy repeatedly asking each other if they looked all right and whisking away imaginary spots from each other's make-up.

Next to them stood an out-of-place man in a battered old Barbour. That would have made him stand out, if it were not for the fact that he was holding eight reins with white geese on the end of them. Not only this, but the geese appeared to be wearing cream bow-ties.

'Fuck me!' Angus and I exclaimed at the same time.

'I'm never getting married without geese,' I said.

'I hope they don't blow up in the explosion,' said Angus gloomily.

'Well, that would sort lunch out for me, given I don't have a place at the reception.'

Angus examined his watch, and I caught sight of it.

'God,' I said, retreating beside Angus. 'He's going to do a last-minute special on us and give everyone heart attacks.'

'Hmm,' said Angus thoughtfully.

Mookie slipped over to join us.

'Hello there!' I kissed her.

'I got them,' she whispered.

'It's OK, there's no one around – you don't have to whisper.'

She opened her Chanel bag to reveal two small cylindrical objects.

'Although I'm not sure you'll rally need them now, will you? Oh, and have you seen the geese?'

We all stood around until the vicar came out, and started hustling people inside. 'I'm terribly sorry, he'll be very embarrassed when he turns up, but I do have another service at two, so if you wouldn't mind awfully . . .'

I didn't mind. It was freezing outside. Angus grabbed hold of Nash and said something about 'sending the car round' which I didn't catch. Then we followed the crowd inside.

Inside, the church was just as beautiful as outside but faintly . . . well, über-wedding. Wreaths and ribbons decorated every area, and there were about five thousand candles. Rose petals covered the carpet and there was a floral tribute of their initials intertwined, a theme which was reproduced on every pew and on the elaborate Order of Service I was being handed. I was so taken aback, I couldn't answer the question 'Bride or groom?'

'What?'

'Are you a friend of the bride or the groom?'

I looked helplessly at Angus. 'I don't know,' I said.

'Groom,' said Angus. 'So you can sit beside me,' he added, when we got inside.

The organist was playing something extremely elaborate, and we sat down at the very front – Angus beside his mother, and me beside Angus. Being in the front pew felt odd and a bit wrong, but I didn't argue. I studied the Order of Service. From the looks of things, this was going to be a four-hour wedding.

'Kahil Gibran! How original!' I whispered to Angus. He raised his eyes.

'I think she planned the service.'

I looked at the fuchsia garlanding which obscured the altar. The large bible had a set of intertwined initials on it.

'You're kidding!'

From the other side of the church, Mookie waved and pointed out the fire alarm. We nodded back at her. The excitement was still there, in the pit of my stomach. The church filled up, and Jof the photographer, for want of something better to do, came and took pictures of the congregation, with reference to his little black book and the prettier of the blondes. People's heads kept turning, and the vicar wandered up and down the aisle in some trepidation. Nash was nowhere to be seen.

'What is going on?' I whispered to Angus. He shrugged again. I turned to look at his mum, but she didn't seem too perturbed; she was holding her hymnal quite calmly. I didn't know what to say to her, so I peered around the church again. Everyone was whispering and giggling. It was ten past, quarter past. I saw Amanda's mum. I don't know if the Priory did her much good, as she looked pissed to me. She was picking petals off her corsage and swaying.

I wondered if Fraser had had an extra stag night, and was even now on a train from Aberdeen. 'Have you tied him up somewhere?' I whispered to Angus. 'You'd better not have.'

'I promise you, I have no idea where he is,' he whispered back. The entire congregation was shuffling and looking at their watches. It was twenty past, then twenty-five.

Suddenly, the doors at the back of the church burst open with a crash. As one, we turned round to see. Framed in the door stood Amanda.

She did look beautiful. The dress was white, but seemed to have been overlaid with gold. The cut-off sleeves emphasized her toned arms and delicate shoulders, and the skirt reflected her every move and clung to her like gossamer. She was wearing a pure white stole round her shoulders which looked like – surely not? – fur. God, it couldn't be polar bear, could it? But the effect was stunning.

Her face, on the other hand, was quite different. She was stone white and looked furious. Everyone was silent. She stalked slowly up the aisle – not quite as poised as usual. Several of the bridesmaids had shuffled in behind her, but had stopped short at the back of the pews. The organist started playing 'Here Comes the Bride', but someone obviously slapped him, as the keys stopped immediately with

300

a dying hiss. Amanda advanced, pale and set. And stopped in front of us.

'Where the hell is he?' she hissed at Angus.

Angus looked straight back at her.

'I swear, I don't know.'

Her voice rose, and reverberated throughout the church:

'You fucking bastard, you've been fixing this from the start. You do fucking know. Where the fuck is he?'

His voice was gentle, not victorious. 'I'm sorry, Amanda. He didn't tell me anything about this. Honestly, if you think I knew, do you think I'd be here? He might just be late.'

'He's not fucking late,' she spat. 'You're all fucking morons, the whole fucking lot of you.'

She turned to me. 'Oh, the collaborator. You sad cow. I heard all about you. At least I made it this far.'

I was trembling from the attack, but in no position to say anything. Embarrassed, I looked around me.

Amanda turned back to Angus. As she did so, I caught sight of something and gasped: at the back of the church, behind the bridesmaids, silhouetted against the wintry churchyard, stood Fraser. He was wearing his hunting tartan, and a fresh baggy white shirt, and looked as if he'd just strode in from the moors. His mouth was set in a hard line, and he was listening intently. No one else had noticed him. Amanda was still in full flow and commanding everyone's attention.

'You can tell your idiotic, stupid, lanky, lousy brother that the next time he'll see me is in court, when I'm suing him for the cost of the wedding. If you can remember that, you stupid, provincial, sheep-shagging moron. God, to think I nearly got hitched into this repulsive family!'

The guests murmured in horror. Angus didn't say anything, but looked at her steadily. Infuriated, she took her

301

huge themed bouquet and hurled it at him – and hit me by mistake . . . Well, I think it was by mistake.

A collective gasp went up from the congregation as I staggered backwards, then came upright again. I put my hand to my head, and it came away with blood on it, from the thorns. I suddenly felt giddy.

Amanda sneered and turned to go, like the wicked fairy at the feast. Then she faced the crowd.

'You bunch of bastards!' she yelled bitterly. Her Woking accent was back in all its glory. 'You're loving this . . . you're –'

Then two things happened. Her voice trailed off and her eyes became fixed as she focused on the back of the hall. Everyone followed her gaze and turned round. Except for me, because I knew who she was looking at.

The second thing that happened was that Amanda shrieked, and her shriek rapidly turned into a hefty coughing fit. The other side of the church from where we were suddenly started to choke, as a mass of dense smoke rose up . . .

I looked at Angus. His eyes were alight. 'Come on,' he whispered, 'get the grannies out . . .'

After that it was chaos. Everyone began piling for the door. There were hollers and yelps as loving couples trod over each other in their efforts to escape. One of the tall candles fell over, and it looked as if we might have a real fire on our hands when someone's over-priced synthetic Barbara Cartland hat caught the flame. A huge squawking went up as the geese took to the air to escape, and the man in the Barbour ran back into the church to rescue the birds.

I had already spotted the side entrance and fumbled my way towards it, pushing as many people as I could. The flowers – no doubt sprayed with terribly flammable perfume – were now ablaze, and as I herded people through the door, I caught

302

sight of Angus doing his thing with a fire extinguisher. Amanda's mum stood in the middle of everything, wobbling as if she didn't know where she was, and I was relieved to see Mookie drag her away by the arm.

The vicar was dancing about outside in agony for his church.

'God, I wish I was a Catholic,' he said. 'Then I could drink the Communion wine.'

'It's fine . . . sir –' I didn't quite know what to call a vicar – 'I think it's under control.'

'You'd think this would be a nice change from all the normal boring weddings, ken,' said Nash, who was nearby doing a headcount.

It didn't look that way as worried, upset people hung about outside, coughing and fretting. I could hear a fire engine. Oh my God – what if we were liable for this and all got put in prison?

However, just as I was thinking this, a final belch of smoke came out of the church and Angus emerged, coughing violently.

'The fire's out,' he said. 'It's OK.' He looked like he was going to pass out, and I ran up to him.

Meanwhile, Amanda was striding past the whispering crowd, talking to no one. Jof, with the scoop of his life, snapped shots all the way, until she threatened to punch him, and he could tell she meant it. The eight bridesmaids – several with goose-poo on their frocks, I noticed – were huddling in a circle outside the church, having been unceremoniously informed by Amanda to 'Fuck off – you won't be fucking needed.'

Fraser was nowhere to be seen – you couldn't even see a car driving away. It was as if he'd vanished in the puff of smoke.

303

No one was daring to approach Amanda, who turned round, surveyed the war zone – smoke still drifting across the ground, and the small groups of hostile-looking people – and pushed herself into the gleaming limousine.

Her dad ran after her calling, 'Sweetheart, sweetheart, I'll make it all right, don't worry. I'll pay to have him killed – whatever you like.'

But she ignored him, slammed the door and indicated to the driver to get the hell out of there.

The big car purred past the arriving fire engine. I rubbed the rapidly forming scab on my forehead. This was turning out crazy.

'Glad you came?' muttered Angus, taking me by the arm.

'Well, it's different . . .' I said. My voice trailed off. Standing nervously at the other end of the churchyard, looking my way, were two very familiar figures.

They started to move towards me as soon as they realized I'd spotted them. I looked, petrified, at Angus.

'Don't worry,' he said. 'You should talk it out. You'd have to, sooner or later.'

He pushed me forward gently.

Fran looked tired and ravaged. She smiled at me reticently. I didn't return it. Alex had put on the fake swagger he always did when he was worried about something.

Eventually, we were facing each other. I stood with my arms folded.

'Hi,' said Fran.

'Hi,' I said back.

'We . . . well, I didn't think you'd talk to us on the phone.'

'Correct.'

'But we knew you'd be at the wedding.'

'Wasn't much of a wedding,' I said.

'So we saw.'

'Oh, so you're a "we". Well, that's good to know.'

Fran swallowed hard.

'Of course we're not, Mel . . . I mean, I'm not . . . and he's not . . . and it's all . . .'

I forced myself to ask.

'Since when? Before you went to America, or when?'

Alex spoke up: 'No, of course not.'

'Oh, so just at the party, was it?'

He hung his head.

Everything, horribly, fell into place. How could I have been such a fool?

'It was the night I twisted my ankle, wasn't it?'

Fran looked pained.

'Tell me.'

'I'd gone round to see Charlie and he wasn't back yet . . .' started Fran, but she didn't have to tell me any more. Charlie hadn't been there and Alex had, and he was never averse to anything on a plate.

I snorted and rubbed more dried blood from my forehead.

'God, the – How could you both? What the fuck were you up to at my dinner?'

'I'm sorry,' said Fran. 'I knew he was . . . moving in because of me. We had to talk . . . and then . . .'

I shook my head in disbelief.

'But you're . . . you were my best friend.'

'I know. I don't know . . .'

I took a step backwards and looked at Alex.

'Well, I suppose . . . he's all yours.'

Alex looked defensive and ashamed now. He knew the

decision had been made for him. He wasn't in control here. He couldn't make the choices.

Fran looked no happier. She turned briefly to Alex, who was staring at the ground, and then to me.

'I think I'd rather have you,' she said to me. 'I'm so sorry.'

'It's a bit too late for that.'

'Think it over?'

Her face was so pleading, so miserable. I wasn't too happy either, but at least I knew. Fran shook her head sadly. Now she could have Alex to herself, it didn't look like she wanted him any more.

I shrugged, and moved backwards again. Angus was waiting for me on the other side of the churchyard. Amanda's dad had walked about the congregation, announcing loudly that as he'd paid for a slap-up meal, we might as well enjoy it – and, amazingly, people were getting into their cars and going on to the reception. I couldn't imagine why, although perhaps I just didn't need a good scandal when I was in the middle of my own.

I saw Alex go to take Fran's arm. She shook it off painfully. I couldn't imagine the two of them together. For the first time, I felt sorry for her.

Against the traffic leaving the churchyard, a sports car screeched to a halt right in front of us. I looked to see what this latest diversion was. A tousled figure leapt out of the car almost before it stopped, and dashed over to Fran. I moved for a closer look. Good God – it was Charlie.

'I knew you were coming,' he yelled. He went down on one knee. 'Please, don't torture me any more. You don't love this son of a bitch –' indicating Alex.

'No, I don't,' said Fran. Alex, amazingly, looked surprised at this announcement.

'I couldn't let you come here, with him! It's tearing me apart. Ever since that night . . . I adore you, Fran. You're meant for me!'

'But you're a violent, upper-class, drunken, moronic toss-pot!'

'I know! And you're a violent, drunken, deceitful bitch! We're made for each other! Come on! Come away with me now . . . we are going to disappear somewhere to make violent, drunken, moronic love until we . . . burst!'

I looked over at Angus, who was shaking his head in disbelief. Fran looked at Charlie, looked at Alex, then looked straight at me.

'Ah,' she said, in those precise, trained tones. She turned back to Alex.

'I believe I'm off. Goodbye, darling . . . it's been interest-ing.'

'What!' said Alex. He looked devastated. 'Where the hell are you going?'

'I have precisely no idea. Goodbye, Melanie. I am sorry. I really am. Maybe one day we'll be able to be friends again.'

'Maybe,' I said. I couldn't help smiling.

'And remember what I told you about those nice McConnalds. Bye, Angus!'

She waved to him, and he waved back heartily.

Then Charlie and Fran leapt into the little sportster. Fran wrapped her scarf round her head like Audrey Hepburn and put on a big pair of sunglasses.

'Goodbye, everyone!' she waved regally. The car shot out of the churchyard and up the road, making a hell of a noise out of the back of the exhaust.

Those of us left behind just stared at each other. I couldn't help it. I suddenly started to half laugh, half cry all at the same time, making an unattractive snorting noise.

Instinctively, Alex moved forward to put his arm around me. Before he had a chance, though, Angus was there too.

'Excuse me,' he said stiffly to Alex.

Alex looked embarrassed and stood back.

'Sorry.'

Angus put his warm coat round me and led me over to the car. Alex watched us, then turned and walked away.

'Are you OK?'

'Yes! – snort – I'm just . . . hysterical! I'm sorry! I'll be OK in a minute.'

He opened the car door and sat me sideways out in the passenger seat.

'Here,' he said, and reached for his sporran, bringing out a little hip-flask.

'I brought this along for Fraser, in case he needed it. Take a wee dram. You'll feel much better.'

I took it, snorting mightily, and took a sip. The warm liquid seemed to make its way through my whole body, bringing a glow and some calm. My breathing slowed down, and I returned to normal.

Angus came round to the driver's side, and we sat in the car together in silence for a bit.

'What should we do?' he said, eventually.

'Hm?'

'Well, what are you thinking about?'

'Fraser,' I replied truthfully. 'I mean, where is he? What's he doing? I suppose this probably means he's not getting married, doesn't it?'

My unpredictable heart started beating again.

Angus turned to face me.

'You're thinking about Fraser?'

'Ehm, yes.'

'Not . . . Alex, or, ahem, me?'

I looked at his sweet face. There was real worry in his eyes.

'Ehm, well, you know, Fraser's been through . . . God, it must have been awful, I don't know how he must be . . .'

Angus heaved a great sigh.

'I think about you all the time,' he said simply.

I stopped talking mid-babble and looked at him again. I didn't know what to say. I knew what I wanted to say – how he was the sweetest, most honourable, nicest, cutest man I knew, but that I was . . . I couldn't . . .

'But', he said, 'you're in love with my brother.'

'Don't be ridiculous,' I said immediately.

'Ah, yes, but unfortunately you are. I thought you liked me, but it's only because I remind you of him.'

'That's not true,' I said fiercely.

'Aye well, maybe.'

'Definitely. I like you for millions of reasons, and that's not one of them.'

'Only like?'

'No, I love you. Just, you know, not in that way.'

'The way that you love my brother.'

I didn't say anything. I couldn't think of anything.

'I knew, you know – probably before you did,' said Angus. 'You light up like a candle if he's within a ten-mile radius. But I'd always thought there'd be a chance . . . even a tiny chance. And I knew Frase was determined to go through with this whole ridiculous thing, so . . . God, selfish of me, really. But I had to give it a shot. Despite myself, I really liked you and I'd hoped . . .'

'What do you mean, you knew?' I interjected. 'There's nothing to know.'

But I was so intrigued.

'It was obvious. Remember that night we took him the tape? I think I know why you were sad that night.'

'That's not true . . .' It was true.

'You couldn't bring yourself to think about him, so you made friends with me.'

'That's not true, Gustard.'

'You even use his name for me.' His fingers fiddled on the dashboard. His ears were flushed.

'Angus, whatever else might be true, I made friends with you because I really like you. Because you're funny and smart and interesting and attractive and kind. And the rest of it . . . I never led you on, I don't think. I'm sorry . . . I mean, I don't think I did anything.'

'No, you didn't. I'm sorry. I should be a more graceful loser.'

'Oh God, it's me that's the loser. I've lost everyone, you know. And Fraser isn't going to want to see me. Look at all the shit he's got on his plate. The last thing he's going to want to do is pick up with one of Amanda's buddies. In fact, he's probably over at Amanda's right now, apologizing and planning the whole thing all over again.'

'I doubt it.'

'So, please, don't make me have to lose you as well, by saying that I used you. Because I promise I didn't. Or, if I did, I didn't mean to. I'm sorry.'

He looked at me suddenly. The twinkle was back, if a little dimmed.

'Did you . . .' he started. 'Did you ever even consider it?'

'Every day,' I said, almost truthfully.

He smiled.

'Come here,' he said, and pulled me to him. We hugged one another for a long time in the front of the car.

Seventeen

Eventually, we pulled apart.

'What are you going to do now?' he said.

'I really want to go home. Are you going back to London?'

'Actually, my mum's gone to the reception. So I'd better go and see everyone, especially as I'll be the only male McConnald around. It's a flak-taking exercise.'

'Do you think your mum was pleased?'

'Pleased? She'll be delighted. She'll be even more delighted to be over there drinking champagne and eating vol-au-vents at Mr Phillips' expense.'

'He can afford it. Ehm, could you give me a lift to the station?'

'It'd be my pleasure.'

Angus put me on the slow train back to London. He stood on the platform waving until the train pulled away, the sunlight

311

glinting off his hair. I watched him until he grew tiny, then out of sight, then sat back in my chair with a sigh.

The woman opposite was staring at me strangely. Straining to see in the filthy train window, I realized I still had blood all over my head and mascara running down my face. Nice.

Suddenly, I realized I couldn't go back home; I was barred for Linda's big secret project. Jesus! Oh, fuck it. I didn't care if she was entertaining the Coldstream Guards in there, it was my home and that's where I had to go now. It wasn't my fault that I'd been to an imploding wedding. I'd stay in my room all day. Linda could cope.

I looked for a handkerchief in my pocket, before realizing that I was still wearing Angus's coat. God, the sweetie. It smelled reassuringly masculine, and there was indeed a handkerchief. It was embroidered in the corner with F.A.M. It was Fraser's, not Angus. I felt a bolt go through me. This was his. I clasped it like the most precious stone. I put it to my nose, but it only smelled of laundry, which I suppose in some ways was quite a relief. I dabbed a little at the blood and the mascara.

The woman opposite me leaned over. She was about fifty and a bit wholemeal-bread-looking – she was wearing lots of shawls, shoes that looked as though they'd been hewn from wood, and had thick wiry hair. She was attractive, in a fifty-ish kind of way.

'I'm psychic, you know.'

Oh God. Nutter on the train! Just when I needed it least. I looked around the carriage for help, but everyone was studiously ignoring us – of course! This was a British train, what could I have been thinking of?

I nodded dismissively to her and wished I had a newspaper to hide behind.

'I'm picking up very strong vibes from you.'

'What, vibes that I don't believe in psychics?' I said, trying to smile politely and get her to shut up.

She smiled. 'Well, that's OK. Lots of people don't. I have trouble myself, some days.'

I stared out of the window fixedly.

'There's trouble in your life.'

'Yes, well, that's probably a good average for everyone.'

'It's OK,' she said. 'Alexander loves you. Go to him.'

I sat bolt upright.

'What did you say?'

'I said, he loves you. Go to him.'

'No, no, no. You don't understand. Did you say Alex? He's a total pig. Are you by any chance a reverse psychic? Are you Australian?'

'No,' she said. 'Sometimes I get the message and I have to pass it on. I can tell it meant something to you. So, there it is.'

'It meant complete crap to me.'

'Well, sometimes that's what your head says when your heart says different.'

'No, sometimes that's what mad people say when you meet them on the train,' I muttered sullenly.

The psychic sat back, satisfied that her work was done, and I stared out the window, thinking furiously.

How on earth could she have known about Alex? I wouldn't put it past him to have set it up, the slimy little toad. But how could he have known I'd be on this train . . . this carriage? I shook my head fiercely to clear it and tried to concentrate on something else, anything else.

Like Fraser. As if the dam had burst, the lifting of the embargo let it all come flooding in. My angel in the snow. Striding like Mr Rochester from the church – I hadn't actually seen him do that, but I imagined it that way. His lopsided grin, his gentle eyes, his ready laugh . . . as London gradually came into view, through the suburbs and the railway stations. I couldn't possibly . . . well, I'd thought . . . but it was his wedding day, for Christ's sake. I couldn't hope to – I mean, he was probably trying to patch things up. After all, he'd turned up, hadn't he? Half an hour late, but he'd been ready and willing to get married.

Probably not the best time to ask him out.

At Waterloo, I moved through the crowds like I was swimming underwater. I knew I looked beyond ridiculous in my pretty dress and ruined face, but I didn't care. I just wanted to go home, pure and simple.

I caught a cab back to the flat. The street was quiet. It was bitterly cold, but inside Angus's coat I felt warm. I could, I supposed, go back to bed. Ignore the day altogether. It might be the sensible thing.

I crept up the stairwell and knocked quietly on the door before unlocking it with my key. Linda was there in an instant.

'I'm sorry!' I said through the door. 'I'm really sorry. The wedding went really wrong, and I didn't have anywhere else to go . . . Please, can I come in?'

Linda opened the door a crack and regarded me suspiciously.

'I might have known this would never work,' she said dolefully. But, reluctantly, she opened the door and let me in.

'Thank you!' I said gratefully. 'I'll keep out of your way, whatever you're doing, I promise. In fact, I'll go to bed straightaway and stay there until you say I can come out. In fact, probably longer.'

'It's OK,' she said. 'You might as well go join your friend in the kitchen. We've been having a nice chat.'

Friend? Chat? I had no idea who she meant. Suddenly very nervous, I walked towards the kitchen door. Maybe Fran had returned early from her little adventure. Despite everything, I wouldn't mind her around to talk to just now.

Slowly, I opened the door — and the sight that greeted me surprised me so much that I couldn't say a thing, for once.

It was freezing in the kitchen — the window was open, as were the fridge and the freezer doors, I noticed. All around the large room stood different model animals. There was a giraffe, a pelican, a wallaby — all large, and lovingly fashioned. They were brown, and so delicately made, that they appeared about to fly off, or gallop — as if they had been caught in filigree for an instant in mid-motion.

The kitchen table had been brought back in. Fraser was sitting at it. He looked tired and drawn, but he smiled at my amazement.

'Aren't they stunning?' he said. I nodded.

'I rather think your flatmate hides her light under a bushel.'

I turned to Linda.

'You did these?'

She blushed furiously and shrugged.

'What are they made of?'

'Chocolate.'

I span in amazement.

'All these are chocolate? Like Topics and Flyte and stuff?'

'I sculpt,' she said shyly. 'They're being picked up today for an exhibition. I practise small, but you have to put them

315

together really quickly, otherwise it melts. And now it's hardening off. They're picking them up soon.'

'Jesus!' I looked around at the edible menagerie. 'They're absolutely gorgeous.'

Linda smiled. It was such a rare sight to see that I grinned right back. Then Fraser grinned at me. In an apologetic, lopsided kind of a way. It was like the reverse ending of *Reservoir Dogs*.

My heart plummeted to the bottom of my shoes. I moved closer to him. We were gazing at each other as if we'd been hypnotized.

I sat down opposite him at the table.

'You can eat the tortoise, if you like,' said Linda shyly. 'It came out wrong.'

'Thanks,' I said, 'but it's too beautiful to eat. Well, for a tortoise.'

And I kept gazing at Fraser. Realizing something was up – poor Linda, could I never let her be at home in her own house? – she retreated.

There was a silence.

'So?' I said flippantly.

He hung his head.

'So, you were right all along?' he said.

'No, that's not what I was asking . . . That was a "So, what happened?" so.'

He looked at me.

'You know, I never wanted to get married.'

I arched my eyebrows at him.

'Really, I didn't. It all happened so quickly . . . and after we got engaged, I started to realize . . . just how wrong it was. With a little help from you and my brother, of course.'

I looked down. 'Huh.'

'And the wedding was arranged before I'd had a chance

316

to blink. I felt . . . well, we were betrothed. I'd made her a promise. It would have been wrong to break it off, just because I'd changed my mind.'

'No, it would have been kinder. In the long run.'

'Maybe. Anyway, every time I tried to bring it up, she'd brush over it. Said we'd be fine.'

'I don't think that it was necessarily only you she wanted.'

'No, me neither.'

He sighed.

'I sat up all night last night. I don't even believe in God, but I nearly started to. Just for someone to give me guidance.'

'Medieval knights used to do that.'

'I know. It's very sore on the knees.'

'And? Didn't it help?'

'No. I sat there for ages, dozed off, woke up again – for hours. And then, by about eleven o'clock, I just thought: it's too late now. I'm a big cowardly bastard and I have to take what's coming to me. It was my punishment for not facing up to it earlier.'

'Huh.'

'And I didn't think she'd – well, do what she did. I thought she'd wait, and bollock me for being late.'

'She must have known deep down as well.'

'I suppose so. Ouch.'

'What?'

'Nothing. I just feel "ouch" every time I remember those things she said. Oh, and poor you!'

He touched my head and I suddenly became very conscious of what a fright I must look.

'Oh, no, it didn't really hurt. I just got scratched by the thorns.'

'She could have had your eye out.'

317

'Well, you know . . . anything to help.'

He smiled, and stroked the scar tenderly. I shivered.

'But, apart from that,' he said, 'I think she did me a favour. I got out of it, and it was nobody's fault.'

'Well, except for the fact that it was *your* fault.'

'Yes, God, you're right, aren't you? It was completely my fault. I suppose what I mean is, I'm glad I'm not the one who came across as a heartless bastard. Because I'm not one, really. Well, I don't think I am.'

'I don't think you are either.'

His hand still rested on my forehead.

'Why did you come round here?' I asked.

'To see you,' he said simply.

'Oh.'

He looked down and took his hand away.

'You and Angus . . . I'm sorry, I know it's completely none of my business, but is — was — well, anyway, there's not anything going on, is there? He said there wasn't, but I thought he might be trying to spare my feelings. He's like that.'

'I know,' I said. 'And no. There never was, really. I was . . . well, I hope I didn't hurt him. I think one of the reasons I liked him — not the only reason, because then I really, really liked him, you know, I think he's brilliant . . . But, well, I think, well, he kind of reminded me of you.'

His mild eyes blinked twice in surprise.

'Is that true?'

'Yes,' I said, swallowing the lump in my throat.

'You . . . well, me, well, you know . . . ?'

'Ehm, yes,' I said, trusting that that was the right answer.

His grip on my hand tightened and he brought his other hand down to cup my cheek. Outside the window, the snow was falling again.

318

'Eventually I realized . . .' he began. 'I realized that I was terrified you'd be with him, and make him happy and not me. I was so jealous.'

I gazed up at him.

'You were jealous? You were getting married!'

'I know. It just didn't seem fair to me that he got you because his timing was on and mine was as off as it could possibly be. As if I didn't have enough to worry about.'

I couldn't believe I was hearing this. I put my hand over his hand.

'I met a psychic on the train,' I said, smiling. 'I didn't believe it. Total nutcase. Do you know, she told me to go back to Alex.'

'You did,' said Fraser.

I looked at him enquiringly.

'Alasdair. It's my middle name. It's Gaelic for Alexander.'

I pulled out the handkerchief. D'oh! F.A.M. That mad woman had probably seen the 'A' when I was clutching it like a maniac, and gone for the educated guess. Unless, of course . . . I looked up at him, shiny-eyed.

Almost in slow motion, we began to touch each other on the arm and the face, discovering each other for the first time. I felt his strong shoulders through his white shirt. All the hairs on his forearm had raised themselves up from the cold air, and the closeness of us. I tentatively touched one of his buttons.

'If I cry any more, I think I'll go blind,' I muttered, trying to hold back.

'That would explain what you see in me then.'

'Ho ho ho.'

Suddenly I felt his strong arms clasp my waist, his grip tighten. The expression on his face was tentative, excited, nervous, unsure — well, actually, fairly sure.

319

I looked straight at this man.

'You know, if this was a book,' I said, 'it really should have ended with a wedding.'

'Not necessarily,' he said. 'It could just have ended with a kiss.'

And it did.

Epilogue

We wanted to sneak away immediately. We had a lot to discuss and a lot to do. Somewhere in the country, we thought, where we could walk, and talk and, well, the other thing. I was lit up like the Christmas lights outside. I grabbed together some warm things in a bag and we made our way to the door. On our way out, I heard the phone ring. Linda picked it up.

'Oh,' I heard her say. 'Mel!'

'I don't think I want to get that, do I?' I said to Fraser.

'Don't tell them I'm here either,' he said.

'Oh my God. I haven't even thought about trying to explain it to people.'

'Shh . . .' From behind, he put both arms around me and leaned on my shoulder. 'There's plenty of time to worry about all that.'

'Mel!' Linda yelled. Linda yelling! What a day this was turning out to be. 'It's somebody called Nicholas! He wants to know if you're free this . . . hang on . . . tonight or the rest of the weekend?'

I raised my eyebrows at Fraser. He shook his head vehemently.

'I think that's going to be a "no", Linda,' I said.

There was a pause. Then she popped her head round the door.

'He's asked me out instead!' she said breathlessly.

'Oh . . .'

Well, how bad could it be? He was well off, he had a nice car, he was tall, he wasn't . . . well, he wasn't the heart of pure evil, and Linda needed to get out of the house.

'Why don't you go?' I said kindly. 'He's all right. It could be fun.'

Linda looked at me quizzically.

'That eight foot, wanky, dog-breath accountant? What the FUCK do you take me for?'